Unlikely Ghosts

Unlikely Ghosts

Edited by JAMES TURNER

Taplinger Publishing Company
New York

First published in the United States in 1969 by
Taplinger Publishing Co., Inc.
29 East Tenth Street
New York, New York 10003

Library of Congress Catalog Card Number: 71-82688

SBN 8008-7940-6

Printed in the United States of America

CONTENTS

35569

INTRODUCTION

Fifty years ago human beings suffered from a peculiar form of conceit. Individually they thought themselves immortal. They recognized death, of course—in others. But, for oneself, death was unthinkable.

In order to bolster up this conceit the ghost story was invented so that, in the moment of reading it, a man could be certain that he was right in believing in his own imperishability. It followed that ghost stories were serious; the after-life which they portrayed a *fact* while the story lasted. Such flimsy evidences of immortality, ghosts, were not to be mocked or laughed at and people actually believed in such phenomenon as, for example, the Angels of Mons. They believed because *not* to believe was to come hard up against the thought of their own death, of their own mortality. This is the reason people still spend money on spiritualist charlatans. The thought of their own dissolution is unbearable.

But two wars and the continuing danger of annihilation have quite changed our outlook on immortality and on ghosts. It may, also, have changed the ghost's outlook on us. Where, before, he went about clanging chains, now he realizes that no one is likely to be impressed by such stagey effects. In short, the ghost has become as absurd today as he was serious yesterday. There is little of the world left for him or her to haunt.

Further, since he had nothing to lose but his chains, it has been necessary for him (if he is to haunt at all) to find his place in the modern world, to adapt himself to a world in which satire has almost destroyed him. In order to exist at all the ghost has had to accept the possibility of his shade becoming a laughing matter, a shadow not to be taken seriously, a jest. In short, the ghost has been brought down to our level. No longer able to frighten us, no longer supernatural, he has been sensible enough to take refuge in comedy, begging us, if only by our gentle laughter, to acknowledge his existence.

And, in this, the ghost has been lucky. Nowadays, serious

ghost-hunters approach the site of a haunt armed with every conceivable kind of electrical equipment, listening device, tape-recorder and so on. It is rather like philosophy. You can no longer be a philosopher without being a first-class mathematician. Nowadays you cannot hope to track a ghost without being an expert electrician. How the ghosts must laugh!

In his own defence then the ghost has had to retreat into something no longer recognizable to the serious hunters. Into comedy. For, of course, who better than a spectre to understand the fact that the ghost was never an example of an immortal? A ghost is unlikely at the best of times and I don't believe the ghosts in this collection would have a place in a genuine psychical researcher's folio.

But that is not to say they are not possible—just.

THE VISITATION OF AUNT CLARA

by Kate Barlay

Somewhere in the world I have, or had, rich relatives—
according to some members of my family. But if so, I never had
their address.

My paternal grandfather lived in the Bachka, in Hungary, the
black-soiled, fertile land where the earth grew gold. Wheat, golden
wheat, heavy with the hard grain, each head hanging humble when
ripe. And there was golden corn on the cob, standing like
sentinels in the heat of the dying summer. Everything was there to
create wealth—except that the family fortune vanished in the 1848
Revolution. My father's and my mother's, too. The ancient house,
with its cool corridors, thick walls, vaulted ceilings, and the veranda with its pillars and redstone floor, curtained with lush green
creepers on the garden side. This house went up in the flames of
the Revolution. I only saw pictures of it; but to me it was so real,
I could have touched it. One day, the church bells rang out the
alarm as the house and the whole town burned under a pall of
smoke, sparks scattering everywhere, blown by the south-eastern
wind, and the Russian horsemen galloped across the great plains,
crushing to death Hungary's bid for freedom.

After all this was over, my father's family was never well-off.
They had to start a new life. A smaller house was built on the site
of the old one. When I was very small, I once visited this house,
but by then it no longer stood on Hungarian soil, for the country
was carved up after the First World War. It was a long time before
things had settled down sufficiently for my parents to go there, and
by then grandfather was very old and had had a stroke. He sat
there in his wheelchair, with his white hair and beard looking like
a patriarch. On his little finger he wore a ring with the family
crest. The ring fascinated me and I asked him to give it to me.

Grandfather looked at me gaily, his blue eyes watering at the
corners, and said, 'My little chicken, I will give it to you after I

die.'

My small heart gladdened at the prospect. I stroked his face and said, 'When will you die, Grandad?'

He burst out laughing—so hard he started to cough.

'Ho-ho, not so fast, little chicken! I shall die, but I won't let myself be hurried. The pity is, I shan't be able to leave you as much as I would have liked.' He paused for a moment and a far-away look came into his eyes. When he continued he seemed to be talking to himself. 'Once, so help me, I had the chance to win back everything. I had fabulous luck. If it hadn't been for that black-guard Bela . . . that scoundrel, that good-for-nothing . . .'

Grandad's face grew purple. Grandmother came in and stopped him.

'Again! Really, Sandor, won't you ever get over it! You haven't set eyes on my brother for forty-eight years! Goodness knows where he is now.'

'I hope he's in a good hot place!' Grandad muttered.

Grandmother didn't say anything after that, but silently pushed his wheelchair out into the garden. There he dozed off, near the flower bed where the huge poppies grew, their fleshy petals soaking in the warm morning sun, innocent, proud, while inside the ped-uncle the black seeds harboured opium. And, though Grandad's sleep had nothing to do with this, it became deeper, as if he had been drugged by the sweet poison contained within the flowers. But at times he called out, 'Clara? Are you here?'

Grandfather always expected to hear from his sister Clara, though she had been dead for goodness knew how many years!

Something was deadly down in the Bachka. The inertia. Bees buzzed among the flowers. Time seemed timeless. I played with a kitten. Soon the noon-day bell would peal out and the huge noon-day meals begin. Everything seemed the same, yet the dice was loaded—against the house and the garden, against Hungary, and against my inheritance, though Grandad put all the blame on Uncle Bela for everything.

Uncle Bela was Grandmother's younger brother. The way I pieced it together afterwards, it all started one noon, just as Jutka, the big, hefty maid whose braided hair was plaited around her head like a crown, put the enormous soup tureen on the table.

As the church bells pealed out the last strokes, Grandad opened the front door, hung up his hat, put his walking-stick in the stand, and walked into the dining-room. Grandfather stood at the far end of the table, stirred the soup with the ladle and started to serve. The children sat down and chanted in unison, 'Kiss your hand, Papa!'

There were six of them—Grandma was sixteen when she married. This was all the children said during meals, unless their father addressed them. Grandad ruled with a rod of iron. His walking-stick was not just something to lean on. Its handle was of silver and carried his initials—a symbol of his authority, a fine malacca cane to be used, if need be, on the backs of his sons. Its thickness didn't bother him! His children feared him as fire, and his wife served him like a slave.

Grandad said grace, then tasted the first mouthful of soup. Grandma waited, spoon in hand. The children waited, too, spoons poised near their hungry mouths. They all looked at him.

'Good!' Grandad pronounced. 'Just enough rice and not too thick.'

It was chicken giblet soup. Cream and chopped parsley floated on top of it. Grandma smiled happily, and everyone had started to eat when the door burst open and Uncle Bela came in.

" 'Day, brother-in-law! 'Day, Melinda!' He patted some heads as he passed the children, who all grinned—they adored Uncle Bela. He threw his hat with deadly accuracy to land on a wine cooler on the sideboard, pulled up a chair and sat down.

'M'm, my favourite soup!'

Jutka came in without prompting and handed a soup-plate to Grandma who filled it without a word.

Grandad shook his head. 'What is it this time, brother—as if I didn't know! Lost at cards?'

Bela guzzled his soup noisily. 'Your finger-tips should be gilded, Melinda, the way you flavour everything. Just right! Brother-in-law, you are lucky Melie married you.'

Grandad gave him a dirty look.

'Also, you are dead wrong! I don't want any money from you. On the contrary, I want to put some in your pocket.'

Grandfather's expression spoke volumes, but he only waved his hand as if to chase away a fly. 'Bah!'

'I'm selling National Lottery tickets,' Uncle Bela continued, unabashed. 'With a little luck, you'll be rich. I've bought some myself,' he added temptingly.

Crops were bad that year. Hailstorms, late frost, drought, the lot. Grandad had worry in plenty. But that didn't mean he changed his habits. As usual when in a tight corner, he was already negotiating the sale of a piece of land with one of the big landowners in the neighbourhood.

'You, Melie?' Bela turned to his sister. 'Won't you buy a ticket?'

Grandma shook her head without answering. Instead, she changed the subject. 'Bela, won't you get a proper job, dear? You ought to settle down. Kate cries her eyes out over you. She's heard about that new girl cashier at the Café Ocean. You ought to put things right with her at once. She has plenty of money and her father will give you at least three hundred acres for a dowry. Besides, she is beautiful, a good churchgoer and in love with you. . . .'

Grandad rapped the table. '*Melinda, nicht für die Kinder!*'

Bela grinned. 'Thanks, brother! It would spoil my favourite lunch if I had to listen to sermons!' He looked at the beans and pork chops approvingly as Grandma heaped his plate with the second course. 'Nothing makes a man feel better than good Magyar cooking. My favourite dishes would be the death of the Austrians, curse them!' The '48 Revolution wasn't forgotten and the skin still smarted under the old scar tissue.

Jutka brought in the sweet, a boiled concoction that resembled ravioli but had a filling of plum jam and ground walnuts, with sugar scattered over it. It was called monk's ear, and by the time it was finished everybody felt a bit distended round the waist. A marvellously nourishing sweet, but a deadly enemy of work, requiring several hours of diligent and devoted digestion. The maximum effort afterwards would be, say, a game of dominoes or cards at the coffee house called the Ocean. At least, that was where Uncle Bela went. Grandad withdrew to the bedroom for a nap on the sofa at the foot of the large double-bed.

It never became clear which was responsible for Grandad's

dream, the second helping of monk's ear, Uncle Bela's talk about winning the National Lottery—or even, perhaps, some supernatural power. What one believes depends on one's inclinations. But it is a fact that when Grandma went into the bedroom she found, to her amazement, the entire front of the cupboard covered with huge numbers in chalk!

Grandad was asleep, snoring peacefully. In the firm belief that one of the boys had done this dreadful thing out of sheer devilment, Grandma hastily wiped off the numbers with her own lavender-scented handkerchief before Grandad awoke and beat the erring child to death.

Sure that the last traces of chalk had gone, Grandma quietly withdrew to the sewing-room to do some mending. It was there that Grandad found her when he burst in excitedly half an hour later.

'Who wiped off the numbers from the wardrobe?' he demanded in a wrathful voice. 'Who dared touch my numbers?'

Grandma was astonished. '*You* wrote on the mahogany wardrobe, Sandor? But why?'

'Don't cross-examine me! Answer!' roared Grandad, his blue eyes blazing.

'Yes, I wiped them off. How could I have dreamed . . . ?'

Grandad sank into a chair, his anger ebbing away under the blow. 'It's all over, Melie. All gone. I'm absolutely positive it was the right number.'

Grandma looked at him as if he had gone mad. 'Really, Sandor, I . . .'

'Listen! You remember Clara, my dead sister?'

Grandma nodded. 'Go on, what about her?'

'She visited me. In my dream, only I'm not certain it was a dream, dressed in white from head to foot. She looked exactly as I remember her, except that her face was luminous. She took a lottery ticket from her handbag and handed it to me. She said she wanted to help me. "*This* number," she said, "will win. Stick to it, brother, and you will be rich." Then she waved to me and disappeared into the wardrobe. I came to myself with a start, but I could still hear her voice saying, "Don't forget! Don't forget!" So I whipped out a piece of billiard cue chalk I happened to have in my waistcoat pocket and made a note of the number—at the very spot where she had disappeared. Then I sat down on the sofa to recover myself. But I must have fallen asleep again.' Grandad shook his head as if even he couldn't understand what had happened. 'I don't believe in ghosts and I'm not superstitious. But Clara was so alive, Melie. So *alive!*'

Grandma was very sorry about the lost number and did her best to apologize and to comfort Grandad. When he was himself again he went out to the Café Ocean, not forgetting to go by way of the banks of the Danube to make sure none of the boys had gone swimming instead of to school. The river was low and the wooden bridge spanning it at that point, deserted. The broad stream was empty, too, and though it was only the beginning of June, the heat of the Hungarian summer enveloped the landscape. A horse whinnied in a near-by field.

Grandad nodded, turned away from the river and went on to the coffee house, reassured that all was well and that the natural order of things prevailed.

Spending the afternoons at the café, drinking a *capuciner* and playing cards befitted his station in life. Was he not a member of the landed gentry? There was the old bailiff to keep an eye on things, and the peasants were there to work. It was equally normal to sell a piece of land when things got tough. Still, what a queer dream he'd had!

Inside the Ocean it was much cooler. Apart from the entrance, the place was almost hermetically sealed. It was darker, too, and above the marble-topped tables the mirrors glittered dimly on the walls. The air was stale and stuffy with tobacco smoke which had eaten into the very walls and furniture, and even the old dress-suit of the waiter. Figures like dummies sat draped on the chairs, reading the newspapers in their bamboo frames. In one corner sat a few of the regulars, playing cards.

The only bright spot in this vapour-laden atmosphere was Mancika, the cashier. There she sat, enclosed in a semicircular wooden structure on a kind of pedestal, at her elbow a glass bowl filled with lump sugar, on the shelves behind her bottles of liqueurs. Apricot brandy, glistening like gold; green walnut brandy; cherry brandy. Even champagne. Whenever the ancient, flat-footed waiter had an order for a *capuciner*—which was a black coffee with just a dash of milk, served in a tall glass—he would shuffle first to Mancika. 'Sugar and *capuciner* for number four.' And Mancika would place two big lumps of sugar on the small round metal saucer waiting on the shining metal tray, and then at once make a note of the order in the ledger she kept open before her. Book-keeping was simple at the Ocean.

Bela stood at her left, leaning against the wooden structure that enclosed Mancika. He was a tall young man. But he had to look up to her, which he did with adoration.

'What lovely white shoulders you have, Mancika!'

Mancika giggled. She wore an embroidered white grenadine blouse, pushed down invitingly. The puffed short sleeves left her white round arms free. Her hair was very dark brown, almost black, shiny and alive and done into a large bun at the nape of her neck.

'What a nice slim waist!' Bela went on softly, caressingly.

Mancika turned her head away from him, showing her neck as she did so, where her hair grew short and escaped in soft ringlets from her bun. 'Too bad you let that clown of a count put his arms around it. Don't deny it. People saw you. Aren't you ashamed, Mancika!'

Mancika turned crimson and looked Bela full in the face, her dark eyes flashing.

'Why should I be ashamed? Goodness gracious me, things like that shouldn't be taken seriously. A man's a man, even if he is a count. I couldn't hurt his feelings. Anyway, I'm not married to you. Really, you expect too much. But even if I were—and I don't presume to that—I wouldn't give my husband sweets every day. I wouldn't spoil him, or he'd soon loathe the sight of me. Besides, it's nice to have admirers.' Here Mancika broke down to the point of tears. 'He ordered twelve bottles of champagne,' she whispered. 'Do you want me to lose my job!'

Meanwhile, Grandad had taken his seat among the card-players and, striking a glass on the table with his signet ring, ordered a *capuciner* and an apricot brandy. Mancika had to get busy and Bela went over to join Grandad for a game. But he was pale and his hands were moist as he shuffled the cards, and he hated Grandad for interrupting his discussion with Mancika.

That same evening, Grandad found it necessary to say something about Bela to Grandma. 'That young ass of a brother of yours is getting himself talked about. The way he carries on with Mancika, the cashier at the Ocean. He'd better not get into any scrapes with the count. It would be a fine thing if my brother-in-law got into trouble for such a girl!'

Grandmother, of course, agreed with every word he said, and the matter wasn't raised again for a week or so.

Then one night after a dinner of Transylvanian sour cabbage and poppy seed strudel, Grandad had another visitation from his dead sister, Clara. He slept heavily, but tossing about, and didn't hear when Grandma got out of bed in the middle of the night and went to the window.

Somebody was throwing pebbles at the glass. She drew aside the curtains and in the pale moonlight saw Bela with Mancika.

Bela whispered, 'Let us in, Melie, please!'

Grandma looked anxiously over her shoulder towards Grandad, but he only muttered something in his sleep and turned over again. Grandma quickly put on her housecoat and, silent as a shadow, slipped from the room.

'For mercy's sake, what happened?' she asked.

Mancika burst into tears. 'Bela beat up the count because of me,' she wailed, 'though as God's my witness, I love only him.' She clung to Bela.

'The old scoundrel! He's lucky to be alive,' Bela growled threateningly.

Grandma clutched her head. 'Jesus Maria, what have you done! He was going to buy a piece of our land. The deal won't go through now for sure! . . . Still, poor child, poor child. You're shivering!' And with a little smile she murmured, 'I'm sure the Count asked for it!'

Mancika clutched at Grandma's hand and kissed it.

'Melie, please put her up for the night,' Bela pleaded. 'She'll go at dawn before anyone gets up.'

Grandma nodded. She was still young herself at the time, only six years older than Bela. But she was motherly, even then. She put her arm round Mancika's shoulders and led her from the sleeping garden into the house. Bela stood watching them until they disappeared, then he turned and vanished under the shadows of the trees.

Grandad was having a visitation. . . . Clara was remonstrating with him. 'You didn't buy that lottery ticket, did you? Don't you believe I know what I'm talking about? I'm going to give you the number again. Perhaps it won't make you as rich as Croesus, but it will give you a little peace, a little time, a little ease. . . . You won't have to sell the land, the land, the land. . . .'

Grandfather's heart ached. He loved his land and didn't feel like selling it. He squinted in his effort to see the number Clara was showing him. At first he thought he saw it, then he didn't. Then, ah, yes, he did. Quite clearly! He sat up with a start, threw himself out of bed, rushed to his jacket, took his notebook from a pocket and wrote down the figures while they were still fresh in his mind. He returned the notebook to the pocket, went back to bed and immediately fell asleep. . . .

He awoke whistling and happy, and was having breakfast on the veranda as usual when Bela arrived.

'Good morning, brother-in-law,' he greeted Grandad.

'Morning,' said Grandad. 'What's up? You're around early today.'

Bela sat down and poured himself a cup of coffee with a generous portion of cream. He seemed thoughtful as he stirred the sugar. Then he said deliberately, weighing every word, 'I'm going to get a job—start afresh.'

'You didn't sell any lottery tickets?' Grandad twitted him. 'As it happens, I have a customer for you.'

Bela didn't rise to the bait. 'I'm not interested in such things any more. It's a mug's game.'

'Oh, I wouldn't say that,' Grandad protested, and fished the little notebook from his pocket. 'Look, I have a tip. This number is going to win. I'll give you five forints and you stake this number for me in Szabadka.'

For a moment, Bela looked at Grandad in amazement, but then lost interest almost at once. 'Nonsense,' he said. 'How could you have a tip? The draw isn't crooked and isn't till tomorrow.' He shook his head. 'You can't have a tip on this. It isn't like horses.

Don't waste your money.'

'Don't you worry about whether I have a tip or not. Just do me the favour of getting a ticket for me in Szabadka.'

'I don't know if I'll have the time today, brother-in-law. I'm very busy, and Szabadka, you know very well, is five hours' drive. . . .'

Grandad hit the table with his open palm. He always had a quick temper. 'You make the time!' he shouted. 'It's the least you can do.'

So Bela took the money and wrote down the number which Grandad read out from his little book. 'All right,' he said. 'Money down the drain. Please yourself. It's your loss.'

A moment later Grandma came out and Grandad, who had finished breakfast by this time, lit his pipe and got up. 'I'm going down to the stables,' he said. 'Wonders never cease, Melie. You've got a reformed brother.' He winked and went off, whistling.

As soon as he was out of earshot, Grandma whispered, 'Bela, she was gone by morning. Where is she now?'

'In my dogcart, under the trees just outside the garden. I'm taking her with me. We're going to get married.'

Grandmother clasped her hands together. 'If you marry her, Sandor will never forgive you. A cashier girl!'

'That can't be helped. I love her and I'm going to marry her. Melie, I shan't see you for a long time. Thank you for everything. You have been a good sister to me. Don't cry.' He leant forward and kissed her cheek. Then, as he was about to go, he remembered something. 'Melie, here are five forints,' he said, smiling. 'Buy something for yourself—it's money that would have been wasted anyway. Don't breathe a word of my plans to a soul. I need time.'

He waved to her and, his footsteps echoing on the red tiles of the veranda, he was gone.

Grandmother was very busy that day. She was making cherry jam. One of her sons was bitten by a dog, and Grandad unexpectedly brought home several friends to celebrate. He didn't tell Grandmother what the celebration was for, but she knew he could always find a reason for celebrating if he felt like it. Grandmother wasn't in the habit of asking too many questions.

While she rushed around all day, her thoughts were with Bela and Mancika. Where were they? Where would they go? She looked sad and absent-minded, but nobody asked what was troubling her. All her life her hands were never idle; her light footsteps sounded all day around the house. But she was silent. As always, it was her way to help, not burden others with her own problems.

The count had sent a letter cancelling his offer to buy the land. But Grandad didn't seem to care, and celebrated instead. For this Grandmother was grateful since the count hadn't mentioned the incident with Bela. She went to sleep while the men were still singing on the veranda by candle-light. Grandfather didn't like lamps. He stuck candles in the necks of empty bottles. Every empty bottle meant a new candle and as the night grew deeper the veranda became lighted with every passing hour.

'He who drinks good wine can't be a bad man! Hey-ho, we'll never die! Drink, friends . . .!' The moths, attracted by the light, swirled round and died in the flames.

Grandad awoke with a big aching head around noon. The veranda was freshly scrubbed, the tiles glistened, and Grandmother placed a tall glass of sour cabbage juice in front of him as he sat down in the very seat he had used the previous night.

'Did Bela call?' he asked.

'Not yet,' said Grandmother, looking away. In her apron pocket was a note she had received that morning.

> Dear Melie, We are going abroad. The world is full of opportunities. I hope—no, I am certain I shall make a fortune somewhere. Don't show this letter to anyone. It would mean trouble if we were discovered before we left the country. The count has influential friends. I hit him hard. Your loving brother, Bela.

And beneath his name, in a childish hand, was written 'Mancika'.

The note burned Grandmother's pocket, but she did not breathe a word about Bela's departure. Grandad was too restless to notice the guilty look on Grandmother's face. He decided not to wait till his afternoon visit to the Café Ocean to see the newspapers.

The result of the lottery would be out by now and he had great faith in Aunt Clara. He was elated, almost excited, and, fortified by sour cabbage juice, already felt much better.

'I think I'm going to the coffee house to see the papers. Tell Bela to join me there when he shows up—and tell him to bring my ticket with him.'

'What ticket?' Grandma asked naïvely.

'Melie, what does it matter what ticket? If I say tell Bela to bring the ticket it's evident he must know about it. So tell him to bring it.'

Grandmother nodded obediently. Grandad put on his hat, took his malacca cane from the stand, picked up his gloves and set out.

The Café Ocean was in a turmoil. Nobody sat at the cash-desk to take the orders and hand out the lumps of sugar. The head waiter was trying to cope with about a dozen people—an unusually large crowd—who had all come to read the newspapers and see the results of the lottery.

Grandfather sat down and after waiting for a few seconds tapped with his heavy signet-ring on the marble-topped table. He had to tap quite hard before the sad flat-footed waiter came hurrying up, bringing Grandfather his favourite paper, ready to take his order.

'What will it be, sir?'

'*Capuciner* and a double apricot brandy.'

'*Capuciner* and a double apricot,' the hoarse, tired waiter's voice repeated to the head waiter who was now filling the role Mancika had abandoned. Grandfather opened the paper, then folded it, took out his pince-nez and was about to start reading when the waiter placed his order in front of him. He nodded, took a sip of the brandy, put on his pince-nez and started to examine the column of numbers.

The next moment, with a great sweep of his arm, he knocked over the coffee in the tall, steaming glass.

'I have won!' he shouted with joy. 'The big treble chance! I have won! Here it is. Right on top. My number! Champagne for everyone. It's on me. We'll drink to the ghost of my sister Clara!'

The head waiter, the waiter and all the regulars crowded round him at once. While the waiter mopped up the spilled coffee, Grandad shook hands with all the well-wishers. Then he looked towards the cash-desk which Mancika used to grace and asked, 'Where's the girl? She likes champagne, too, that little one. . . .'

The head waiter cleared his throat and after a small silence supplied the information: 'Mancika has left. She's gone for good. . . .' He cleared his throat again. 'She's going to get married. She's gone abroad.'

Grandad laughed. 'She's a sly one. Who was the fool who took her?'

There was an awkward pause, then the head waiter replied with yet another reluctant little cough, 'Your brother-in-law, sir.'

Grandad shot from his seat. He grabbed the head waiter by the lapel of his shabby tailcoat. His eyes blazed.

'It's a lie!'

'No, sir . . .'

'When did this happen?'

'Early yesterday morning, sir. They took a train to Budapest to get married—and went on from there. Mancika left a note to tell you. She has no family, so she felt we ought to . . .'

Grandad had changed colour. He released his grip on the head waiter's tailcoat and sat down heavily.

When he spoke his voice was quiet. 'It's all over. He never bought that lottery ticket . . . and I won! That's the pity of it all. I won! . . . Hell and damnation! Clara will be disgusted. She'll never visit me again.'

Grandad looked round at the people gaping at him. He reached into his pocket and threw a banknote on to the table.

'Champagne for everyone, just as I said. . . .' And he walked out of the coffee house.

Uncle Bela's name was never mentioned in front of Grandad again—only in whispers behind his back.

For a while Grandmother received letters from him. From Vienna, then from Berlin, later from London. The last note said they expected a baby and might go to America. Perhaps at last Uncle Bela did make a fortune, and successful people become forgetful. But Grandad did go on hoping for a visit from his sister Clara.

The old house in the Batchka has gone. Taxes and bad management took it after my grandparents died in the alien land that was no longer Hungary. The Second World War finished off what was left of the silver, the family portraits and the furniture. But I still have the number of that lottery ticket. And it is nice to think that, somewhere in the world, maybe I have rich relatives. And of course, who knows, any day now I might have a visitation from my great-aunt Clara.

EVERYTHING A MAN NEEDS

by Ronald Blythe

Margery Nethershole had confidence, self-assurance, call it what you will. Her poise was obvious and challenging, and people and arguments less poised, although not necessarily wrong, collapsed at her approach. Sheer presence allowed her to win usually half the battle, occasionally all of it. It was something, of course, which one would get used to after fifty-odd years and Margery had got used to it. When life was rough, she was shining and smooth, like a lighthouse in a gale. She had always been called reliable and now that springy grey curls advanced across the still mainly chestnut masses of her hair her role of wise woman increased. The demand for her services on committees and in personal difficulties grew. There was no problem, great or small, on which she withheld her advice. Her method was to beam a powerful common sense on every complexity, with the result that she scarred not a few lives whose terrors called for a less drastic approach. In any case, people never blamed her when her *mana*, as she liked to call it, didn't work; they blamed themselves for lack of faith or for not understanding her instructions. And so her name remained the natural conjunctive to any emergency in central Suffolk.

A problem shared is a problem halved was one of Margery's favourite axioms and all round Ipswich there could be seen faces entirely concerned with these half-problems on the one hand, and the fact that Mrs Nethersole knew the whole secret on the other. To do her justice, there was no need for this latter anxiety. Information where she was concerned was a strictly one-way traffic. She collected confidences as other people collected rare or strange objects and was congenitally incapable of giving them away. Experiences and confessions were packed inside her like shale, an instant stoniness fossilizing them the minute she received them. It was strange that there were those who doubted her discretion, though less strange, perhaps, that those whom she had helped should hate her, as one sometimes hates a seducer. 'You can tell me *anything*,' Margery would say, fumbling in her bag for a Goldflake and coughing comfortably, and, amazingly enough, people did. They talked, she listened. If she saw herself as anything it was as the local sin-eater, but a growing number of people saw her as a kind of walking file in which, in a moment of madness, they had thrust their reputations. An inescapable O.B.E. for social services did nothing to lessen the fact that she was human and one victim of her charity had a recurring dream in which Margery appeared as a piggy-bank from which he could only regain what was once his alone with a knife.

Only one person understood Margery's secretiveness and this was Perpetua Cranmer, her friend-housekeeper since before the war. They had actually met on Abdication Day in the Charing Cross Hotel, recognizing in each other the peculiar happiness which follows a blessed release.

'I thought it was for the King,' said Perpetua, indicating Margery's black.

'Heavens, no!' smiled Margery. 'It's for Alfred. Or was. But I'm wearing it today because it suits me.'

'Alfred?'

'My husband.'

'O, I am sorry. Was it a happy release?'

'I expect so. It is usually reckoned to be, isn't it?'

'I didn't wear·black for Mummy,' said Perpetua. 'She asked me not to—to save the money, you know.'

'Do go on,' said Margery.

'I shouldn't be telling you all this. It is such an imposition. I mean you don't know me. . . .'

'But I do know you,' said Margery. 'Besides, it helps to talk and you can say things to a stranger which you cannot say to even the dearest friend.'

'How understanding you are,' said Perpetua, and she then told all there was to know about herself, which was very little. When she had finished, she ordered more hot water and invited Margery's confidences in return.

'But I wouldn't dream of boring you with them,' cried Margery.

And she never did. They had shared Penault Fayre, their house on the edge of Ipswich, for thirty years and all this time the only things which Perpetua had been able to discover about her friend had been such odds and ends as had accidentally sagged into view, like the hem of the oyster silk slip which Margery inevitably wore under her tweeds. Naturally, Alfred provided the greatest mystery. Who was he . . . *who*?

'He worked in Dunbury, Fife and Loman's.'

'A solicitor?'

'Just. He died before he began to really earn.'

'He must have been young?'

'Oh, he was—we both were.'

'He must have been, well, more than just a solicitor,' persisted Perpetua. She had lived with Margery for years before daring to hold this conversation. At first she had imagined that the subject filled her friend with pain but there was soon plenty of evidence to prove that this wasn't so.

'He was just a young man,' said Margery. 'They're all much of a muchness, you know!'

Perpetua refused to believe this, but having no evidence to support an argument, she broke a cotton indignantly against her teeth. She wanted to say, an ordinary photograph would tell me all I need to know. Your wedding picture, Marge. But years of reserve prohibited any reasonable discussion of the subject and Perpetua was left, more often than not, with a miserably embarrassing flush induced by a special look, half-playful and entirely too knowing, which her friend turned on her when she stumbled into talk about men. Sometimes she thought of Alfred *with* Margery—no, she didn't mean just that, but simply the two of them, young and companionate. And Alfred sitting for his finals. Fancy having to do that the year one died! Time heals, they say, and time had healed the place where Alfred had been in Margery's life so totally that there wasn't a sign left of his existence. Not a snapshot nor a collar-stud. Perpetua had looked, not once but scores of times, turning over the papers and oddments in Margery's desk and hoping to see his signature. Margery bore his name of course, and no wonder, for else she would have had to revert to Miss Catt.

'He was part of you,' said Perpetua accusingly. She was suddenly Alfred's champion, his remembrancer.

'Don't be too sure of that!'

'Oh?'

But Margery was not to be drawn. She stood up, banging threads and fluff from her thick skirt with the hand upon which Alfred's rings glittered feebly.

'Come on, Perp. Get the booze out—and stop ferreting.'

They drank their sherry like medicine and then went into the kitchen to begin the dinner. The kitchen was warm and lofty, with a scarlet rug in front of the Aga and a buttoned Victorian armchair full of sleeping kittens. Old wooden cream platters were heaped with withered Cox's Orange Pippins and flaking ropes of onions swung from bacon hooks. There were endless labelled canisters, all of them containing what they said they did, and in generous quantities. A *jardinière*, besides its usual burden of plants, held a load of freshly made marmalade and a torpid cat. Crates of beer and wine lay under the dresser and a huge straw-coloured table whose pale sweet grain eddied in the lamplight stretched itself purely across the scrubbed brick floor.

'Mmmm!' murmured Perpetua appreciatively, entering her kingdom.

'We live well, is that what you mean?' asked Margery. Her friend thought she noticed a change of inflexion; some clouding or maybe brightening in Mrs Nethersole's voice, causing it to sound like the voice of a stranger. The eyes, too, while retaining both their customary shape and expression, contained some new intelligence which Perpetua could not fathom. Surprisingly, it occurred to her that the sensible, practical front had slipped and that she was looking at a revealed, an exposed Margery. It was the merest momentary displacement, rather like when one of their colour-slides went crooked into the projector and brought the garden out flaring like Africa on the screen.

'As some kind of compensation, perhaps?'

The non-typical sharpness of this brought the familiar Margery hurriedly into focus.

'Maybe. But we don't have to go into it. After all, we are not the usual kind of women who, er, share, are we . . . ?'

It was more a statement than a question.

'No, we are not,' said Perpetua so distinctly as to make it clear that, this hitherto tacit fact having been uttered, there was no need ever to mention the subject again. She was stripping a chicory head leaf by leaf and now she rejoiced in the mutual silky coolness of her fingers and the plant. Behind her, she could hear Margery laying the table, bonking down their heavy silver on the spotless wood, chinking glasses, sounding slapdash but achieving perfection. Order! I love it! That was what Margery said—this, in fact, was her creed. Alfred, the marriage, it had all been tidied away. Order. This was all it was. Perpetua had pondered that it might be so before but now it convinced her. She could have hugged Margery, except they never hugged. Or touched. Or even shook hands. Order. Sweet, immaculate order. Feeling happy, she leaned over and switched on the kitchen wireless. It was the same instrument on which they had listened to Churchill and ITMA. A group thumped away. Shopping around she found an announcer offering selections from *The King and I*.

'That's better,' cried Margery, 'let's have some real music!'

She had finished laying the table and was crouched over a big Boot's diary on the dresser, checking over tomorrow's engagements. The Bench in the morning. School governors at two. Then nothing until six, which was Library Committee. One got a fairly clear day like that sometimes; she wondered what she would do. Perpetua, glancing round at her, saw only the stalwartness, the large beam and the contradictorily small, pretty feet. Margery's face was in the shadows. It hung down over the page, the faintly swarthy flesh pulling away from the bone and creating soft fresh planes. Her mouth in this absorbed, leaning-forward stance was pouched and greedy like a child's. Her thick lustreless hair swung out in fat scimitars which hid her ear-rings. Body at this moment was definitely one thing, and mind, indicated by the ballpoint with which Margery was scrawling in further appointments, another. Bare neck and arms flowed out of sight with great richness. Something in the very reality of such an ignored corporeal wealth proclaimed an unlooked-for and unthinkable defeat of an intelligence which had hoarded it so matter-of-factly. There was no surface tremor, no discomfort as it is so curiously called. Nothing to suggest to Margery or to anybody else that she would act as indomitably out of character as in it.

*

Two days later Margery returned from Ipswich with a pile of shopping which included some garment or other, judging by the softness. Breathing heavily and carefully, like a singer, she whipped it open and tossed what it contained over to Perpetua, who caught it with a little scream of pain.

'Sorry, I forgot. Men's shirts are always full of pins.'

Perpetua spread the shirt on her lap with one hand and sucked her finger. The heavy salty taste of blood filled her mouth. The small, decided injury, the shirt and Margery's ordinary face left her feeling more stupid than astonished.

'I just went in and bought it,' said Margery like a teacher chivying a child in the direction of the required answer.

'Compulsion . . . perhaps ?' asked Perpetua in an attempt to say what she imagined Margery would have said had she done such a thing.

Margery laughed (her safe old laugh). 'I didn't lift it, love. I went into Whithers and asked for a man's shirt, size fifteen, and bought it.'

Subsequent action and its sharp corollaries stem from a small moment when conspirators decide to see eye to eye. Perpetua did not say 'Why ?' She said, 'Whithers—isn't that the outfitters near the bus station ? They don't know you there.'

'That's right, they don't.'

A long pause while Perpetua's blood flowed, disgustingly filling her nail.

'It's for—Alfred ?'

'Alfred's dead, isn't he ?'

Teacher was back again.

'Oh, I don't know!' said Perpetua crossly. 'Who then ?'

'That is exactly what we have to decide. Who and what, though chiefly who.'

Perpetua's tight, waxy face relaxed.

'Oh, Marge, it's a game!'

'If it is, I've had my turn,' said Margery.

Perpetua thought hard, like when she played Scrabble. Her first move would show at once whether she understood the rules. 'I'll put it in his room, shall I ?' she said.

'Who's room ?'

'Thomas's.'

This time she scarcely had to think at all.

'Thomas's room will do,' said Margery, adding, 'Only knock before you barge in.'

Perpetua hesitated then left the kitchen and went upstairs. The bedroom doors were shut all round the landing, her door, Margery's door, the bathroom, the guest-room. He wouldn't be in the guest-room if he actually lived with them, would he ? There were two more spares. She chose the first.

'He was out,' she announced, returning slightly puffed.

'Never mind,' said Margery. 'He won't always be.'

About a week later, Perpetua went into the spare room to air it and noticed the shirt lying on the bed. It was slightly damp and the room itself ached with its sealed uselessness. The curtains were faded on the folds and the leather buttons on the rolled-up mattress were curled and crinkled like perished flowers. There was a thin, pervasive smell which she could not name. It was the smell of poverty. At first she only put the shirt in a drawer, opened the windows and laid the mattress flat. Then came sheets and pillows; a great Turkistan rug for a bedspread and the duelling prints from the top of the stairs where they could not be seen. Hangers in the wardrobe. A lamp. Some books. She was like a child playing houses and dashing off to fetch a thing the moment she thought of it. She was putting the finishing touches when Margery arrived. She was carrying something in her hand and appeared more surprised to see Perpetua than the transformed room. She laid it on the dressing-table.

'What is it ?'

'Shaving soap.'

Perpetua's face set up a desperate fluttering, like a bird on the point of being dispatched. Making a room comfortable in one's own house, that was one thing, but to buy shirts and shaving soap . . . Then Margery looked at her with that steadying, special look which was full of the wise, broad view of things, and which she usually reserved for youths she was about to sentence for three years' Borstal training, and Perpetua understood. She opened the little drawer under the looking-glass and displayed her father's set of razors, seven in a blue velvet case, one for each day of the week.

'Very thoughtful, dear,' said Margery, 'except a young man of twenty-four is bound to use a safety.'

Not long after this, perhaps not more than a month, Thomas was safely confined within the margins of a game. The actual rules remained implicit, mostly because both Margery and Perpetua disliked the idea that they were playing to rule, although it was hard to see how else they could play at the moment. Besides, the excitement came only in moments of over-play. Breathless after such a moment, and with a little creeper of veins suddenly appearing on the sides of her emphatic white nose, Perpetua would exclaim, 'What a couple of fools!' Meaning the two of them with whatever it was delivered to the room, which stayed damp and strictly uninhabited so far as it was concerned. During this time, each of them learned the great importance of the casual move. After all, Thomas was not a doll to be shaped and stuffed and attired, although it was his clothes which presented his first great test of faith. Their cost. It was scarcely credible. The Oxfam baby thrust at Margery with his broomstick legs and, with an urgency not entirely despicable, her car called for an exchange. There was money in the bank but there were also priorities.

Perpetua thought she was just being logical when she declared, 'If he is—you know what I mean, Marge—*if* he is, he would come first. Naturally.'

Margery flew at her.

'If! If?'

Perpetua flinched and then had a brainwave.

'I know! He can have some jeans and pullovers from Marks and Sparks.'

'Who can?'

'Tom. You know, that teenager we've got upstairs. Also, we'll have to get him a record-player and a motor-bike and . . .

'You've made your point, Perpetua. Tom or Thomas, we don't get him for nothing, is that it?'

Perpetua did not answer. She was staring at her friend with the

large faded eyes in which the vitality came and went like a faulty
street sign. 'Marge,' she whispered, 'I've got to know something.
Thom . . . as, is he . . .' Her brain began to throw out words for
Thomas and one of them rolled straight off her tongue. '*Is he a
gigolo?*'

There was a second when it looked as though Margery's stern
hand would strike Perpetua. Instead, her head bent down and
down until her face was so close to Perpetua's that all she could see
was a pouch of powdered fur. The pouch was open and through the
crimson slit she was screaming at Perpetua under her breath, a
sound so thin with temper that it hardly had the strength to be
heard. She imagined something like 'dirty bitch', except who could
believe that Margery would say words like that? Yet Margery had
got to be made upright and audible again. The slap set Perpetua's
hand stinging as if she had pushed it into nettles and all her fingers
had left a birthmark-pink negative on Margery's cheek. There was
lots of life in Perpetua's eyes now and a wonderful energy in her
painful hand. She would have liked to have slapped Margery
again and only kept herself from doing so with great difficulty.
After falling back in a chair in a frumpish sitting position, Margery
rose, looked at her watch and went out to the garage. The car
crunched round under the window and, whether out of saintliness
or habit, Margery toot-tooted. The pink fingers on her face had
turned into a kind of dahlia.

She drove to Hunter's right in the middle of the town and
bought a two-piece suit off the hook. Her behaviour was superb.
She was refusing to cheat, even when there was no one to watch
her. She took her time. She did not say it was for her nephew, nor
did she flinch when the proprietor, who was a colleague on the
Library Committee, bustled over to give her his special attention.
From her handbag she took a card on which were the sizes of an
eleven-stone man which she had copied from the Ideal Weight
Chart in a colour supplement.

'He really is stock!' remarked the assistant. 'They're usually
just stocky when they think they're stock, but he's *stock*, your
friend—husband, madam.'

She went on buying, shoes, socks, pyjamas, underwear, just one
of everything. The proprietor passed and re-passed with pro-

fessional indifference. The assistant now and then ran his tongue along the edge of his top teeth. When she had finished he stuck down the packages with Scotch tape on which was printed 'Everything a man needs'.

'There, everything,' he said.

She drove home and Perpetua helped her put the clothes away in Thomas's room. They worked silently in an atmosphere which was stifling at first but which later grew more and more lax, until by the time they returned to the warm drawing-room their peace had reached the stage of a delicious nervelessness. In the midst of tea, Perpetua, thinking of the pale colours, the fresh blues and greys, said,

'He's fair then?'

Margery nodded and answered, 'Is that all right?'

'Oh, perfectly,' said Perpetua. 'Marvellous,' she added.

'All so excellently fair!'

'Is that a quotation?'

'Coleridge,' said Margery. Swallowing a mouthful of cake and staring at Perpetua with eyes which said, nosey-parker-there-won't-be-any-peace-until-I-tell-you, she murmured, 'Alfred was small and dark.'

'None of Thomas's things would have fitted him, then?'

'No,' answered Margery. Her voice rose and broke on the word. It seemed to fill her with tumultuous relief. The cruel double-vision of the past few weeks (of which she had bravely not complained to a single soul) vanished as she spoke this resolute syllable and she was back once more to the big plain outline which constituted her usual view of life. Could it be the Change? If it was, she did not intend to tell Perpetua. And even if some such logical excuse for her recent behaviour was not forthcoming, what was there to get upset about? She thought she had been using her imagination in helping others but it was obvious now that some other faculty had been involved all these years and that imagination, or whatever one liked to call it, had been suppressed, causing it to burst out now. These and other arguments for her conduct raced through her mind while at the same time she heard her tongue carrying on a reasonable conversation with Perpetua. She had frankly changed the subject and was describing that morning's embarrassment when Dr Cleary's wife had appeared before her for shoplifting, but Perpetua's huffiness and displeasure could be felt long before Margery got to the part about the court's civilized attitude to the tragedy.

'What's wrong?' she demanded, halting the recital and similarly bringing the analyses, all various, of why she should have gone into the village shop, of all places, and bought a dozen hankerchief's initialled T, to a standstill.

'I know what you're getting at,' said Perpetua. 'I'm not a fool. But just speak for yourself—that's all!'

'I'm speaking about poor Mrs Cleary.'

'Are you—are you sure?'

It was on the tip of Margery's tongue to have the matter settled there and then, but this seemed too harsh in view of what had happened. *What* had happened? A psychiatrist or a parson could offer a thesis if they were asked, no doubt, but what was the use of this when she had the answer within herself and only needed the courage to exhume it! She had been off her chump and old Perp had been damned decent about it. She'd find out why if it meant digging down to Australia! Excelsior! She leaned over and patted her friend on the knee. 'Don't worry, it's all right!' Her big smile ruled everything. 'It's *all right*. . . .'

In her room that night she delved into what she supposed would be termed her subconscious. It was a process or deed which she found quite repulsive but she did it gladly, knowing now that she did it for others. A banana-like moon dangled outside the window, picking out the furniture with its feeble mocking light. Now, what is it all about? Margery asked herself. It was 16 April, 1936, wasn't it? Yes. Why should you be so certain of this— because it was the day after . . . (Yes, go on) after Alfred's funeral. (Doesn't that explain it? Who behaves normally after their husband's funeral; you were not yourself.) I *was* myself, my dreadful, dreadful self! (Nonsense!) No nonsense about it; I obliterated him. (But men don't live on in their 'effects', as the law describes them. You could have given his clothes to a tramp— plenty of tramps in 1936—but they would have gone just the same. Why are you accusing yourself?) I'm not accusing myself, I'm seeing myself. (You looked a bit daft, that was all.) I looked . . . I

looked wicked . . . (Oh, for God's sake!) *I did!*
'Did you call?' asked Perpetua through the closed door.
'Goodnight.'
'Goodnight . . .!'
Then it was the day after Alfred's funeral and she was in the semi-detached in Reading, opening windows at first to get rid of the stench of the wreaths and then opening Alfred's wardrobe, and his chest of drawers, and his stud-box, and his Minty book-case, where his school prizes were only separated from Roman Law by a run of Sappers, and then she was carting all this stuff into the garden in order to get it *out of the house*. There was a mountain of it. She had to run backwards and forwards half the day before Alfred was out, all out. Marrying her and then dying! Dying all the time they were married and then—dead. And all this stuff to hide his flimsiness: golf clubs, and fishing rods, and the Hilary term photograph with Alfred fourteenth along in the back row, and, help! one of those B.S.A. bicycles with a laced-up chain case—what on earth was she to do with that? Oh, the horror of seeing his suits in flames and his braces jumping in the heat like snakes. His shoes sizzled like meat and his umbrella burned like a martyr, cloth first then ribs. The explosion of his watch in the incandescent glory which such mediocre possessions had so strangely created really did mark the end of Alfred. It was beautiful, poetic! Margery had told herself at the time. Although it could not have been for else how could she have spent thirty years repenting her bonfire? She now forced herself to recall every memorable minute of it with such completeness and totality that she was left charred and ashen herself. Poor Alfred! He had made her put it all back. Had haunted her, she supposed. She tried to think of him, of what he looked like, but all she could see were a pair of rather stubby hands and heavy shaving shadow. Pig! she told herself. She must sleep now. Tomorrow she must talk to Perpetua.

*

Her intention had been an honest confrontation, a clean break, but these were checked by the daring of Perpetua's latest move. She had picked up the letters from the mat in the usual way and was waiting for Margery to sit down at the breakfast table before sorting them out. Margery sat, her relief smothered in foreboding. The bulk of the letters were for her, as usual. Two were for her friend but there were two more, and these Perpetua placed against the toast-rack. Her brow was shiny with achievement and a pulse throbbed busily in her naked throat.

'Oh, no!'

Margery's despair sounded like wonder to Perpetua; that was the way she was thinking. 'Of course, I had to give him a surname first,' she said.

The letters were circulars from *Reader's Digest,* and the National Gardens Scheme, and they were addressed to Thomas Home, Esq., Penault Fayre, Flint Drive, Ipswich.

'But what the hell will the postman think ?'

'Its pronounced Hume.'

'Perp, concentrate!' Margery's disappointment was making her shout. 'What are they going to say at the Post Office when they sort my letters and then, er, his ?'

'What does Mrs Ellis say when you buy all the pipe tobacco ?'

'He is going to give up smoking,' said Margery meanly. And we are going to give Thomas up, she longed to add, but she needed time to explain all this and she had to be in the centre of the town by nine-thirty. I'll tell her tonight, she thought. She was sitting in the car and rubbing a space in the dust on the windscreen with Kleenex when Perpetua's pleading face appeared.

'Smoking is one of his few pleasures,' she said accusingly.

Margery did her best to see beyond the mask—it must be mask, surely ?—Perpetua was a bit withdrawn, as they called, but she wasn't daffy. Nothing showed. It was Perpetua's ordinary bare morning face before she covered it up with cosmetics.

'But the expense, darling. . . .'

'He can afford it. You seem to forget he earns two thousand a year.'

'At twenty-four ?'

'Yes. It's great, isn't it! He's going a long way, that boy. You'll see!'

'I must get on, too,' said Margery, tugging at the choke. The waste and destruction had found its way into the lighthouse and was thundering around. There was a seething and bursting disorder. 'What am I going to do?' she asked the Golly mascot bobbing against the window. '*I* don't know what to do!' She felt ponderous and stupid. This feeling reminded her of her childhood and the dismal realization of being too big to join the game. She drove past the old part of the cemetery where the gravestones staggered about like bad teeth. That was what Alfred's grave was like she imagined. She had not been near it since the day of the funeral, although she had got them to put up a cross. She could be a sentimental old hypocrite and go and see it, she supposed. Perpetua needn't know. And, anyway, it would get her away from the house. The idea hardened into an intention. The uproar in her head died down. The policeman on traffic control saluted her trimly and received her commending nod. I acknowledge you, too, Alfred, she thought. I do—Guide's honour!

That evening she explained her plan with deliberate vagueness to Perpetua.

'Just a couple of days in Berkshire, you know. Take the car, look around. . . .'

'Visit old haunts?' added Perpetua. 'Oh, I don't mind, I've got lots to do. I'm out all Saturday evening, anyway. They're doing *The Knack* at the Rep. Thomas is going to be away too.'

'Is he?' said Margery with automatic interest. She could have bitten off her tongue. She heard Perpetua telling her, with incredible elaboration and conviction, how Thomas was going bird-watching at Minsmere and how pleased he was with his new field-glasses.

'How much were they?' she asked shakily.

'Its no use having a cheap pair,' countered Perpetua.

'How much?'

Perpetua was offended. 'You'd better ask Thomas.'

'Listen—listen! You've got to listen. There isn't a Thomas. Do you understand? *No Thomas*. He doesn't exist, he didn't exist. Ever.'

'I understand all too well,' answered Perpetua coldly. 'You decide when people exist and when they don't—or even if they ever did. Like your husband.'

Margery felt the raw blush eating its way up her neck and across her face, making her ridiculous and hideous. It was the 'your husband', the implacable relationship between Alfred and herself. Perpetua saw the ugly blood-flooded skin and was immediately shocked and contrite. She couldn't apologize: her lips twitched soundlessly. But her eyes were strained with regret and her hand flew out to Margery's like a cold white bird and held it awkwardly. Margery squeezed it. How were you to know where the most naked nerve lay? she was telling her friend in this rare contact. She went upstairs to pack. What on earth did one wear for a night in Reading? She would drive out to the Downs afterwards or perhaps to Windsor and look at the Castle. When she got home on Sunday she would set to work on the whole problem, even if it meant talking to Dr Healey.

The drive down was easy, miraculously easy, it taking her a little under four and half hours to reach April 1936. For the dim road took the same twists to the cemetery and the weathercock on the chapel spire caught her eye just as it had then. The evergreen smell and the sharp gravel under foot were identical. Countless little numbers inscribed on tabs shaped like the ace of clubs sprouted in the grass, making her think, as she had then, in big, sad, obvious and satisfying terms of mortality. She made her way instinctively, pride refusing to let her inquire at the office as to the whereabouts of the grave. She remembered it as being a long way and she also recalled passing a remarkable stone, a kind of undertaker's Rock of Ages which looked as though it weighed a ton. And there it was, only riven. Or something had happened to it. It was fallen on its back with its wet base stuck with snails for all to see. Other monuments were cavorting themselves with equal abandon. They had toppled and cracked or simply gaped, as at the Resurrection. And suddenly the cemetery was not silent any more but was full of struggling, gesticulating men, talking and writing things down. Bewildered, her heart thudding, Margery walked through their midst to Alfred's grave. His cross had snapped off and the marble wound shone frostily in the sun. A fringe of sour grass hid Alfred's name. She knelt and pulled it up by the roots. 'Alfred Nethersole,' she read. Said. Many times. The men clambering about near her drew back. They included two policemen and a photographer. It's all right, Alfred, thought Margery, they think I'm praying, I expect. But I'm apologizing. I'm sorry.

She tried to remember Alfred's face and a vacant splodgy horrible thing wordlessly introduced itself. She saw for the first time the extent of her destruction. Pity struck her like a brand.

'Alfred!'

A policeman and a workman were leading her to a seat. They guided her feet round scattered lumps of granite and through crushed flowers. She could hear the larks singing against a babble of indignation.

'What happened?' she asked.

'Vandals,' said the policeman shortly.

'Must want a job!' said the workman. 'I mean desecrating the dead, what could be worse than that?'

*

Perpetua began to dress for the theatre at six. Margery always laughed at this 'dressing' which wasn't dressing in fact but a glorified fixing and arranging of Perpetua's ordinary quiet clothes, and the addition of a gold bangle and a fob watch, plus her mother's rings. 'All for Ipswich!' she would mock, only kindly. What she failed to realize was the importance to Perpetua of what preceded the dressing, her spoiling, as she liked to describe it to herself. She bathed and did her nails and pumiced the little depilated patches on her legs. She took her time to fix her well and carefully dyed hair—tinted, she called it—in a clever facsimile of Katherine Mansfield's fringe and chignon. They could have been sisters, somebody once said years and years ago. But mostly she sank into a leisurely and unconceited appraisal of her own flesh. Its contours beneath the blanched, glowless skin had an arrested, immaculate quality. The immutability made her so grateful. None of the taken-for-granted things had happened to it. Women of her age—fifty-three—resigned themselves to appendicitis scars, Caesarean puckers, limp breasts and livid groups of vaccination marks but she was untouched. She wore a sleeveless navy-blue sheath and her three-strand pearls. She felt—it was one of her favourite words—svelte.

The novelty of being alone at Penault Fayre pleased her. She walked about trimly in her high court shoes putting out lights and checking the heating gauges. A mackintosh hanging in the hall

made her think, 'Thomas!' Her cool and certain feeling at once
left her and a troubled exciting sensation took its place. Her
eyes widened and her hand reached for her necklace in a swift
guarded gesture. She could feel her breasts against her bare arm;
they disturbed her by their new sense of obvious largeness and
warmth. She was no longer svelte, with its concomitant reassur-
ances of grace and restraint, she was perspiring freely and her
suspender-belt seemed to drag and claw at her legs. Thomas's
room was dank—it was always dank, whatever one did to it. It was
on the sad side of the house. She opened the lower sash and the
early spring-night smell came pouring in. A pair of tangerine
coloured pyjamas lay on the bed. She tucked them under the
pillow to keep them from getting damp. The open book on the
bedside table was *Born Free*. She closed it, marking the place with
an envelope. At the bottom of the long drive, just before she turned
to walk up the lane to the bus-stop, she glanced back and thought
how lonely the house looked and yet how rarely she left it. 'I don't
touch it, somehow,' she told herself. 'But Thomas does—he's
there all the time, even when he is at Minsmere. I know it and
Margery knows it. . . .'

The Rep let her down—or she let it down, what did it matter,
the fact was that what she had come for and what she was offered
bore no relationship in her mind—and this was a habit it tended to
repeat. She felt stupid sitting in the front stalls with a group of
mostly middle-aged women with blued hair and powdered necks,
and watching a boy and a girl in jeans bickering on a mattress. She
had 'gone to the theatre'. Such an action suggested some kind of
magic and beauty in return for her money but the girl, who was
grubby and plain, was shrilling, 'Rape! Rape! Rape!' like an ulula-
ting native. At least Margery wouldn't be waiting with the Horlicks all ready and a 'I can't think why you go if you don't like it'
and her own mean answer of, 'If I stop going to the Rep I
wouldn't go anywhere!' She smiled her way through the departing
regulars in the foyer and got a taxi. The short drive home was the
biggest treat of the evening. Instead of Horlicks, she gave herself
a whisky, then made up the Aga. A hint of the happiness she had
felt earlier on returned. It was a joy and a privilege, as her mother
would have said, to have a real home. Not a flat or one of those

estate developer's boxes but Penault Fayre on its tree-swathed hill with its rich Victorian decorations and silence.

Silence. That was because of no Margery and thus perfectly understandable. And no Thomas. Only herself. She filled a hot-water bottle and went upstairs. Owly was calling—she must tell Margery. Pussies were sound. That *daft* play—and after all those marvellous reviews she had read! There was a scraping noise and then a creak. She listened intently and heard it again. Thomas's window! She had left it open. With the zip of her dress open at the side to reveal a long petal-like slash in the tight silk, she hurried next door.

The light blazed before she touched the switch. She saw the pyjamas first, more and more of them until their waving brilliance seemed to fill the room, and then the door slammed behind her and her head was being thrust back into the choking folds of the dressing-gown hanging against it. 'Thomas! Thomas! Thomas!' she shrieked against a barrier of gagging wool. What was the use? she asked herself just as she thought she would faint. Who could hear? Then her face was free and she was panting and gulping in the close stale air, and words, like a whispered shout, were beating against her ear.

'How did you know? How did you find out? Who told you? *Who told you?*'

'Thomas . . .' she gasped weakly.

'You heard it on telly, didn't you? Didn't you?'

Oddly enough, the blow steadied her. She struggled up from the floor with an elaborate knowledge of what she was doing. She heard Thomas say, 'I'm sorry about that, missus, but you asked for it and you got it.' She could see his face now, fair and damp and rather tired. His hair stood up in a ferocious spike and his blue eyes maintained a constant vivid motion. He was nearly pretty but hard. 'Now, missus,' he was saying.

'Miss—Miss Cranmer.'

'Listen, old doll, how'd you find out? Tell me.'

'This is Thomas's room and so you are Thomas.'

The blue eyes ceased their mad dancing and became fixed and still. She returned their flat concentration and repeated, 'You-are-Thomas. Aren't you?'

'I see,' he said, his voice quiet and drifting now, 'I'm Thomas and this is my room, is that it? Let's get things right. Is that it? Is it?'

She nodded, relieved. She had subsided into a crouched sitting position at the foot of the bed.

'And what happens in Thomas's room, eh? I bet you haven't seen Thomas lately, have you?' He laughed. His mouth with its wet red flesh and fine teeth hanging over her had the richness of a cave. The laugh stopped abruptly and her head was being forced to look down at something which lay in the palm of Thomas's hand. It was one of her father's razors. It was open and rocked lazily to and fro against the life-line. 'Just so you realize,' Thomas told her. 'Because I've got to eat and if you touch the phone or call out . . .' and he drew the blade in a flashing little arc just above her pearls. What would Margery do? she wondered. She knew what Margery would say—something sensible.

'Get back into bed,' she said. 'You're getting cold.'

'Or cool, perhaps. Like you, eh?'

He put the dressing-gown on and then the slippers. The clothes pulled him together somehow.

'Are you an American?' she asked. His accent slipped about and worried her, the voice avoiding identity, as it were.

He looked vaguely pleased and said, 'Lead the way, lady,' like a Hollywood gunman.

She broke two eggs into the pan. 'Go on until I say when,' he murmured, standing close behind her. She broke another and he said, 'When.' She also cooked some bacon and fried bread. The greasy breakfast smell in the middle of the night—it was only a little after eleven, actually, but the twin sensations of strain and ordinary behaviour reminded Perpetua of the war, which always went on most after bedtime—revolted her. She had to make a great effort not to be sick. The heat from the Aga met her in waves and she gripped the rail unsteadily. When he first touched her she thought it must be to stop her from falling. Then she felt the hand inside her dress, rapid, searching.

'Don't,' she breathed.

'Not now—later? Is that what you mean?'

She remained rigid, hardly able to create a pulse-beat. That this could—would—*must* happen to her was unbelievable. Had never entered her thoughts. She must protest, explain. He had to understand! She turned and shook her head soundlessly. He kissed her and wiped his mouth on his cuff.

'Say thank you,' he said. '*Say thank you!*'

'Thank you.'

She watched him eat. The eggs disappeared in halves and afterwards he ate a lot more bread and a whole pile of fruit. Perpetua had never seen anyone eat so in her life before; it was animal but it wasn't ugly. The cats had woken up and sat blinking and detached. He threw them scraps and they ignored them.

'This is a nice loving house,' he said, 'a real nice loving house.'

She sat staring, sometimes at the young man, sometimes at the grain ridges of the table, wondering what to say. Now and again he caught her look and once he winked, an incredibly coarse gesture in the context of his rather blank good looks. She picked up his plate and carried it to the sink. She had fastened her dress and now she began to wash up with mechanical efficiency. He sat watching her with languid patience but when she turned to the Aga with a damp cloth, he dragged it from her hand and said,

'Uh-Uh! That's enough.'

She flew at him. Her hands thumped against his chest, making his laughter jerky and breathless. 'No-no-no-no-no!' she was shouting, just like somebody she had heard recently. It was the heroine in the play. He caught both her wrists at last and held her away from him, easily and conceitedly without apparent effort. Speaking quietly and in a natural Midlands voice, his mouth parted in a deliberately sweet smile, he said, 'Listen, doll. Who came into Thomas's room stinking of scent and whisky with her dress all undone? But never mind *that*. Who is stupid enough to let a scared old girl go charging off to the neighbours?—that is what we have to consider.'

'I wouldn't betray you, Thomas.'

'You won't get the chance to, doll.'

Grasping her shoulder with one hand, he switched off the lights and, in a dream, she accompanied him up the stairs and into the spare room. He transferred the key and locked the door. Then he pulled off the dressing-gown and slid into bed. 'I leave at six,' he said. 'What are you going to do ?'

Perpetua stood looking down at him, quite motionless. She was conscious of the cold stippling the skin on her arms and of a sour distinctive smell from which there was no escape. Disturbed birds scuttered in the guttering outside. The young man breathed with a profound regularity and depth which suggested near-sleep; it was nearly one o'clock. I can't just stand here, she thought. I can't just stand in this room for five hours! Her fear had gone and she now felt the incredulous annoyance of someone who had lost the last train and for whom there was no other choice but to sit on a bench until it was light. Her unbelief communicated itself to the young man and he grinned. Then he put an arm outside the bedclothes and patted the space by his side. Total refusal seemed to make her enormous. She thought she must look absurd, horrible, and bent forward in a mixed gesture of attempted recovery and extenuation. His hand reached out and grasped her arm.

'You *can't* stand there all night, can you now ?' he said.

She shook her head. She couldn't. For one thing there was the terrible light bulb swooping out of the ceiling and almost hypnotizing her with its harsh filament, though most of all there was the cold. There was, too, her draining will-power which was reducing her reactions to a puppet's responses. This could not be happening to her, *it could not*, thus how could she greatly care ? She switched off the light and lay beside him. All the landmarks of her conscious identity were obscured. She was crashing through a black and fantastic forest where tense and unwanted sensations were thrust upon her. Her hair was torn and pressed across her face and sometimes she was eating it. There was invasion and outrage and sometimes the most ordinary conversation as though nothing had happened—was happening—at all. For instance he said, 'I shall have to change sides, my arm has gone to sleep,' and she said, 'I'll put the hot-water bottle on the floor; that'll give us more room.' The birds chuck-chucked and clawed the eave the whole time. The room wasn't properly dark because the grey night seeped through the comfortless unlined curtains. She could see her pearls, phosphorescent on the dressing-table, and her stockings, pale as dust. She could not sleep—wouldn't ever sleep again—but he slept. He hissed faintly and sadly and occasionally caught his breath in a muted sob like a baby. The hours dawdled by, taking every second of their time and with them wandered the vast unwanted leisure of her thoughts. No recollection of any happening in her life occurred to her without a full-scale analysis becoming attached to it. Margery appeared and reappeared in her relentlessly exposed confidence as a great shutter, a wall, a dense hedge, a swooping baton commanding her occasionally ranging free-notes to cease. There was no longer anything to feel grateful for. She ate, breathed, that was all. So did a maggot.

Cocks were crowing now. How medieval that sounded and who ever listened? The morning lay deserts of time away and so far without a hint of an horizon. Where their bodies touched there was careless moist agreement, the kind of humanity which the flesh itself took for granted. Not because of this but because her tumbling dreams made her uneasy, she dragged herself up into a sitting position, saw, incredibly, her breasts like suns and snuggled down again. She could see him lying in profile with his lips slightly parted and silver spit glittering as he whispered his way through sleep. He smelled acrid, institutional. Where had she noticed this odour before? In a class-room? No, in Nissen huts during the war. That was it. During the war and during the year she spent in the W.A.A.F. before Margery got her out with 'pull'.

'What are you doing?' he asked without moving, without opening his eyes.

'Only getting comfortable.'

'I was asleep.'

'I'm sorry.'

'You keep on being sorry, don't you? Life is just life. You don't change it or stop it by being sorry.' His eyes were still closed. The mouth was hardly enough awake to frame the words.

'I'm sorry . . .' she began before she could stop herself.

He giggled, turned to her and pulled her against him.

'There you go.'

'Are you never sorry then?'

There was a pause this time, not his usual snap response. 'Not now—not yet, is what I mean. But I will be. I mean you can't live and sit still, and if you live you make things happen. Funny things sometimes. Good things and bad things.'

'You're quite a philosopher,' she said without irony. Yet the remark displeased him. He turned from her abruptly and even in the uncertain glaucous haze of earliest morning, with the things in the room mere hulks of darkness, she caught the look on his face as a hardening of the mouth and eyes thinned the expression down to the mean and glinting one she had seen in the kitchen. But now, instead of fear, she felt pity. She patted his shoulder and then his hair. Awkwardly.

'Go to sleep,' he said. 'You got what you wanted, didn't you?'

Incredibly, she did sleep. The merciless images chasing one after the other through her brain tore away into blankness like a fractured film. She awoke to the inconsiderate sound of the bath running and of drawers being opened and slammed shut. He was robbing, of course. She clutched her hands together and felt the rings. Her necklace and her watch lay where she had left them. What was it then?

'What are you looking for?' she called.

'Blades.'

'They're here—in the little drawer under the mirror.'

He chatted while he dressed.

'You'll be on that buzzer to them the minute I've gone, won't you, doll?'

'The . . . police?'

'The police,' he mimicked. He was pulling clothes out of the wardrobe, feeling the material of the suit, choosing socks. She might not have been present. 'And then,' he said, 'when you've told them all they'll want to know, you will be a very interesting lady in the neighbourhood. You think about that, doll. Think of the look on the beak's face!'

'Where will you go?' she asked.

'Harwich, maybe: get on a boat.' He put on the jacket and turned to face her. 'There now, how do I look? More like Thomas?' He looked transformed.

'Things could be better for you if you got abroad.'

'A new start?' he mocked. 'But better than never making a start, eh? Poor old doll!'

Her eyes filled with tears. She lay there letting them roll to the sides of her upturned face. She had not removed her make-up and scraps of it still adhered to her skin with cruel irrelevance.

'Poor old doll . . .' he repeated thoughtfully, staring down at her. He left the room and returned with her handbag. He must have noticed it lying on the dresser last night, she told herself. 'Now *I* am sorry about this,' he said, handing it to her, 'but we can't spoil the sailor for a haporth of tar, can we?' She gave him five pounds. 'I'd better have a spot of loose, too,' he said. 'For the bus.'

'There's some silver in the baker's jar on the dresser.'

'Thanks.'

She looked past him, deliberately not seeing him.

'I did ask,' he reminded her. 'I asked, you asked . . . for what was there for the asking.'

'Go away—*go*!'

She heard the back door bang and hurried to the window. He was swinging down the drive. After a few yards she saw him stop, glance back at the house and shake his head incredulously. She went into the bathroom. There was water everywhere, grey suddy water in the primrose basin and still steaming water in the bath itself. Blobs of shaving soap spattered the floor. Her immediate thought was to clear everything up before Margery returned—in time for lunch, she said. What was she going to tell her when she discovered that the clothes had gone? What was she going to tell her anyway? Would Margery go to the police? In a way she was the police. Her imagination reeling, Perpetua began to clean and tidy, at first with a certain plodding efficiency but after a little while with an unnatural rush which made her clumsy and confused. Soon she was running about the place, frenziedly putting it to rights. She was brought to a halt, not by the actual surprise, but by the harsh confirmation of the bundle which lay under the bed. The shoes were worn down at the heel and the trousers and jacket of thick grey flannel were each stencilled on the inside with 'Thomas, J. N.' and his prison number. There was a striped, collarless shirt and a pair of grey socks with reddish sweat-stained soles. She carried them into the garden, holding them away from her. Her face was now dragged into a knot of hysterical loathing. That it was of herself merely intensified the revulsion. She envied the brilliant simplicity with which the foul things and the foolish things, the prison uniform and what was left of 'Thomas', pulverized in the flames. The bed-clothes roared their purification and blazed thankfully in a tent of light. When it was all over, when the room was stripped and it and her strength had been crushed, Perpetua crouched in it. Her mother's rings itched on her scorched hands and ashes powdered her brow. She wasn't weeping when Margery found her. Just sitting still and thinking that there was no substance in her life to burn anyway.

Margery looked at the smuts, looked at the hollow spaces and then saw the murderous smoke blowing outside in the garden.

'Alfred . . . Alfred . . .' she said.

THE ETERNAL AMATEUR

by D. G. Compton

It was lucky really that the end wall of the west wing finally fell out early in June, since this gave us the whole summer in which to see about getting it mended. None of us was living in the wing at the time—not even the less domesticated children—but the missing wall was nevertheless visible from the drive and my wife decided that it would give visiting tradesmen the wrong impression. (Or the right one, depending on your viewpoint.) So a working party comprising Mr Pennington-Ashleye and some of the older children was started, using sand and cement and stones, and some pieces of timber from the old stable block.

Great-great-great-grandfather, for whom the west wing had always formed a favourite stamping ground, was as usual of no help at all. He resented bitterly the changes in his routine that the work made necessary. In his view everything should go on in exactly the same way for ever—after all, he intended to. Almost hourly he would come to me with complaints: about the noise, about Mr Pennington-Ashleye, about the dirt, about Mr Pennington-Ashleye, about the children, about Mr Pennington-Ashleye again. It was hard to make great-great-great-grandfather understand how much times had changed, that Mr Pennington-Ashleye was not the product of a press gang, and that both keel-hauling and suspension from the yard-arm were no longer strictly legal. I began to dread the thunderous stamping that heralded great-great-great-grandfather's approach.

'Willy ? Willy—ah, *there* you are.'

I was rarely anywhere else.

'What's the matter now, Grandfather ?' As usual, he had chosen a bad moment. 'I am rather busy, you know.'

'It's that cur Ashleye. Rank insolence. He's just asked me for a "borrow of my telescope".'

'I'm sure he wasn't serious. He knows the old and the new

don't mix.'

'Some bird in the woods away to the nor'-nor'-east,' he said. The old man peered over my shoulder at what I was doing. 'When I offered to attempt an identification myself he had the nerve to call me a dirty old man.'

'It's a contemporary phrase, grandfather. Quite harmless.'

'Personally I'd never have suspected him of knowing the difference between a gannet and an albatross.' He jangled his medals and pointed down at the table. 'Bishop to King's four,' he said. 'Pins the Queen so you can come in on the beam with your Knight.'

'Thank you very much, Grandfather.' He only does it to annoy me, so I try not to give him that evil satisfaction. 'Actually I was considering a subtler move with the King's Rook's Pawn.'

'No future in it, Willy. What you want is the big guns, bang-bang-bang. And don't try to side-track me. Ashleye will have to go.'

A distant rumble of falling masonry seemed to indicate that Ashleye had already gone.

'He means well, Grandfather. Just young—a bit high-spirited and all that.' I considered the old man's suggested move. 'We'll get him to wear his hair back in a cue—take you back to your days on the quarterdeck.'

'You don't patch a rotten timber, Willy—you tear it out.'

Bishop to King's four was undoubtedly the answer. If I won the book token I'd have to share it with Grandfather. I wrote the move on a postcard, addressed the card and left it on the hall table to go with the other letters. In a day or two somebody would probably remember to post them. I rarely won anything, but the possibility had kept me going through many a rainy fortnight.

'I'll have a word with him at once, Grandfather. I'm sure he didn't mean any harm.'

'Weak, Willy. You're like your father. And his father before him. And the one before that, whatever his name was. God knows where they got it from. . . .'

The stamping departed in the direction of the library. It has always surprised me how such very noisy footsteps can manage to leave no mark at all in the dust and the toffee papers over which they pass.

I decided to approach the west wing from the garden side, in case Mr Pennington-Ashleye's efforts had seriously weakened the remaining structure. Some of the children were sliding down a large heap of rubble, out of the side of which projected buckled winkle-pickers and two short lengths of Day-glo sock. Other larger children were gathered round a cracked transistor radio, trying to make it work. A broken ladder leaned against the five-hundred-year oak, and several pieces of bent scaffolding.

I suggested tentatively that we might dig out Mr Pennington-Ashleye. I was told that his other end was breathing very nicely.

Walking round to the far side of the pile of rubble, I discovered that this was indeed so. Mr Pennington-Ashleye's head and shoulders had been protected by a window frame wedged diagonally. He had his eyes shut, and he was softly whistling some way-out progression to himself—trying it for size, as he called it.

His manner irritated me, and I shook a scurfy shoulder.

'Man, don't bug me.' He opened his eyes. 'It's Lord William. I thought it was one of the kids.' He indicated the weight of rubble on his chest. 'It's done it again,' he said. 'I reckon we can't of got the angle right somewhere.'

'Pennington-Ashleye, you've been taking the mickey out of the Admiral. This makes life difficult for all of us and I wish you wouldn't.'

Nothing weak about that, I thought.

'Christ—the old man gives me the needle. "That wall's crooked," he says. "They didn't build walls like that in my day," he says. Lucky I didn't put the boot in, I say.'

'It seems to me he was probably right,' I murmured, unsnagging my plus-fours from the end of a splintered floor-board.

'There's some things a real gent just don't say, Lord W.' He closed his eyes again, the better to concentrate on his whistling.

At this point an explanation of Mr Pennington-Ashleye's position in my family is probably advisable. By deeply felt moral convictions the young man was a layabout. Speaking of the debt the older generation owed him for the mess the world is in, he claimed as his just due everything that the Welfare State had to offer. This idealistic attitude however was in direct conflict with his naturally industrious temperament. He was a man who could not bear to be idle for a moment. An early riser, he was—like myself—never happy unless fully occupied. So he worked as general handyman for Lady Clewes and myself, on the strict understanding that he never received a penny in wages: in this way he remained technically unemployed, fully eligible for National Assistance, and receiving in full the debt Society owed him.

Unfortunately the friendly basis of his employment did allow him a certain degree of freedom in his relations with the family. In particular with great-great-great-grandfather, who invariably treated him like some recalcitrant midshipman. Thus I myself was always between the devil of not wishing to lose Mr Pennington-Ashleye's free services and the deep blue sea of great-great-great-grandfather's recurrent exacerbation.

Leaving the young man to be dug out in due course by the children, I returned to Grandfather. I found him in the library with my wife.

'I've spoken to Ashleye, Grandfather. He says he's very sorry. He has no head for heights, and he says being up the ladder must have made him delirious. He doesn't know what can have come over him.'

'Lout like that ought to be up reefing the royals. Soon see if he was delirious or not. I've scraped better than him off the poop.'

It will be clear by now that the old Admiral was a thoroughly exaggerated character. This was inevitable—a hundred and fifty years of repetition had caricatured his vocabulary and attitudes beyond all reason. Which accounts for the ludicrous over-playing of ghosts in general.

'Anyway, Grandfather, I doubt if he'll be up the ladder to bother you again. After this morning's fall it seems to be rather broken.'

'Which raises the only relevant point in all this shim-sham.' Lady Clewes snapped her teeth and got out a ball-point pen. She counted notches on its barrel. 'Today marks the fifth time that the construction methods of Mr Pennington-Ashleye and the children have proved faulty. It will soon be winter. We must face the fact, William, that not only the west wing but the whole house is urgently in need of repair. Things fall off it continually. Small things, admittedly—gargoyles, cornices, chimney copings—but these are but symptomatic of a deeper malaise.' She clicked the pen's point in and out several times, like a snake's tongue. 'Something will have to be done,' she said.

Thora is a great believer in getting things done. As for her own person, she gets that done yearly in one encyclopedic visit to a beautician in Cheltenham Spa. I gazed at her, trying absent-mindedly to gauge how near she was to her next overhaul.

'I shall speak to the children,' I said. 'If they can be persuaded to climb about the upper parts of the house exterior for a day or two, that ought to dislodge any loose particles. Mr Pennington-Ashleye can sweep up the pieces and construct some sort of rockery with them outside the servants' hall.'

'You have a superficial mind, William. What of the deeper malaise?'

Great-great-great-grandfather snorted. He'd been out of the conversation for so long that if I'd thought about it I'd have said he was failing.

'You beat about the bush, Henrietta. Plain fact of the matter is the old Chase is falling to pieces. Another five years and there won't be one stone left standing.'

Henrietta was one of my father's aunts. Grandfather has been dead too long to care.

'Not one stone left standing, Henrietta. Won't worry me, of course. To me the old house is just as it always was. Which is the only reason I stay.'

He went out through the door. If you know what I mean. I turned to Thora.

'Perhaps I ought to ask Mr Pennington-Ashleye to buy a plumbline and some more cement.'

'He is not a builder by trade, William. And the children are as little use at construction work as they are at anything else. We need professional advice, and professional craftsmanship.'

'I quite agree, my dear.' Not even great-great-great-grandfather disagrees with Lady Clewes. 'I'm rather busy myself—several pressing matters to attend to. Would you see to it for me, Thora my dear?'

I returned to my study and to the correspondence with Podolkin.

My reply to his last was already three days overdue. Rook to Queen's Knight's three. It contained overtones of Weng T'eng Fu that were going to take some meeting.

The followed Tuesday I was still considering my answer to Podolkin when Lady Clewes entered the room, propelled from behind by a small man in a blue bib and brace. He carried a tee-square and something faintly resembling a sextant. He was obviously a man with a flair for joists and a real genius for under-pinning. He had a pencil behind each ear and one of his shoes was calibrated in inches with white paint.

'William—this is Mr Struss. I've asked him to give us his advice on restoring the Chase. He's quite an expert in these matters.'

'Blenheim, Hampton Court, Chatsfield—you name 'em, I've saved 'em.'

We shook hands convulsively. I suggested that the Chase was perhaps too humble to be worthy of his attention.

'Be it ne-er so humble, my Lord, there's no place like home. And a home what's fell down is no good to man nor beast. Struss to the rescue!'

Rallied a little by his battle-cry, I followed him on an inspection of the house. His cheerfulness as he scribbled in a big red book was infectious. Everything about the house that had seemed pre-viously to be a cause for deep depression now took on a new light. The dismal crack in the portrait gallery wall prompted in Mr Struss a happily hummed rendering of the 'Post Horn Gallop'. The sag in the roof of the Great Hall made him do something amounting to a small dance. While the smell that came as we passed the door to the cellars caused him to embrace Lady Clewes and kiss her on both cheeks. I was cheered. The man was an optimist, an enthusiast, a continental, a man after my own heart.

As we were on our way along the passage to the only leaning billiard room in Britain—'In the world I'm sure, your Lordship—if you don't mind my correcting you'—we met great-great-great-grandfather. I made the introductions.

'Grandfather, this is Mr Struss who is going to help us mend the Chase. Mr Struss, this is Admiral Lord Clewes, seventh Baron Clewes.'

'He doesn't look very strong,' the old man remarked. 'I should send the bailiff out for someone a little sturdier, if I were you.'

Mr Struss was unabashed. Perhaps his previous employers at Blenheim, Hampton Court and Chatsworth had been equally feudal.

'It's not brawn that counts on a job like this, my Lord. It's brains. The proper harnessing of the modern miracles of science. You've no idea what can't be done with pumped concrete.'

For myself, I could think of dozens of things that couldn't be done with pumped concrete, and hardly a single one that could. Great-great-great-grandfather was similarly unimpressed. He eyed the tools of Mr Struss's trade with open scorn.

'If you are planning to take a bearing on the sun, Mr Struss—that was the name, I believe?—I can refer you to the astrolabe under the observatory dome. If you know how to use it. The house lies three points north of due west, and the height above sea-level (God bless it!) is—'

'The house ain't going to lie three points north of anything at all, your Lordship, if you don't let me get in soon with the old pumped concrete.' Mr Struss was fighting back. 'Straight for Davy Jones's Locker it's heading, if you recognize the reference.'

The Admiral disliked being interrupted. He also disliked being met in battle on his own ground. He gathered his dignity about him like a corset and swept by without another word. In the intensity of his affront he failed to go round his great-great-great-granddaughter-in-law, but went though her instead. Unfortunately Mr Struss noticed.

In the main we tried to keep grandfather's peculiarities within the family. With blood relations fanning out from a basis of forty-three cousins, visitors from outside were rare and hardly necessary. Besides, in front of gas-meter men and the vicar grandfather had always been very careful.

We had however our drill in these matters. When Mr Struss had duly paled and fainted dead away, we carried him between us along the corridor and laid him out—his feet higher than his head—on the only leaning billiard table in Britain. He revived slowly.

We were kindness itself, showing every consideration yet

managing to convey at the same time that we both thought he had been drinking but were too well-bred to say so. He pulled himself together, taking our lead in not mentioning the Admiral. Later he would come to believe that he must have imagined the whole episode. He sat up on the edge of the billiard table and cleared his head by doing sums in the big red book. The figures comforted him, restored his confidence.

'Eight and a half thousand,' he announced, cheerful again.

'That's very interesting, Mr Struss?' His meaning escaped me.

'Five in advance. Three and a half when examined and approved.'

'There's no accounting for tastes, Mr Struss.'

'Others may be cheaper, your Lordship, but where's the service? Where's the experience? Where's the background?'

Idly he trundled red up the table and watched it slow down and then return to him. I realized he was talking about money, thousands of pounds. He was giving us an estimate.

'It's been very kind of you to call, Mr Struss. My wife will show you to the door.'

'Seven months, I give it. Eight at the most. Then—dust and ashes. Dust and ashes. . . .'

He climbed up the floor of the billiard room to the door.

'A fine old house, my Lord. Not another like it in the county. Seems a shame it should all come to dust and ashes.'

As he followed my wife out of the room he contrived to slam the door so that an Australia-shaped patch of plaster fell heavily from the wall above the fireplace. An owl peered through, and several bats.

To concentrate on poor Podolkin was hopeless. As I stared at the board in the silence of my study a crack seemed to spread across it, a crack identical to the one in the wall of the portrait gallery. If I lifed my eyes in thought I seemed to see the bulged ceiling of the Great Hall. And continually to my nose came the mud-flats smell of cellars. Even great-great-great-grandfather had known that the place was falling down. And now Mr Struss with his seven months. Dust and ashes, dust and ashes. . . .

In the end I could stand the worry no longer. I called a family conference in the small banqueting hall.

'Family—we are in urgent need of five thousand pounds.' A few of the younger children applauded and were shushed by the others. 'Without such a sum of money the Chase will collapse to dust and ashes, and we shall all be homeless.'

'Eight and a half, I thought the estimate was,' Thora put in mildly.

'Five in advance, the rest when examined and approved. I imagine we could stave off the day of approval almost indefinitely.'

'Five thousand pounds is a lot of money, children.' Thora's ball-point flicked from side to side, mesmerizing them. 'All piggy-banks will be brought and emptied on the table.'

Fourteen hundred and fifty-nine pounds were gathered in this way, which, when added to my own bank balance, made a grand total of fourteen hundred and fifty-nine pounds, eighteen shillings. The necessary five thousand was still a long way off. I threw the meeting open to suggestions.

The children muttered among themselves for some time, but came up with nothing except the thought that we might perhaps apply to the National Trust. I told them I had done that years ago, at which time I had been told—politely—that I was hardly national, and certainly not to be trusted. It seemed unlikely that anything would have happened in the interval to change this opinion. Mr Pennington-Ashleye, who is always included in these family affairs since he is probably the brightest of a bad lot, contributed the idea that we should throw the house open to the public at five shillings a time—and a fortune to be made in ice-creams on the side.

'For people to pay to come and look at it,' Thora replied, 'a house must be either one thing or the other. Either a beautiful historic home or a total ruin. The Chase is not quite either.'

'Quite right, my dear. I'm sorry, Pennington-Ashleye, but I fear people would simply not pay to come and look at it.'

Great-great-great-grandfather cleared his throat.

'They would pay to come and look at me, however.' He gazed around, delighted with the stir he had caused. 'It would mean my giving up my amateur status of course, but I've been a dilettante for too long. Desperate situations call for desperate measures.'

He struck a Napoleonic attitude on the long-demolished

minstrels' gallery.

'I am willing to appear before the public, Willy, on a twice-nightly basis for as long as may be necessary to put the finances of the family on an even keel.'

'Grandfather—' Thora fixed him with both her eyes at once—'you told us you didn't care if the Chase fell down or not. You told us it was always the same to you, whatever happened. You said that was the only reason you stayed.'

The old man replied in a chokey voice. He appeared deeply moved.

'I got to thinking, Henrietta. . . . About the solitude. . . . About the wind whistling through the bare rafters. Gone for ever the warmth of human company. . . . Gone for ever the bright fireside, the cheery greeting. . . . All of it gone, gone for ever.'

Gone for ever the people he could shout at and nag into early graves. But it was the wrong moment to be carping.

'But grandfather,' said the children, 'you *couldn't*. Wouldn't it be prostituting your art or something ?'

Where they learn these words I can't imagine. The comic papers have evidently changed since my day.

'Nonsense, children,' I put in quickly. 'Grandfather's quite right. Desperate situations call for desperate measures. If the audience reaction of Mr Struss this morning is anything to go by, your Grandfather has a very real talent, a talent that for his own sake he has hidden for too long. Self-expression is a universal right, children—we must not deprive your poor Grandfather of it. We must not, and we will not.'

'Instead of ice-cream, hot dogs,' said Mr Pennington-Ashleye. 'I know a bloke with half a million sausages he don't know what to do with.'

Through all the excitement of the preparations that followed great-great-great-grandfather played the prostituted martyr, though I knew damn well that he was going to enjoy every minute of it.

We advertised The Haunted Chase extensively, promising a genuinely ghostly apparition to every customer, with a money-back guarantee. We let the cobwebs round the house grow thicker than ever in preparation for opening night. Mr Pennington-Ashleye supplied a trio of brindled cats with more than usually piercing voices and the children spent the whole of the day before manu- facturing ghastly bloodstains on the main staircase. It was only when Thora remarked on the paleness of the youngest that we discovered where they'd got all that blood from.

Opening night was clear, with the moon expected to rise half- way through the first house. Mr Pennington-Ashleye was doubling the duties of car-park attendant with service on the hot-dog stand and Thora had three coppers of bottled coffee bubbling in the staff wash-house. The children had borrowed a gang of skulls—I never discoverd where from—and were fixing candles in them ready for when the lights would fail at a prearranged signal. Great-great-great-grandfather was pacing his room, sternly rejecting the vulgar suggestion that his head would look more impressive removed and carried in the crook of one arm. For myself, I was with deep regret incommunicado, locked in my study and wrestling with the problem of Podolkin.

Although I was therefore unfortunately forced to miss the proceedings, Thora repeated them to me very fully that same night and I'll pass her account on more or less as I received it.

At six-thirty the audience began to arrive in large numbers, offering satisfactory comments on the sinister decreptitude of the establishment. The children had been warned to keep a look-out for souvenir hunters and were able to rescue several banister rails and a length of haunted carpet. At seven o'clock, when the visitors were evenly distributed about the safer areas of the upstairs, all the lights went out as arranged. The cats were prodded into voice and Thora started up the wind machine down in the basement. A gratifying number of the spectators fainted immediately and were in many cases not revived by their companions in time for great-great-great-grandfather's triumphant progress. They missed a lot.

The old man was superb. He'd mustered a luminosity that none of us would have believed he had in him. He chose to use the old pre-Georgian floor-levels so that sometimes he appeared to be walking on the stumps of his knees while at other times he was a good three feet above the visible boards. Ignoring his audience entirely, he paced solemnly along the corridors, groaning as if all the cares of the world were on his shoulders, and disappearing into the wall at strategic moments. In the library he ascended a tight spiral staircase long since gone, and vanished into the ceiling. And just as the audience was imagining that the show was over, he reappeared in the latticed moonlight by the landing window, his telescope mournfully to his eye, the silvery light falling on him and round him and through him, so that he cast no shadow on the pale boards beneath his feet. From there he dematerialized very slowly, till nothing was left but his sighing along the musty passages. And the candle-light flickering on the borrowed skulls.

A performance that might have bordered on the farcical had been lifted by his artistry to something that was—and these were the only words for it—strangely haunting. Strong women broke down and cried.

It was the high point in great-great-great-grandfather's whole career, moving, poetic, inspirational. When the lights were turned on again the audience revived itself gluttonously at the hot-dog stall and drank the coppers of coffee dry.

In the interval between shows, while Mr Pennington-Ashleye was guiding one set of cars out and the second set of cars in, Thora went to great-great-great-grandfather's room to offer the old man her congratulations. She found the door firmly locked and heard the sound of arguing within. After rattling the doorknob anxiously for some minutes she was finally admitted. The admiral was in the company of two strangers, a forbidding captain of Marines in full regimental blues (*circa* 1946) and an equally massive lieutenant of Hussars in white doe-skin breeches (*circa* 1833). For attempting to turn professional without proper application to the Governing Body, Admiral Lord Clewes, seventh Baron Clewes, had had his resident's licence suspended and he was being withdrawn to base immediately. He might appeal at a later date against the Governing Body's decision, but there was little chance of his appeal being successful. Service etiquette had been seriously affronted. The lieutenant of Hussars flourished a musket several feet longer than he was, and presented arms.

Instead of the show they had come for, the second house assembling at that moment on the ground floor was treated to the ignominious departure of the star performer under close arrest.

He was conducted, protesting, in a hurried and somewhat furtive manner down the main staircase, across the small banqueting hall and out on to the terrace where a coach and four was waiting, soot black horses and a coachman in a huge black tricorn hat. For good value the captain of Marines had not thought of opening any of the various doors that had stood in his path. With a tumbril rumble the coach departed into the night, taking the old man and his escort with it. The road away from the Chase was strewn for several miles with cars that had dived into the hedge to avoid being run down by a ghostly coach. Some of the drivers mentioned four black horses with sparks issuing from their nostrils. Others had heard the voice of an old gentleman raised in angry argument from the coach's interior.

I hope, for his escort's sake, that great-great-great-grandfather's journey was not a long one.

In spite of the change in programme, not one of the audience demanded his or her money back, and those who had not yet paid hurried eagerly to Mr Pennington-Ashleye to do so. Among these latter was a Swedish psychic researcher who was so excited that he offered to buy the Chase there and then for twelve thousand pounds. Mr Pennington-Ashleye pushed him up another four and a half and then settled, invoking the now departed spirits to be his witness. The Swede superstitiously kept his bond.

We live in a more modest mansion now, and some of the children have begun to go out to work in a near-by small-arms factory. It was, I suppose, fortunate that Mr Torkelsen should have approached Mr Pennington-Ashleye, rather than myself or my wife, since both of us would have felt morally bound to tell him that great-great-great-grandfather had been deported never to return. The ignoring of such an obvious moral duty would have weighed heavily on us for the rest of our days. I rewarded Mr Pennington-Ashleye with a testimonial so nobly phrased that it should ensure his never even being offered another job again, whatever the Labour Exchange may get up to.

I sometimes pause—half-way through the Castiglioni End Game, maybe—and wonder if great-great-great-grandfather really knew what he was doing when he risked offending the

Governing Body for the sake of the family. I rather think not—he was the sort of man who would assume that things like regulations applied always to the other fellow, never to him.

DIARY OF A POLTERGEIST

by Ronald Duncan

It was my usual habit to leave my office in Berkeley Square at five-fifteen precisely. But that particular evening it was well past six-thirty before I walked to the lift. The reason for this lapse was that it was the day before Christmas Eve. There had been a mild impromptu party: we junior partners had indulged in no more than a couple of whiskies each; our secretaries had had a bottle of sherry between them. But it had been sufficient to relax us and give the illusion that there was something to celebrate. Somebody had mysteriously produced a box of crackers; and, before I left, paper hats had already appeared. I had sidled towards the door unobtrusively, fearful that 'Auld Lang Syne' would be imposed at any moment. I was feeling far from festive, having had an unusually bitter quarrel with my wife that morning. In the circumstances, I didn't want to be home late. If I were, I knew she would suspect that I had been to see Janet. And since I was innocent I thought I might try to avoid being punished for a pleasure I had not enjoyed. So I hurried towards the car park and then drove as quickly as I could through the Christmas traffic towards the A.4.

The journey to Maidenhead usually took me an hour. But on the Slough by-pass I ran into mist rising from the river and had to slow down to a crawl. I found some music on the car radio. Then I began to trail behind an Esso petrol lorry, keeping twenty yards or so from its tail, content to let its driver penetrate the fog. I was careful not to get too near the lorry in case it should brake suddenly. There was ice on the road. But with it as a pilot, I was able to relax and listen to the music. But in counterpoint to it, I could hear the discord of the morning.

Like most serious quarrels, it had started by something infinitely trivial. One of our mutual friends had made the mistake of sending us a Christmas card which had been addressed only to me.

'I see your friends think you're no longer married,' she had said throwing the envelope into the marmalade, 'or maybe you've told them that I'm dead?'

I had stirred my coffee vigorously.

'Is that what you've told them, that I'm dead?'

'No,' I had said buttering my toast, 'anybody can see you are in your normal good health and full of your usual resentment.'

'And whose fault's that?'

That question had gone unanswered. It was one that didn't require a reply. I knew better than to speak when I was spoken to or to mistake a soliloquy for a conversation. But that morning my strategic silence had made her even more angry.

'The trouble with you,' she had screamed, 'is you are either faithless and unpleasant, or faithful and more unpleasant.'

'Yes.'

'Yes, what?'

'I will mend my manners and be as pleasant as you are.'

'Are you telling me you intend to start up with Janet again?'

'No, I haven't seen her for six months. . . .'

'. . . four.'

'And I don't where she is.'

'You expect me to believe that?' she'd screamed, knowing it was true.

I was not unaware that I was being punished now because I had deprived her of the justification for punishing me.

'You expect me to believe that?' she'd repeated.

Now suddenly the Esso lorry came to a standstill. I slammed on the brakes: I reached for the handbrake too.

After this fright, I ceased going over the row of the morning and listened only to the music. I drove on unthinkingly as though with an automatic pilot. I did not stop until I got out of the car to open the gate at the end of the drive. As usual, cursing the hasp. Then I garaged the car and put the paraffin lamp under the bonnet, collected my brief-case from the back seat, and closed the garage door. Actions which I'd repeated so often I could perform them in my sleep. Then, as usual, I put my hand in my pocket five paces from the door to find my latch key so that I had it ready in my hand as I reached it.

I put my case on the hall table, hung my coat up then went into the sitting-room. The room was empty. I went to the foot of the stairs.

'Darling,' I called, 'come down and have a drink.' There was no answer. But I stood there, waiting. I felt no resentment in spite of the things my wife had said to me that morning. I am not an unkind man. Indeed, my kindness to my wife can be proved by the fact that I never believe a single word she or any woman says. And when I saw her coming down the stairs, I went up towards her, intending to embrace her, hoping that she felt as little resentment as I did. But to my surprise she walked past me coldly. I followed her into the sitting-room. She ignored my presence. This was ridiculous. I thought we'd had squabbles enough before, without making a war of it. But tonight there was no breaking the ice. She returned my smile with a stony stare. She didn't look particularly angry any more, just bored. After a few minutes of this awkwardness she stood up and switched on the television. With feigned interest we listened to the news. Then just as the next programme started, the front door bell rang. I made a move to go to open it, then saw my wife going to the door too. She still had not spoken to me.

'Don't bother,' I said, 'I'll see who's there.'

But she came on and shoved past me rudely as she drew back the latch.

A policeman stood there.

'Mrs Staniforth?' he asked.

'Yes,' my wife replied.

'May I have a word with you?'

'Come in,' she said.

I followed them back into the sitting-room and went to the sideboard to hand the man a drink.

'I'm afraid I have to give you some bad news,' he said awkwardly. 'Your husband has had a motor accident.'

'Is he hurt?' she said anxiously.

'I'm afraid he's dead.'

I almost dropped the bottle, then turned, to hear him say: 'It was about an hour ago. His car had skidded beneath the back of a stationary petrol lorry. He was killed instantly.'

'Nonsense,' I said, 'do I look dead?'

But neither of them listened and neither looked at me.

For the next ten minutes I had to stand there listening to the bobby mouthing platitudes of sympathy for my wife's grief which she did not feel. True, there were tears in her eyes. But she could always weep to order.

Then, eventually, she showed the man to the door, and came back to the room. She went straight to the mirror to repair her make-up.

I went up behind her. I saw to my horror that I had no reflection there. It was a personal loss. Feeling so sorry for myself I had some sympathy for her too. I bent to kiss the back of her neck. And as I did so my reflection appeared briefly as though it is that only love defines us. Seeing my features fleetingly in the glass beside her own, my wife cried out. But did not weep now there was no one there to see her tears.

*

My first reaction on realizing I was, though dead, still conscious, was one of irrepressible hilarity. This mood was heightened by seeing the mock grief about me which my sudden, if not sad, demise had caused. After drying her eyes and repairing her mascara, my wife had run upstairs and changed into mourning. She knew black suited her, especially in her underclothes. When she was suitably dressed, I had stood by her side doubled up with unheard giggles, as I had listened to her phoning round our relatives and friends to share her news and milk them of their sympathy. Not for me, of course: those who grieve, grieve only for themselves.

My next reaction was of sober exhilaration as I realized that death was something I need no longer fear. And I felt free, with all my senses and appetites still intact, yet without a tedious conscience to restrict them. I had no sense of responsibility except to myself. I valued my life, now I no longer had it. Though I was dead to others, I felt most alive in myself. The only thing I lacked was a sense of time. Perhaps this was necessary since I now had to bear the weight of all eternity? But within what had seemed to me only a few seconds since the bobby had left the house, I saw my solicitor, and my brother, Charles, enter the house. They were joined by my wife in my study. All were in mourning. They helped themselves generously to my whisky. Then my solicitor began to read my will. I enjoyed watching their mock approval at hearing of the small bequests I had made to others. With this succulent pleasure before me, I failed to notice anything untoward in the procedure. It was not until I heard my solicitor reading the final clause, in which my executors were empowered to defray my funeral expenses from my estate, that I realized I had omitted to attend that final ceremony.

'Unless my wife has any objections,' the man continued, 'I wish that my body should be cremated.'

I wondered if she had objected? I guessed not but instinctively glanced in the looking-glass above the desk to see if my hair was singed but there was no image there. The thought of the flames brought a cold shudder down my back. I resolved to find the urn which contained my ashes then sprinkle them facetiously on my head. For the dead feel no remorse for the sins they have committed, only for those temptations they needlessly overcame.

Busy as I had been with observing, if not attending, my last obsequies, I had failed to notice that there was no validity in any of the orthodox Christian threats concerning the after-life. Indeed, since I was still conscious, I refused to regard my life as past, though I could see, as country people euphemistically put it: I had passed beyond. But it was comforting not to see Saint Peter hanging around in the flesh as I was sure he'd prove a disappointment after El Greco's portrait of him.

I was in no doubt what I wanted to do next. My impulses in death were as definite as they had been in life. I now felt consumed with unusual malevolence. The sight of my pompous self-righteous brother Charles when my will was being read had focused these feelings against him. I had always resented him. When we were children, he, being two years older than I, got a bicycle before me: he was allowed to smoke and stay up for dinner while I was still treated as a brat. My hatred was as well rooted as it was natural. It had grown at the university where he had patronized me, and then flourished into full flower when, at my father's death, Charles had inherited the small estate in Somerset which I had loved and he had despised, and had then sold it

without offering it first to me. With a private income and a flair
for small talk, he had gone into politics, not out of any zeal for
reform, but from self-conceit, choosing his party, not from conviction, but only with an eye as to which one was likely to obtain
power and further his own fatuous advancement. While I, on the
other hand, had had to go into business and had the humiliation
even in my own obscure suburb of being known as Sir Charles
Staniforth's younger brother. He had been knighted when he had
become Minister of Education. It would have been more appropriate if they had made him a Dame. For in addition to his
financial advantages, Charles was ambivalent, ambidextrous and
homosexual: three valuable attributes in contemporary society.
Yet, in spite of his predilection for his own sex, and his smug
relationship with Geoffrey Mortimer, his private secretary, he had
always managed to censure my heterosexual infidelities, safe in the
assurance, I suppose, that from his way of life there could be no
illegitimate issue. As for his boy friend and toady, Geoffrey, I
hated him even more than I did Charles. This was because I knew
he really despised my brother and it made his fawning attentions
to him all the more nauseating. My impulse was to pay them a
visit as an invisible guest, especially as they were giving an important dinner party to which, alive or dead, I would never have been
invited.

Charles's residence was in Tite Street. When I appeared, or to
be accurate, arrived, the guests were just going into dinner.
Amongst these I observed the Prime Minister and his lady; the
leader of the House of Lords; a bishop, and various other leaders
of the New Establishment. A more pompous parade of hypocrites,
bores and prigs I had not seen. They had bestowed honours on
each other and covered themselves in cant. As they seated themselves at the splendid Sheraton table resplendent with the family
silver, of which I had only an odd pepper-pot, I longed for an
Hieronymous Bosch to be there to paint the hideous features
which lay behind their supercilious masks.

My brother had placed the Prime Minister at the head of the
table and, as host, had taken the far end with Miss Maude Smith,
the Minister of Transport, on his left and Lady Hartland on his
right, with the Foreign Secretary on the other side of her. Lady

Hartland had reached such eminent company, not by virtue of birth—she had suffered from the social disadvantage of not being a barmaid born, but sired by a backwood Earl, nor had she intelligence to recommend her; her only attributes were two aggressive protuberances in front and a couple of curvaceous buttocks behind. Carrying these features everywhere, she was welcomed wherever she went. Men with one eye on her milk ducts or her nates praised her as a conversationalist or wit, women were silenced by her vacuous effrontery. Knowing everybody and nothing at all she had become a TV personality. In the diplomatic language of the Foreign Secretary, she was 'a dish'.

As I surveyed the assembly sucking their soup, I realized that my intentions were no less than to reveal Geoffrey Mortimer's true nature to my brother, to unmask my brother to the world, to bring down the Government and reduce the dinner party to a shambles, if not a riot. But I wanted to have fun: I wasn't going to do it all at once. Indeed, I did nothing very alarming at the start, except to stand near the butler when he was serving the turtle soup to the Prime Minister's squaw and then gently steer the ladle into the lap of her dress. But unfortunately the man corrected its direction before it could reappear loaded with her breast.

But when the asparagus had been served I got busy: harmlessly touring the table and as each guest raised a piece to their mouth, I guided the buttered end either into their eye, their ear or down into their collar. After this course, they all looked a pretty messy lot. Neither dignity nor mascara is much improved with butter.

Next, while a cliché of sole was being served, I descended under the table to see what, if anything, was going on down there. Feeling particularly childish, no doubt engendered by the perspective, I amused myself by tying the episcopal boots together by their laces and then gently caressed Miss Maude Smith's calf with the point of my shoe till she was sufficiently encouraged to wrap her leg round Geoffrey Mortimer's. Then turning round I observed the Foreign Secretary lay a podgy left hand just above Lady Hartland's right knee. This didn't surprise her or me. But it gave me an idea when I saw my brother's right hand idle beneath the table. They were, of course, eating their sole with a fork alone. So firmly I placed my own right hand on Lady Hartland's other knee and then as it were observed which of these two crabs might crawl to shelter first. Presumably her ladyship must have been used to such attentions while she dined, for I could hear her chattering away above me quite unconcerned. This blasé attitude to our joint assault annoyed me. So I placed my other hand in between her thighs. For a minute she seemed only to respond to the contact; then presumably noticing that the men on either side of her were still using their only free hand to hold their fork, Lady Hartland concluded that the third hand came from the other side of the table. She struck out with her right just avoiding my spectacles and catching Geoffrey Mortimer, who sat opposite her, a mortal kick in the crutch, causing him and his chair to fall over backwards. Even so, I did not remove either of my hands, nor did the Foreign Secretary take his paw away from Lady Hartland's garter. With three hands upon her and only two arms within reach, she now emitted a horrible shriek.

'Its bad enough to be groped by the Cabinet,' she said standing up, 'but I'm damned if I can tolerate being raped by the Holy Ghost.'

'Dear, dear,' said the bishop and was then silenced when he noticed that I had removed his crucifix from the chain round his collar and replaced it by the more appropriate symbol of a corkscrew.

Hearing Lady Hartland's accusation against his colleagues, the Prime Minister playfully threw his bread roll at his Foreign Secretary, unfortunately missing him and catching Miss Smith so firmly in her open mouth that when she removed the roll her dentures still adhered to it. Now this example from 10 Downing Street occasioned the subsequent Battle of the Rolls in which bread bounced from pate to pate or was forcibly stuffed by the ladies down one another's corsage. This brawl incited the servants who, not to be outdone by the guests, went round the table squirting syphons of soda on to bare backs or napes of necks.

It was then that my brother revealed himself as both a man of action and a resourceful host: bellowing above the din, he announced that he intended to give a recital of Chopin. Being of a sadistic nature, he always enjoyed inflicting this upon his guests. They, now without any ammunition left to express their reaction to their host's threat, rose to their feet and followed us both from the room.

Immediately the quieted company was seated and when coffee had been served without incident Charles strode with feigned bashfulness to the concert grand. As usual, Geoffrey stood at his side to turn the pages and with subtle gestures of patronizing approval indicate that he himself had taught Charles everything he knew. While he played the Polonaise I did nothing more than cause Geoffrey to turn two pages together. But my brother knew the piece so well he was not thrown except for tempi and a mounting irritation against his protégé. After this piece, he began on one of the Études. I allowed him to get into the run of the piece, then brought the lid of the piano down on to his hands when Geoffrey's fingers had happily strayed near enough to it for him to be blamed.

'You clumsy bugger,' Charles shrieked, dancing with the pain from his wrists.

'You old queen,' Geoffrey countered. 'It serves you right. Now you won't be able to carry on with Lady Hartland any more.'

This witty exchange also ended in a brawl in which somehow Lady Hartland's necklace was broken. When she bent to pick the pearls up I approached her from behind and dexterously reached for the hem of her skirt which I slit up to her buttocks, then with one hand I pulled her black panties down and with the other stuck a head of celery in between her legs just as my brother came to her assistance, and consequently stood there blamed for the whole, blushing like Lady Hartland's pretty bottom which I had playfully slapped. Complete chaos now ensued. But I got bored with my evening as a poltergeist and promised myself not to repeat it. It was far too easy making those who were ridiculous appear as absurd as I knew them to be.

After leaving the shambles of Tite Street, I next found myself in my bank, Cox & King's, at the bottom of Pall Mall. I suppose I wandered in there with the vague intention of taking advantage of my condition and absconding with a few thousand pounds. I sat on the counter for some time watching clients coming in to exchange one paltry piece of paper, and stuffing other bits of the same material into their wallet. And when one of the cashiers had a slab of new fivers before him I teased the poor fellow by taking half of them, intending to slip them into my pocket. There must have been £500 or more. But they were bulky and, realizing suddenly that I had no need of valid currency, I stood up on the counter and scattered the fivers like confetti over the astounded clients. But I didn't feel generous: I felt an all-consuming sense of indifference. In this mood, I walked up Bond Street. How often had I done that before stopping at one shop or another to admire a scarf, a picture or a piece of furniture which I could never afford, and then hurrying on empty-handed? But this time I went straight to Asprey's: they had been displaying a gold and platinum cigarette case there which I had lusted after for months. I took it out of its case, admired its chasing and delicate workmanship, and was about to put it into my pocket when I realized something: I had not smoked a single cigarette since my demise. The shock of this nearly killed me. I had always been a compulsive smoker. I had not even wanted a cigarette. And now I remembered something: my wife had always said that she would never believe I was dead unless a lighted cigarette was placed in my mouth and I failed to draw it. I now found myself replacing the case. To me it had become a bauble. I hurried from the shop and crossed the road, and went towards the Burlington Arcade where there was a little shop whose hand-painted silk ties had always arrested me. But now I found I had passed this shop unaware of its window. My mind must have been on less substantial things. Irritated by this apparent lapse into abstract thought, I retraced my steps deliberately and stared blankly down at these tawdry bits of cloth which, only a month ago, had attracted me so much. Suddenly a sense of panic seized me. I had found I had lost my desire to smoke; could it be that I was now losing interest in all material things too? I felt indignant at the thought. But glancing at the other objects in the shops in the Arcade convinced me this was true. Even jade, which I always admired, now interested me less than lumps of unfashioned clay. This realization did not give me a sense of liberation but of resentment. It is one thing to achieve spirituality by abnegation, fasting and other self-imposed disciplines, quite another to find this condition forced upon one, especially without any religious belief as a compensatory illusion. Having lost one vice had I also been deprived of my others? What of my natural appetites ? I now recalled that I had not eaten since, but I could not answer that for I had no more sense of time than Cleopatra's Needle. I now ran to put this to the test. My direction was easily chosen. It had been my habit to treat myself occasionally to my favourite dish of crab meat at Rayner's Bar at the top of the Haymarket. I ran down Piccadilly towards this place: fear, not hunger, pursuing me. As usual, George stood behind the bar opening oysters. They were Imperial Whitstables. Normally I would have eaten two dozen at least. Now plate after plate passed over the counter before me and no greed arose. At this failure I felt saddened beyond words, and outraged too, like a Las Vegas croupier who wakes up from a trance to find he has involuntarily become a Yogi. Astounded, I reached over the bar and helped myself to a great dollop of crab meat, and then taking some brown bread and butter, I retired to a corner. It was a test, a question of life or death to me. I heaped the fork with the brown crab meat and slowly lifted it to my mouth: not only did the saliva fail to meet it, my mouth refused to open. And sitting there I began to weep noiselessly. At least my tears still flowed. Then I realized there was one appetite which surely had not forsaken me. I stopped weeping and smiled to myself as I got up and strode vigorously out of the pub, taking the first car I found at a parking meter. I drove straight to Janet's mews cottage in Gloucester Place, causing some alarm to drivers in the traffic who were unused to seeing a Lagonda propel itself or weave so dexterously round Piccadilly. I did not find my condition extraordinary. After all, I had long been of the opinion that many of my friends were dead and didn't know it.

Such is habit, that even now as I parked the car, I found myself making up excuses to give to my wife. Catching myself at this again pleased me: at least my invention had not left me. Feeling comparatively cheerful again, I let myself in with my latch-key.

Janet was nowhere to be seen downstairs. I called up. There was no response. But I knew she was in: her handbag was hung over the back of a chair. I guessed where she would be: upstairs taking a bath. Janet was a compulsive bather. And I recalled that the geyser was so noisy she would not have heard me. I opened the bathroom door: there she was with her giant sponge lying on her pretty belly. It had been months since I had seen that navel. I found myself flooded with affection for her and glanced at the mirror now confident that my reflection would be there—but the glass was covered in steam.

Janet now got out of the bath and sat on its edge, her legs outstretched before her. As she reached for a towel I let her take me into her arms. I kissed those lips I had so often kissed and my tongue imitated what I performed below. Was this what they meant by rigor mortis? I always knew sex would be my last sense to go. I had thought that Janet had responded to my passion. But later, as I lay within her arms, I realized that she was not even aware of my presence. She perceived that she was sexually excited but doubtless explained this to herself as being due to some erotic fantasy which had passed through her fertile mind. How often, I wondered, had I ploughed such a futile furrow be´ore?

Janet was never a girl to hesitate to put inclination into effect. 'Henry,' she called coquettishly, 'come and dry my back.'

A young man walked obediently into the bathroom wearing my dressing-gown. I now suffered the humiliation of seeing my mistress lifted out of my own arms and carried manfully into the bedroom. I had been nothing but an aphrodisiac for another.

With the agony of a voiceless Rigoletto deprived of his strangled cry, I stood there and watched them make love before my eyes. And I wept again, not for my loss of love, but my loss of pain. The beast with two backs filled me with no revulsion, just indifference.

Then, as if I had not suffered enough from my lack of suffering, something occurred which makes even the dead die again. Standing there watching my beloved in her playful transports I saw her visibly age before my eyes. The apples of her breasts drained of their pretty pout. Next, the thighs sagged, her waist thickened and the neck wrinkled. At first I dared not look at her face. When I did, I saw the double chin, the tight lips of age pursed with wrinkles lying over her toothless gums. And her hair? Oh, pity the dead, who without a sense of time, stand and stare and see on an instant what the living are spared, blinded as they are by the gradualness, the mercy of years.

At this moment of compassion for her, my features must have taken on definition again. Janet, opening her eyes, saw me. She always said she wanted me to be the last thing she saw before she died.

When I left her cottage, I do not know where I walked or for how long. My last recollection was standing on some cliff edge looking down at the interminable breaking waves. With all the earth and all that's on it accessible to me, I felt nothing but consummate indifference to it. That is what death is. And why so few ghosts appear: we are too bored with you all to be bothered to haunt you.

So, I walked into the mist and finally let the yawn of space envelop me.

SALPINGOGRAM

by *James Hamilton-Paterson*

Between the end of the platform and the bookstall stood an isolated hut with a green sign on the door which said 'Lamps'. Inside, three men were sitting on drums of kerosene drinking tea. On the back of the door was a further notice which read 'No smoking. By order'. One of the tea-drinkers, who had just arrived, drained his mug and stretched. A dandruff of ash fell from his cigarette onto his serge-covered knees.

'Better get back to it, then,' he said to the others without enthusiasm. 'One short today, Sam being off and all.'

'Off?' echoed a thin man in a peaked cap. 'We don't do Sam's work without extra, you know that as well as I do, Herb. What's the matter with him? All right yesterday, he was.'

'Jaundice,' said Herbert. 'All yellow, says his wife. Poor bastard.'

'Poor Sam's wife, more like. He'll have to lay off that for a bit.'

'How do you mean?' asked the third tea-drinker, a handsome coloured boy who managed to invest his railwayman's uniform with a certain careless elegance.

'Well, I mean, it's jaundice, isn't it?' reinforced the other. 'Can't do it when you got jaundice, you know. Makes you bloody sterile, ask any doctor.'

Two of the men chuckled sympathetically over Sam's fate. The coloured boy was silent.

'Man, does it always do that?' he asked seriously.

'It does if you don't lay off it. First thing they tell you, that is.'

'Does it take women the same way? My girl's going into the hospital tomorrow,' added the boy inconsequentially. 'She's having a check-up. Sure hope she doesn't get it.'

'What are you so worried about, anyway?' asked Herbert. 'You haven't got jaundice, have you?'

'I did get it when I came to England. Real bad, the doctors said.'

His two companions formulated a question in their brains which, although unvoiced, was none the less posed eloquently by the silence which supervened. Eventually the thin man sniffed liquidly.

'I shouldn't worry, mate,' he said. 'From what I've heard, it'd take more than jaundice to stop you lot.'

Not quite knowing whether to be insulted or flattered, the coloured boy flashed his teeth uncertainly. Nevertheless, there was a measure of satisfaction in his voice as he stood up and reached for his cap.

'I'll take Sam's place today. I don't mind.'

'Can you do tickets?' queried Herbert.

'Sure I do tickets. Simplest thing.'

They ground their cigarettes out on the top of the kerosene drums and left.

*

Lunch had been distributed from squeaky trolleys like iron bedsteads and Cottlestone Ward, women's surgical, now echoed to the clatter of L.C.C. cutlery and uninhibited appraisals of the food. Against the wall at one end of the ward fat Mrs Farnaby was picking at the first meal since her admission that morning. Her jocularity dared one to think that perhaps she was just a little unnerved. Mrs Farnaby's questing fork lunged like a heron spearing fish.

'I suppose they think this is toad-in-the-hole,' she remarked, eyeing the morsel. 'Lot more hole than toad, if you ask me.'

Little Miss Watts rolled her eyes in sympathy from the next bed. She had not been given anything to eat since her breakfast cup of tea; the House Surgeon had called to see her the previous evening and had left strict instructions about not eating. He had also given instructions about her pre-med., but the girl had looked so frightened he had determined to persuade the anaesthetist to see her himself before anything was given.

'You're not missing anything, dear,' went on Mrs Farnaby. She pushed away her plate with a quick movement. On it, the wedge of yellow batter lay stricken in a haemorrhage of ketchup. The flesh on her beefy arms flopped as she heaved herself up on her pillows, at the same time turning towards Miss Watts.

'I envy you, I do. It'll all be over soon. Another couple of hours you'll be back here and then home again tomorrow or Saturday. It's an Investigation you're having, isn't it ?'

Miss Watts nodded. Her rich black skin seemed to be stencilled on to the whiteness of her background. It was like looking at a figure in a negative.

'Yes, that's all it is. Do you think it will ? . . . I mean, does it *hurt* at all ?'

'Good Lord no, dear. Mine's tomorrow and it'll be me third. I've never felt a thing, and I've had some lovely dreams under the anaesthetic. Ted wants another kid and he says he's wore himself out trying. Like stoking a boilerful of clinkers, he says. I says he should worry, who's got to look after it when it does arrive ? All them nappies again. I'll be that glad when the Change comes,' said Mrs Farnaby with light-hearted fervour.

Her neighbour glanced nervously round the ward. The patients all seemed so old: the girl's view was of a sea of grey heads nodding and heaving to the irresistible tides of Parkinsonism. She wondered what women's chronic was like.

'I wish Ray was here,' said Miss Watts in a small voice.

'Your man, is he?' queried Mrs Farnaby with a gossip's keenness.

'Yes. His name's Ray Garvey. We aren't married yet but we're going to be; p'raps in April, he says.'

'And you want an Investigation already ?' mused Mrs Farnaby. 'Not that it's any of my business,' she added unconvincingly.

'I love him, Mrs F., I really do. I want to be a really good woman for him. But Ray's funny about children; he says it's no good to marry a woman who can't get children.' She sighed.

Vexed, Mrs Farnaby automatically folded her meaty arms but was obviously aware of how odd this gesture looked when made lying in a hospital bed and promptly unfolded them again.

'None of my business, of course, dear,' she said, 'but he sounds pretty . . .' She changed gear. 'People have different customs, I s'pose. Where does your Ray come from ?'

'He's from Barbados. He's really smart, that man. He says he'll soon be in the ticket office permanent, instead of just managing the platforms.'

'That's lovely, dear. I'm sure you'll be very happy together. But what's going to happen if the Investigation shows you can't have kids?'

A nurse appeared with a trolley at the foot of Mrs Farnaby's bed.

'You haven't finished your lunch,' she said in a Dublin accent.

'If I had it would have finished me,' came back Mrs Farnaby tartly.

'There's some people don't know when to be tankful,' said the nurse to the ward at large. 'It's plenty of people in the world today would be happy to eat what you've trown back in our faces.'

'If they did they'd mostlike end up in here.'

'An' if it's complaints you want to make,' said the nurse, scraping the gelid batter into a pan of scraps in a marked manner, 'I'll jest ask Sister to step over here.' She crashed the plate on to a pile of dishes and peered at little Miss Watts. Then she turned sharply back to Mrs Farnaby.

'What have you been doing to upset her?' she demanded belligerently. 'Have you been saying things?'

' 'Course I've not,' said Mrs Farnaby, 'the idea of it. A poor young thing like that.'

Little Miss Watts lay back in her bed, tears running silently over her black cheeks onto the pillow. Mrs Farnaby beckoned conspiratorially to the nurse who sidled closer, still looking at Miss Watts. The fat woman lowered her voice which somehow gave her words much greater clarity and carrying power.

'She says her man won't marry her if she can't have kids. Can you beat that?'

'Mother of God, did you ever hear such a ting?' The nurse turned back to Miss Watts. 'Now don't you worry yourself, darling. You'll only send your temperature up and then they might tink you was sickening. They'd have to postpone everyting, you know. Jest you lie there quietly an' I'll bring you a pill.'

She eased her giant trolley into motion and ploughed away up the ward.

'Don't cry, dear,' said Mrs Farnaby. 'You'll be all right, I know you will. And I'm sure your man will understand, whatever happens.'

'We had a bit of a fight last night,' said Miss Watts plaintively.
'Who, you and Ray did ?'

'I've never seen him like that before, and we've been together
about a year now.' Details seemed to make the girl happier. 'I was
working down at the Supermarket when we met. I was on the
registers, and along he comes up to the desk with his basket all
stuffed with tins and bread and that. Took me about ten minutes
to tot it all up, even on the machine. "You must be hungry," I says
to him, "or p'raps you've got a family ?" "I haven't even got a
wife," he says, "I do all my shopping once a month." Then we
started going out together.'

Mrs Farnaby popped a toffee in her mouth.

'Can't offer you one, dear,' she said without obvious regret.
'You don't want it all coming back under the gas. You were saying
about this fight you had with him.'

'Last night,' said Miss Watts. 'He kept on screaming at me, how
come I wasn't . . . wasn't pregnant. And so I said how did I know,
p'raps God didn't want it, us not being actually married and that.'
She rolled her flooding eyes timidly to peep at Mrs Farnaby, as if
fearful that such a personal revelation would be taken as a sign of
unfaithfulness.

'I don't mind, my dear,' said Mrs Farnaby with a degree of
unction. 'I'm a woman of the world myself.' But her airy tone
belied the care with which she filed away this piece of information.
It would go down well at the Launderette.

'Well, and what then ?' prompted the fat woman eagerly, her
toffee stowed like a carbuncle in her cheek.

'Then he started pushing me about and I got mad because I've
always tried so hard to please him, and I said bad things to him.'
Tears of remorse slid down the girl's cheek.

'Anyone would, love,' said Mrs Farnaby consolingly. 'A great
brute of a man pushing you around like that. I'd have done the
same thing too in your place.'

Mrs Farnaby was so obviously not the right size to be pushed
about by anybody that her words of comfort belonged firmly to the
realm of the hypothetical, but Miss Watts was far too distressed to
perceive this.

'I told him I'd done all I could,' she sobbed; 'I told him it takes two to make a baby.'

'Quite right too. My old man used to say however much a hen sits on them, bad eggs'll never hatch a feather.'

Miss Watts appeared uncomforted by the philosophies of her neighbour's father.

'Then Ray got quite crazy. He said I'd got jaundice and that I'd never be any good, and then he knocked me down. That's about all I can remember. He'd gone to work when I woke up yesterday morning. So I had to bring myself here in the afternoon. I left him a note, though, telling him how sorry I was. Oh, I wish I hadn't said all those things to him. I love him and I only made him angry.'

'Don't you worry yourself,' said Mrs Farnaby; 'it probably did him the world of good to be told a few home truths. I expect he's forgotten all about it already. Men are like that. You wait till you've had the operation: he'll come in here all trembling, he'll be that anxious. Just you see.'

The thought of her impending ordeal emptied Miss Watts's mind of her pre-marital difficulties and in their place insinuated a clean jab of fear.

'I'm scared,' she admitted. In a voice of nervous inquiry she asked: 'What do they do to you in the Investigation?'

'Don't you know?' asked Mrs Farnaby in return. 'I'm surprised the doctor didn't tell you: he told me the first time. It's not much, you know.' Mrs Farnaby was not an imaginative woman, but in her sympathy she searched for something that would cheer. 'Why, they don't even take you into the operating theatre.'

'They don't?' Miss Watts looked slightly relieved. 'Then it's not really a proper operation?'

'No, it's nothing, hardly. That old Dr Kildare wouldn't give you a thank-you if they rolled up with an Investigation for him to do. I mean, there's no *glamour* to it.'

'And I'll be asleep when it starts?'

'You'll be having them lovely dreams. Then they take you down to the X-ray department and fill you up with some stuff which shows up in the picture. They take a few X-rays and then the doctor in charge, he takes a look at them and he says: "Them tubes is clear," or "Them tubes is all blocked," depending. Then they bring you back up here and you wake up. There's nothing to it.

And they send you home in a day or two if you're up to it.'

Miss Watts's little black hands were gripping the sheet on a level with her chin.

'You're sure that's all that happens?' she asked anxiously. 'There's no . . . I mean, they don't want to see inside?'

'Knives?' inquired Mrs Farnaby with relish. 'Lord love you, no. There's no *cutting* to be done. Just them photographs.'

'Then why do they put you to sleep first, if it's just X-rays?'

Mrs Farnaby became vague.

'I s'pose it's to stop you being embarrassed, love,' she said. 'Anyway you get these lovely dreams, and all on the National Health. You oughtn't to miss them,' said Mrs Farnaby emphatically.

'I'll have these lovely dreams too?' queried Miss Watts, wanting to make quite certain.

'Of course you will, dear. Why, everybody knows you have lovely dreams under the anaesthetic. It's something they put in the gas. My Ted says so and he's got a friend who's a hospital porter.'

Little Miss Watts was silent. Her hands had relaxed their grip on the sheet but her brown eyes were rolled towards the clock over the ward doorway. It was one-forty-five.

Pudding arrived with another access of bustling and unoiled wheels. Mrs Farnaby sank her dull spoon through custard to the square of flan which lay suffocating beneath. After a mouthful she rejected this offering as well.

'Sheer cheek,' she commented. 'Cold as ice and half as nourishing. And this is what we pay taxes for. It's a crying scandal.'

'Is anything the matter, Mrs Farnaby?' enquired a scrupulously starched voice. The speaker was a tall grey woman with a glinting badge pinned to her chest. Mrs Farnaby's eyes rose to meet Sister's and then dropped to the badge. It seemed to have a mesmeric effect on her.

'Nothings, thanks. I was just chatting to Miss Watts here.'

'You don't seem to have finished your lunch.'

Mrs Farnaby picked up her spoon.

'I'm not really hungry, dear. I expect I shall fancy a little something around tea-time.'

'I have no doubt,' observed Sister. 'However, I shall warn nurse not to let you stuff yourself with bread. What you need is a balanced diet and in any case the doctor's said to get your weight down.'

Mrs Farnaby smiled equably. On a less sympathetic person the smile might have seemed menacing; with fat Mrs Farnaby it was merely a refusal to be put upon.

'I'm not married to the doctor, Sister. My Ted likes me the shape I am: it's the shape he married, after all. It's only Investigation, not slimming I'm here for.'

The ward Sister bustled away and after a short while reappeared accompanied by a slim young man in a white coat from a pocket of which the rubber coils of a stethoscope protruded. Mrs Farnaby prepared for battle but at the last moment they stopped by Miss Watts's bed.

'Just about time for your injection, dear,' said Sister kindly. Miss Watts's eyes widened. 'And this gentleman here's Dr Sargent; he's the anaesthetist who's going to look after you.'

Miss Watts's eyes were glued to the young man's face. He grinned in the way which, he had been told, inspired confidence.

'Is it time?' asked little Miss Watts faintly.

'More or less. How are you feeling? You're certainly a very fit young lady. I just want to listen to your chest again and then I'll give you an injection which will put you to sleep. Then you won't feel a thing until you wake up in here again.'

He reached for her wrist, which she neither gave nor withheld. Resigned tears gathered once more in her eyes. 'Seventeen,' thought the anaesthetist, glancing at the second hand of his watch, 'seventeen. She's just a girl. Ought really to be in the children's ward.'

Mrs Farnaby was up on one fat elbow watching the proceedings intently. Not a detail was missed which could later be retailed among her friends at the Launderette. A nurse approached carrying a kidney-bowl and Sister started to draw the green curtains around Miss Watts's bed. Before she could finish Mrs Farnaby said:

'Wait a minute, Sister. What's your name, dear?'

'Lily,' said Miss Watts.

'Next April,' said Mrs Farnaby very firmly, 'you'll be Mrs Lily Garvey, you mark my words. Now you just lie back and enjoy yourself. Remember me in those lovely dreams of yours and I'll save some tea for you when you get back.'

In the face of vague clinical menace this homely gesture brought the tears running down the girl's cheeks.

'Oh, thank you, Mrs F.,' she said bravely, and then: 'no, please not.' She said this so urgently that Mrs Farnaby was somewhat taken aback until she realized that the girl was addressing the anaesthetist who was trying to remove a band from her throat.

'We won't steal it,' promised the young man soothingly. 'It'll be quite safe here.'

'No, no. Ray gave it me. Please don't take it away, sir. It's to bring me luck. It's made of elephant's hair. Please leave it.'

Slightly startled by the girl's pleading, Dr Sargeant relented.

'Well, I don't suppose it'll hurt if you want it that badly. It's loose enough: quite safe.'

'I love him, sir,' said Lily as if an explanation were needed, and she clutched the brown, wiry strands. As the curtains were whisked shut the last things which Mrs Farnaby saw clearly were Lily Watts's eyes, terrified yet stoical with the love she felt for her railwayman from Barbados. The green curtains ended a foot from the floor and through the gap the fascinated fat woman caught an impression of feet shuffling purposefully round the girl's bed. Her ears caught the clink of instruments against enamel and the low murmur of brief exchanges; her nose detected a pulse-quickening whiff of ether. Mrs Farnaby could visualise the bright needle sliding into the vein and the child's face growing suddenly peaceful, the black eyelids sliding down like blinds in a shop being closed for siesta.

Soon afterwards the anaesthetist left with the nurse, leaving Miss Watts to sleep alone. Sister looked at Mrs Farnaby as she drew the curtains to behind her.

'You'd best be getting some sleep as well,' she said. 'Everyone has a little snooze after lunch.'

'Not likely, Sister; I'm not tired.'

'You're not going to be troublesome, are you Mrs Farnaby?' inquired Sister sweetly. 'It strikes me that you're just a little bit excited. And anyway, if you stay awake I expect you will soon begin to feel hungry. I'll get nurse to bring you something. Which you will take.'

On this firm note Sister left, and soon the nurse from Dublin strode down the ward with a medicine-glass in one hand.

'Here you are, Mrs Farnaby,' she said. 'Down with this and then I'll go and get my lunch and put my feet up.'

Mrs Farnaby hesitated.

'Will you hurry it up?' asked the nurse. 'She'll have our scalps if there's fuss, sure as my name's Maureen.'

Resistance was clearly futile. Mrs Farnaby swallowed the potion and lay back. The tent of her knees collapsed beneath the blankets as the nurse tidied the bedclothes and the bed exhaled the ammoniac breath of the fat woman's secret crevices. Despite herself, the nurse recoiled slightly.

'There you are now, have a good sleep,' she said and marched away.

Just as Mrs Farnaby was on the point of dropping off, two overalled porters came into the ward pushing a stretcher covered in black antistatic rubber sheeting which had been hurriedly draped with a cotton cellular blanket. This was edged into Miss Watts's curtained cubicle and reappeared after a moment's activity. The ward watched in silence: the crotchety, the doddering and the serene turning their heads to follow the stretcher as the little black head of Miss Watts was wheeled through the swing doors and out along the polished corridor.

*

As she appeared in the X-ray department two floors below, Mr Hawkins, the surgeon, glanced at his watch.

'How many this afternoon, Jack?' he asked the anaesthetist.

Young Dr Sargent inspected dials.

'Only three. There were five on the list originally but one's p.u.o. and another's cried off. With any luck we'll be through by tea-time. I hope so: I'm taking Penny to the theatre tonight.'

'*Ernest?*'

'It's supposed to be a marvellous production,' said the younger man defensively. The surgeon slipped his mask on.

'Who's this?' he asked, jerking a rubber-sheathed thumb at the stretcher.

'Lily Watts. I thought we'd do her first: she's the youngest.'

'Christ in Heaven, why are salpingograms always black?' demanded Hawkins.

'I suppose they're all crazy about fertility. This one's engaged, but he won't marry her unless she's guaranteed to produce.'

'God, what a bunch. Oh well, let's get started. What's she had?'

'Pentothal. I gave her five hundred milligrammes; she was a bit jumpy.'

'Right then. Stand by with the gas. Somebody give me a hand.'

Together the surgeon, a sister and two nurses lifted Miss Watts easily on to the X-ray table and slid her down so that her rear practically overhung one end.

'Lord, look at this,' interjected Dr Sargent. It was as if the girl's skull had hinged open. Her long, matt hair had slipped backwards revealing a tight scalp crimped with minute frizzy pigtails. Mr Hawkins poked irreverently at the wig.

'Must have cost her a packet. Genuine hair, that. None of your spun nylon nonsense.'

'Do they all do this?'

'A lot of them. Most of their money goes either on wigs or on having their hair straightened. Quite amazing,' commented the surgeon, straightening up. Interest shifted to the girl's other end. The two nurses grasped a thin black leg apiece and in this undignified posture the sleeping Lily Watts was held defenceless under the glaring lights. In the background stood a radiologist and a radiographer, both of them looking rather sinister in dark glasses which they wore so that their eyes could later adjust to the dim glow of the X-ray screen with the minimum of trouble.

'Speculum,' said Mr Hawkins in a bored voice. The sister handed him the instrument.

'Syringe ready?'

'Yes, sir. Twenty c.c.s all right?'

'Fine. Thanks.' Mr Hawkins grimaced as he carefully introduced the applicator, gently pushed home the plunger and watched the straw-coloured Lipiodol creep down the barrel of the syringe and vanish into the girl's womb. Even now, Mr Hawkins still found it strange that this weak-looking fluid could show up opaque on an X-ray film. It was rather like discovering lemonade to be highly alcoholic.

'Patient O.K., Jack?' he asked Dr Sargent.

'Fine. Plenty of oxygen. She's fit as hell.'

'It's all that exercise,' said the surgeon obscurely. He grinned to himself and the operation proceeded.

*

When Mrs Farnaby awoke the clock said half past three. The ward was quiet and she lay drowsily collecting her wits. Then she remembered and glanced towards Miss Watts's bed. The green curtains round it were not quite drawn to the wall and through the gap she could see the girl blinking sleepily. It was clear that she was just coming round.

'Hullo, dear,' said Mrs Farnaby in her piercing whisper. The brown eyes swivelling towards her.

'Hullo, Mrs F.,' replied Lily weakly.

'How are you feeling, love? Did you have them lovely dreams, then?'

The girl blinked some more.

'I can't remember . . . I think so. But I feel good, all sort of calm and warm inside. And I know everything's all right. Somebody said I was patent.'

'That means your tubes are clear. That's wonderful. Funny how you can hear what people are saying when you're half asleep, isn't it?'

A smile crossed Lily's face.

'My man,' she said softly to herself. 'I'm all right and now Ray'll come and take me to be his wife. Here,' her dark head turned to face the fat woman, 'I want you to have this, Mrs F. It got me through and you've been so kind to me. I was really scared before. It'll bring you luck too.' She undid the charm round her neck.

'Why, that's sweet of you, my dear.' Mrs Farnaby was more touched than she could say. 'But it'll keep for now; my Investigation's not till tomorrow. Wait until you feel a bit stronger.'

'No, I want you to have it now.' Lily put the elephant-hair band on top of the locker between their beds.

'A real gesture, that is,' said Mrs Farnaby. Her voice sounded rather gruff. 'Now you just have another sleep and we'll chat again when they bring the supper round.'

The future Mrs Garvey closed her eyes with an expression of great serenity.

Mrs Farnaby must also have dropped off again because when she woke with a start the ward lights were on and Sister was offering a cup of tea.

'Had a good sleep?' inquired Sister.

'Not bad, ta. I could just do with a cuppa.' Fat Mrs Farnaby hauled herself upright. Then she noticed that the curtains round Lily's bed were drawn back and the mattress had been stripped to the bare stains.

'Where's Miss Watts, Sister?' she asked.

'She won't be coming back,' said Sister gently. 'Do you want the pan?'

'No. Where is she, then?'

' "No, *thank you, Sister*," is what we say in Cottlestone Ward.' Her tone softened. 'I'm afraid it's bad news. Miss Watts died a short while ago. Please don't tell all the other patients, Mrs F., I don't want them upset.'

Mrs Farnaby distinctly felt something like a small lift go down inside her. It reached the foundations of her complacency with a jolt.

'Oh, the poor little girl,' she said softly. 'That young she was, and so sweet too.'

Shocked, she reached out a pudgy hand and picked up the elephant-hair charm Lily had left her and ran it through her soft fingers. It felt wiry and tough.

'Why, Sister? Why did she die? Just an Investigation, it was. What I'm going to have tomorrow,' she added uneasily.

Sister sat on the end of Mrs Farnaby's bed. Even at that moment her professional eye took in the scrumpled paper handkerchiefs and toffee-wrappers in the top of the fat woman's locker.

'It was just one of those things,' said Sister resignedly, 'nothing to do with that. She died under the anaesthetic during the operation. They tried for half an hour to save her but there was nothing anyone could do. You mustn't worry, my dear.' Sister moved nearer, reached out and squeezed Mrs Farnaby's plump hand in a surprising gesture of tenderness. Just as unexpectedly, Mrs Farnaby lost her comfortable self-assurance and clung to Sister's hand. Tears were beginning to filter through the cracks in her composure.

But Sister was not looking at the fat woman's flooding eyes. She was staring at Lily Watts's mascot.

'How did you get that thing?' she asked abruptly. 'That girl was wearing it when she left the ward, I remember.'

Mrs Farnaby gave a mucous sniff. 'But she came back,' she gulped. 'I was talking to her after she had woken up again.'

'Impossible,' said Sister flatly. 'She never left the X-ray department.'

Then, as understanding came, the two women sat holding each other's hands tightly until Sister's frozen stillness and Mrs Farnaby's wails brought nurses running.

*

There were only two men in the 'Lamps' hut but by dint of much smoking and boiling of tea-kettles on a Primus stove they had worked up a comfortable fug. An idealist, thinking that workers should merit their name, might have suspected that it was guilt which made one of them snap at the felt-hatted stranger who opened the door. In fact, it was the blast of cold air which gave an edge to the thin man's voice.

'Public aren't allowed in here,' he said inhospitably. 'Specially when they stand around leaving the door open.' Herbert growled agreement and glared at his tea.

'Police,' said the stranger briefly, still firmly in the doorway. 'I'm looking for a Ray Garvey. Booking clerk told me I'd find him here.'

The two railwaymen, who had been feebly hunched against the fresh air on top of their kerosene drums, acquired a measure of alertness.

'Ray?' queried the thin man in a noticeably more helpful voice.

'He's not been in today, has he, Herb ?' He looked at his mate for confirmation which all three men knew to be unnecessary.

'No; nor yesterday neither. Nor day before, for that matter,' said Herbert. 'What do you want to see him for, anyway ?'

'Well, when was it you last saw him ?' persisted the stranger, ignoring the question.

'Must have been Tuesday.' This time it was Herbert's turn to look to his thin mate for support. 'Today's Friday. . . . that's it; it was Tuesday because it was the day Sam was off with the jaundice and Ray took over tickets. I remember.' Both men nodded.

'Tuesday ?' asked the stranger, removing his hat and coming into the hut. He shut the door behind him and the draught stopped but the temperature inside had fallen considerably. 'Tuesday,' he repeated to himself.

'I might as well tell you,' said the policeman more briskly, 'that we'd like a word with Mr Garvey. Did you know he was engaged ?'

'Oh yes. Girl called Lucy, wasn't she ?' asked Herbert.

'Lily. Lily Watts. They were living together. Did Garvey talk about her on Tuesday ?'

The two workmen looked at each other, their eyebrows raised.

'Don't think so,' said the thin man tentatively. 'Wait a bit, didn't he say something about her going into hospital the next day ? A check-up or something. You remember, Herb.'

'That's it. He said she was going in Wednesday for something small. Seemed a bit anxious about it as I recall.'

The policeman perched unbidden on a kerosene drum and made notes.

'Anything else ?' he asked at length. 'For instance, did Garvey say anything about going away ? How did he seem ?'

'Same as usual. We'd have remembered if he'd said anything about skiving off, don't worry: we're short-handed enough as it is. He seemed more worried about jaundice than anything else. Why all the questions, anyway ? What's he supposed to have done ?'

'Jaundice ?'

'It was just a joke we were having. He was worried he might get it and dry up. You know.'

'I see. Well, their neighbours dropped round on them a couple of hours back. They wanted to find out how the operation had gone and if Miss Watts had got back yet. They found her, all right. She was dead on the kitchen floor.'

'Dead?' asked the thin man. His peaked cap rose up his forehead on shocked eyebrows.

'I'm afraid so. Battered. Our surgeon said she'd been dead two or three days. That would make it Tuesday night, perhaps Wednesday morning. No later, anyway. Garvey's disappeared, of course. Do you know anywhere he might be?'

The railwaymen shook their heads.

'Ray never mentioned any relatives anywhere,' said Herbert. 'He didn't say anything on Tuesday about going off, either. All he said was that his girl was due in hospital the next day.'

'Well she never got there, that's for certain,' said the policeman.

He took their names and addresses and, declining a cup of tea, went out shutting the door gently behind him. Inside the hut the fug began to build up satisfactorily again as Herbert and his thin mate set about boiling the kettle with unaccustomed industry.

THE FOOT

by Christine Brooke-Rose

The victim to be haunted is female. And beautiful. This makes a difference. She has the habit of confidence, but also a greater adjustment to achieve. In the intact body there is a constant stream of impulses bombarding the cortex from the nerve-ends in the muscles, which bombardment is evenly balanced on both sides. But when the body is no longer intact a neuro-muscular imbalance results which throws additional strain on the sensitized cerebrum and upsets the previous state of equilibrium. It is difficult to estimate at this relatively early stage how far her habit of confidence will counter the despair at the adjustment to be achieved and therefore weaken the imbalance in the stream of impulses reaching the cortical areas.

The victim is female and very beautiful, as far as can be judged at present with her eyes closed peacefully in analgesic slumber unaware of pain. It is easy to forget the full extent of beauty when the eyes are shut and the neuroblasts asleep to agony. Eyes open can bring beauty alive with awareness of pain terror despair or anger, not to mention desire and liquid tenderness or even the alluring invitation down the pathways to the womb the tomb the cavern the ebb and flow of time linked to the sun-devouring moon the monster chasm of death and timelessness that draws man like a magnet from the moment he is conscious of a fall a wrench of umbilical tissue rough manhandling tumbling lying in soft cloud sucking at heaven severed weight of body on stumbling legs and fall, fall through the days and minutes. Eyes open can bring archetypes alive but now they are closed on a white ashen face sheathed in pale lanky hair like dead nerve fibres that conduct no pain along pale lanky limbs except for the right leg amputated above the knee. Pity. A thousand pities bombard the cortex from the nerve-ends in the stump-neuroma where the axons proliferate excitedly and send back false messages of pain that find at present

no decoder in the slumbering central image of a limb no longer
there. We have however no room for pity in the haunting game.

It is a proven scientific fact that women have a higher pain
threshold than men. Which makes the task more difficult but
interesting. Men are no challenge. Yet even within this distinction
the threshold varies from subject to subject and from time to time
for there is rhythm in the haunting game as in any other according
to stress fatigue drugs general constitution previous equilibrium
distraction violent activity including sex and the psychiatrist
recommends electroencephalic treatment despite statistics proudly
quoted for example out of nineteen cases eight improved six
relapsed after improvement three unchanged two worse as if that
proved anything and some are unduly sensitive he says in his
report. In every case the treatment improved the patient's attitude
towards the pain so that he or she was less distressed by it. True,
and annoying. But there are ways to re-create distress. Often the
treatment altered the nature of the pain he proudly adds and thus
in several amputees the position of the phantom limb and its
concomitant pain were altered rather than relieved. Yes, there are
ways.

Still, they do make the task more and more difficult. In the old
days they believed merely in conditioning methods, an empty
name for the attempt to raise the threshold simply through the
refusal of those in authority to admit the existence of the phantom
pain. As if one could refuse to admit the existence of a ghost. They
have to admit it now. Unfortunately they also study it, which does
make the task more difficult, even though they do not wholly
understand it yet. Why, for instance, the ghost pain haunts at such
an unpredictable rhythm, leaving an amputee in peace for twenty
years and suddenly appearing, inexorable, excruciating. Or why it
materializes in the phantom shape of the foot only, or the hand,
not the whole limb, although the limb is also a phantom and the
real pain the stump aches in every neurone. And yet it is obvious
that to be effective pain must attack the most active therefore
vulnerable part of the central memory-image, the extremities
once in touch with earth air fire and water, the soles that bear the
whole weight of existence as man transmutes his structural
archetypes from curled to lying to upright position and learns the

shapes of time food light dark play by fingering breasts limbs balls
cuddly animals. But there are other reasons. Ghosts must preserve
some mystery.

If they can. Certainly knowledge is advancing. White sun, for
instance, or audio-analgesia to be more precise can annihilate us if
only for a while. But leucotomy is the great enemy, resorted to
quite openly in cases of intractable phantom pain. Nice word,
intractable, in view of the way we phantoms infiltrate ourselves
down the pathways of pain, down the spinothalamic tract to be
precise, not that I'm partial to words, they can be enemies too, but
I like words that bring alive my task my journey down the pathways of pain, down the spinothalamic tract into which they now
however introduce electrodes in a stereotactic procedure to produce a phantom pain and find out where exactly to coagulate.
Very dangerous. Obviously, since the phantom is not the real one
but electrically raised. The result is only too often spasticism in
the other limb on the same side and loss of upward conjugate gaze.
Eyes open can bring beauty alive with awareness terror pain despair or anger not to mention the alluring invitation down the
pathways to the womb and all the rest. A thirty-year-old woman
not as attractive but still desirable and successfully haunted by an
excruciating phantom in the foot no longer there was very agitated
and importunate said Mr Poole the surgeon but after a leucotomy
she became calm, the importunacy vanished and she only referred
to the pain when asked if it existed. It is true he innocently proudly
adds that she then said it was excruciating. Ghosts must preserve
some power.

If they can. There are still ways of lowering the threshold.
Severe mental deprivation or retardation for example raise it and
the highly intelligent undoubtedly suffer more than the plethoric
unimaginative like the last one a man plethoric unimaginative.
That was a hopeless attempt. It's best to haunt the intelligent.
They are not used to responding fully with their bodies and the
shock is greater.

But it also makes the task more difficult in other ways, though
interesting. The present victim is not only beautiful, pale of
course, ashen pale in all that hair ashen pale from lack of violent
activity including sex but intelligent. She thinks about me, thus

creating my shape, together with its pain, thus giving me existence as a foot, the prettiest foot I have ever been and perhaps was before the leg was lacerated wrenched and crushed in all that twisted car metal because it's hard to tell whether I once was her real foot or not, so completely do I now achieve identification as her phantom foot slim long and gracefully arched and well sprung above a most shapely big toe. That's where I manage to hurt most. But she thinks intelligently about me, in the full knowledge that I am not really there attached to the long space that is her phantom leg also not there. She winds me round with other thoughts like boring details of hospital routine that loom larger than life or intrinsic worth and wrap each phantom fibre of me like a medullary sheath at times. But at times only for I have my rhythm and several other amputees to haunt which would tend to prove that I never was her personal real foot in a full schedule with necessary rest-periods to withdraw my atoms in quiescence before gathering them up into the neuroblasts that will create me anew within her brain along the spinothalamic tract and the efferent fibres down to the neuroma in the stump where the axons of the severed nerves proliferate wildly and send back false messages to the cortical areas that will soon when the strong tranquillizer dies build up from them the central image of a limb no longer there but wrenched and lacerated crushed and cut now cleanly, surgically away, if cleanly it can be called with such tumourous antheap in the stump. And now she thinks about me, giving me strength, existence, and creating my shape, her slim long phantom foot, her unendurable phantom pain.

She cries quietly. I find this very exciting. The imitation neurones I am now composed of agitate their dendrites like tremulous antennae interlacing intermingling or the frictioning legs of flies that swarm as the cell bodies dance through the synapses and I want her to scream.

But she cries quietly. She is not only beautiful but brave, pale of course ashen pale in all that ashen hair like dead nerve fibres that conduct no pain themselves but sheath the white face crisped in a cramp agony of sharp nails driven into the five bones of the metatarsus and the ball of the foot that only exists within the white matter of the mid-brain as greyish white as her face and as crisped in its creation of my shape with its concomitant pain, dear?

—Yes, nurse. It's very bad. But don't give me another injection. I must learn to deal with it.

Not if I can help it.

—That's right dear. I wasn't going to. It's time for your percussion soon.

—Oh no.

—Oh yes. You know it'll do you good.

—But it's agony. And it doesn't help at all.

Alas it does, it is the death of me, although it hurts her real pain in the stump neuroma.

—It's agony at first love. Like wearing the padded cast the day after the operation. But then the pressure gradually deadened the pain, didn't it? It's the same with percussion. You'll see, in time. Like tapping a bad tooth.

—Temporarily perhaps. But it doesn't cure the tooth does it? And the tooth exists, and is sick. Why should banging my stump with a mallet stop the pain in a foot I merely imagine?

Her intelligence will be the death of me, despite the lower threshold it creates to help me.

—And why do I get pain in the imagined foot anyway, and not in the whole leg? I imagine the leg too. And the stump hurts like hell. But that's different, it's real pain, so it's bearable, however acute.

—Yes dear, I know.

—Do you, nurse? Pain is so personal.

—Subjective, dear, that's right. You'll be coming on nicely once you recognize that.

—My foot is an object. Outside myself. It exists.

—In your mind, love. Only in your mind. Mr Poole explained it to you didn't he?

—Oh yes, I know. The central nervous system can't get rid of its body-image, it's got so used to it after all those years. Twenty-two years to be precise. As if that helped. Only twenty-two. Why did I have to go with Denis in his crazy car? I didn't even like him. It's so unfair, it's—

—Now my dear, don't upset yourself. You'll only make it worse.

—It hurts, it hurts, I can't bear it, nurse, please give me something, I can't bear it.

She cries much more than quietly now, she shouts, she sobs, she yells, she gasps. I find it very exciting. The imitation neurones I am composed of agitate their dendrites like made ganglia that arborize the system as the cell bodies dance along the axis cylinder within the fibres of the foot that isn't there, move backwards now, tugging away from the interlaced antennae as if trying to wrench themselves of some submicroscopic umbilical tie anchored into soft tissue, caught into bone, straining, straining to freedom birth and terror of time and space as the impulses race down the fibrils and create me, shape me and I ache strongly, I swell to huge existence that possesses her wholly and loves her loves her loves and hurts her unendurably until the cortical areas can only respond by switching off the supply of blood along the nerves going out of the spinal cord so that she faints.

She looks so beautiful, so white and ashen pale in all that ashen hair like dead nerve fibres that conduct no pain themselves but sheath the white face peaceful now with conjugate upward gaze vanished beyond the slit eyelids to face the darker phantoms of the womb the tomb the cavern the ebb and flow of endless tides linked to the sun-devouring moon monster of chasm death and timelessness that draws the human soul like a magnet from the moment of the first fall wrench of umbilical muscle rough manhandling tumbling lying in soft cloud sucking at heaven severed from weight of body on stumbling legs and fall through days and minutes. Eyes open can bring archetypes alive and love that draws me to her like a magnet as she wakes and there there, love, lie quietly you'll feel better now.

—Yes. Thank you nurse.

As if she had done anything.

—Nurse.

—Yes, love?

—Is it true that children amputated before the age of four don't get phantom pains? Mr Poole told me.

They do like to remind us of our powerless spheres. I feel exhausted, impotent.

—Well, if Mr Poole told you it must be true, mustn't it?

—That doesn't follow. Mr Poole says a lot of things to patients to cheer them up. But like all doctors he's so busy he forgets we're individuals. For instance the other day, during percussion, he said—

—That reminds me, it's time. Are you all right now dear?

She retreats as usual into her obsession with Mr Poole the surgeon the knife-man the castrator. She drowns in Mr Poole, dipping her nerve-ends in soft surrounding tissue as in water oedema, wrapping each phantom fibre of me with a medullary sheath of myelin that winds me round with thoughts of Mr Poole and all that Mr Poole has said in molecular detail to relive soothe stimulate and occupy. I do not mind however at present being thus wound round cut off castrated as a phantom limb for I have temporarily spent my energy in possessing her so hugely hurtfully and I must rest recuperate my atoms while the rubber mallet knocks at her stump neuroma for ten minutes of time until with each knock several hundred unmyelinated nerve-fibres degenerate and after days weeks months curl up and die. But the real pain in her stump does not concern me, being as she so wisely says real therefore bearable. I merely take advantage of its existence in the early stages to increase my shape my hugeness my hold on her, I borrow its pain returning it with impulse interest. I draw my main strength though from the central image of me, so that after months of intimate relationship I am able to create myself out of this central image without recourse to the pain in the stump which may have vanished almost entirely after years or recur just intermittently according to stress and strain but unrelatedly to my sudden visitations. Ghosts have their own rhythms, must preserve independence, mystery.

I am beginning to miss her. It's always a bad sign when I start analysing my methods of self-creation self-absorption more like. She is herself absorbed away from me in Mr Poole, who is gentle manly with silvering hair and sexy eyes he knows just how to use to arouse the right degree of emotional involvement in his patients. He comes into the women's ward saying why haven't you brushed that lovely hair young lady and where's your handbag sweetie there take out your compact and a little lipstick too I like my patients to look feminine even the day after there that's better I thought you were so pretty on the operation table but a little pale as if anyone could look pretty in an oxygen mask. Even the men

respond from submerged rivalry for his good looks frustration
father-dependence and castration fears well founded as he taps
their stumps with a rubber-mallet in percussion therapy talking
softly of problems pains and phantoms and get quite annoyed
when Dr Willett does it instead.

When is she coming back ? Is it ten minutes or ten days since I
last possessed her ? I am losing track of time, always a ghostly
failing when out of sense out of mind. She doesn't think of me. She
is absorbed in Mr Poole's silvering hair sexy eyes and soft words
like young lady I'm very pleased with you which flow even through
the neurilemma across the myelin sheaths of every fibre and send
impulses down the unsolid structures of the fibrils past the nodes
where somehow they transmute into unformulated other words
my little girl my love my sweet good little girl that float their
chaotic particles around the entire autonomous system back up the
spine into the thalamus with no more than a mild thermal sensation in the phantom foot as I grow jealous at a distance in lost space
and time. I should have gone with her. But he would have observed
me. And I was tired. And now I am restless at her absence from
me.

He is explaining to her in a suave and sexy voice that the phantom pain is related to a central excitatory state with emphasis on
the internuncial pool of the spinal cord or in other words my dear
the higher sensory centres, with resulting summation of abnormal
stimuli and a persistence of the pain pattern due to higher-level
involvement. What is summation she asks to hide her confusion
at the word involvement. I'm sorry darling oh he calls everyone
darling it's his therapeutic way you're so intelligent I forget you're
not professional that too is his therapeutic way with her it merely
means the total sum, you know, all the abnormal stimuli working
together at once. And internuncial well you've heard of a nuncio
haven't you, a messenger or ambassador of the Pope, it's the same
with the nerves, they send messengers who gather together in the
internuncial pool, like a typing pool you know, that's why I'm
called Poole, ha, I receive all the nerve messages of all my patients
and I sort them out and soothe them, like the pool of Lethe
darling, so that they don't hurt any more, you see. For a while at
least. Until your next visit.

—You seem intent on building up an emotional dependence in me. If you go on like that I'll get the phantom pain every time I'm due to see you.

—Now don't be too intelligent sweetie or you'll make it worse.

—Why abnormal stimuli working all together? What's abnormal about me?

—Not you darling. You're a normal healthy lovely girl and you will soon be leading a normal healthy lovely life if you're good and do as I say.

The words flow through the myelin sheaths of every nerve and send impulses up and down the unsolid structures of the fibrils past the nodes where somehow they transmute to a normal healthy love life not quite formulated as they float in scattered particles slowly around the autonomous system back into the cerebrospinal and drown in the internuncial pool before reaching the thalamus. She lies calm serene almost euphoric on her bed her open eyes alive with liquid tenderness and the alluring invitation down the pathways to the womb the ebb and flow of time linked to the sun-devouring moon white chasm of heaven and timelessness that draws me like a magnet from the moment I am conscious of my rebirth in desire to re-create my shape her phantom foot and devastate her beauty with my aching hugeness as an intractable phantom pain.

She shall love me want me need me despite her intelligence or even because of. She shall desire me to re-create my shape her phantom foot in her mind for the soft-voiced sexy-eyed attention of Mr Poole the knife-man the castrator of that shape once in intimate touch with earth air water mother belly and bearing the whole weight of her existence in upright position on that shape of bone flesh fibre skin deeply engraved within the cellular composition of the left midbrain at the level of the superior colliculus six millimetres lateral to the aqueduct of Sylvius in the region of the pain pathways. She shall cherish her symptoms.

How strong I was on that first day when she came to from dreamless anaesthetic nothingness and wanted to get up convinced her leg her foot were there after all the surgeon having somehow mended soothed plasticized remade the crushed and lacerated limb that now just dully ached through the still slumbering nerves.

I watched her wake, so beautiful in her pallor sheathed with pale gold like myelin round dead fibres that conduct no pain. And the astonishment hope wonder in her sleepy siren's eyes that seemed to surface from deep waters moving with the sun-devouring moon great chasm of death and timelessness to which man must return drawn like a magnet from the moment of the fall the wrench of umbilical placenta rough manhandling tumbling lying in soft tissue sucking at the day that streams its minutes into weening separation weight of body on crumbling legs and fall through months and years. Even then I knew in a split atom of time bombarded by her beauty that it would have to be the higher-level involvement for my pains and I felt awed but strong with resulting summation of abnormal stimuli my shape quite hypertrophied though slim still in her mind and gracefully arched the prettiest foot I have ever been and perhaps was before her leg was lacerated crushed in all that twisted car metal.

The optic thalamus in the cerebral cortex was working hard and suddenly awake she saw me clear as I stretched my imitation metatarsus long gracefully arched towards the malleolar prominences on either side of her slim ankle up the shapely shin the rounded knee the dimple in the flesh of the popliteal fossa behind the knee till suddenly she threw back the bedclothes saw the stump bandaged into gaping void and gasped, then started moaning like an animal or a woman about to come. It was very exciting. But annihilating. I had existed so strong so hypertrophied and so sensuously detailed till she saw with her own eyes that I wasn't there and I almost ceased to be. But her terror her suffering as she panted galvanized my impulses into the free nerve-terminations of her pain fibres afferent proprioceptive and she screamed, oh joy ineffable. I knew then that the visio-erotic element of her inner eye would always help me despite her intelligence or perhaps because of.

Words are my enemies. The words of Mr Poole and Dr Willett but especially Mr Poole soft-voiced and sexy-eyed with his demands for lipstick hairbrushing self-confidence vanity and his explanations that soothe strengthen her understanding. She winds me round with words that formulate new thoughts of her mother her boy-friends and her job past present future which wrap each fibre of me like a medullary sheath at times. But only at times for I have my rhythm and although too engrossed obsessed too highly involved now with her to haunt other amputees I need my rest-periods, to ache for her recognition of my existence, of my shape as a foot that belongs to her ineradicably and intimately within her cerebrospinal system bombarding it through all its impulse-bearing tracts with an intractable pain. The real danger of words is that they create thoughts which lead to other thoughts and these if stimulating and distracting and absorbing enough may smother me altogether or knock me out like a percussion mallet until my imitation unmyelated nerve-fibres degenerate curl up and die. If she starts thinking constructively about her future for instance. But there are ways. The words of Mr Poole do have a side-effect that helps me, building up as she so intelligently said an emotional dependence from visit to visit the intelligent recognition of which can in no wise prevent. For his soft-voiced and sexy-eyed attention she too often desires to re-create my phantom shape her foot once in intimate touch with earth air water mother belly and bearing the whole weight of her existence in upright position on that structure of bone flesh fibre skin now pierced with sharp nails driven into the metatarsus and the ball of the foot that only exists as an image deeply engraved within the left midbrain as greyish white as her face and as crisped in its creation of my shape she cherishes with its concomitant phantom pain.

—You are cherishing your symptoms my dear says Mr Poole severely with a nevertheless gentle tap on the stump the neuroma almost circumscribed mature now non-proliferating healed and she has never heard the phrase before.

—It means darling that although the phantom pain is undoubtedly real to you the causes are more psychogenic now than physiological, what we call a functional pain. Don't look so insulted sweetie I'm not saying you're deranged nor that you're malingering. Malingering is very rare in this field. But some patients, who are depressive or hysterical, unconsciously prolong their symptoms even for years and years, and suffer genuine agonies that in the end can only be dealt with by sympathectomy, which is not as you might think darling don't look so frightened the removal of sympathy but the removal of certain nerves or rather ganglia in the sympathetic autonomous nervous system, a small local operation. But you don't want more surgery do you, or, for that matter, a leucotomy, that's much more drastic.

—What! Never.

—Well, there you are. That's by way of a playful threat darling since you're not in fact either depressive or hysterical but a normal healthy girl who's had a nasty shock and a nasty operation. Would you like another course of electroencephalic treatment? That gave you some relief didn't it?

—No.

—Well, there's a new thing called white sun, a nice poetic name for audio-analgesia, it's fed into the ear over such a range of auditory stimuli it swamps all the receptors in the brain—

—Shut up!

—I was hoping you'd say that. All right darling calm down. You want to deal with this yourself. You're a good brave girl. You're doing very well with the new artificial limb, I hear from physiotherapy. That's quite comfortable isn't it? Doesn't hurt? Good. And are you occupying your mind?

—Yes.

—Good. What with?

—Oh, thoughts. Ideas.

—Now that's not so good. You mustn't get ideas. What thoughts? You should do something. Prepare for ordinary life. We'll be discharging you soon and you must think of that.

—You just told me thoughts are not so good.

—Smart girl, you'll be all right. Do you have a job you can go back to?

—I was a model.

—Oh. I'm sorry sweetie, you did tell me and so did your mother. Yes. I forgot for a moment.

—You have so many patients.

—That's no excuse.

—As a matter of fact I thought, perhaps, I could write.

—To whom darling?

—Just, write. You know, novels.

—Oh yes. Love stories you mean? Or spies? Why not, there's a lot of money in it. As long as you don't get too excited yourself, tension brings back the phantom you know.

—Well, I wasn't exactly thinking of love stories no she isn't exactly thinking of love stories or spies although I love her and I spy on her through the symptoms which she cherishes a little for the soft-voiced and sexy-eyed sympathy of the internuncial pool in the spinal cord or in other words my dear my little girl my love my good sweet little girl the higher sensory centres with resulting summation of abnormal stimuli and a persistence of the pain pattern she cherishes due to higher-level involvement fear of sympathectomy and white sun swamping all receptors in her brain. She is thinking of me to write about in order to get me out of her system as they call it not sympathetic or parasympathetic autonomous but cerebrospinal out of her midbrain on to paper instead of aching there fifty-three and a half centimetres away from her stump now circumscribed mature and non-proliferating with a phantom lower leg between though painless but undoubtedly projecting out the pain of sharp nails driven into the metatarsus and the ball of the foot that only exists in the higher sensory centres near the optic thalamus with which she sees me in her inner eye visio-erotically lateral to the aqueduct of Sylvius in the region of the pain pathways until I exist again so strong so hypertrophied and so sensuously detailed that I galvanize my impulses up the free nerve-terminations of her pain fibres afferent propioceptive and she starts moaning like an animal or a woman in joy ineffable.

I shall not let her get rid of me with words that re-create my shape my galvanizing atoms of agony on mere paper to be read by careless unsuffering millions vicariously and thus dispersed. I shall possess her and possess her again obsessing her absorbing her growing strong on her distress that excites me and re-creates my shape as her sweet phantom foot with its associated pain intractable unendurable and cherished.

She writes however. She has a Biro pen and a small exercise book Denis brought her. He got off with a broken arm worn in a sling for a while and looked like Napoleon short podgy oddly continental with a thin straight wisp from his receding hair down over his brow but constantly smoothed back and patted down as he says how are you dear and the brow contracts a little with guilt concern embarrassment fear removing the sympathy and any love that might have been with two legs. She uses him but not so much as well she might and he brings her fruit and flowers and books she wants about amputation syndromes not magazines full of models and the Biro pen and the small exercise book that stays closed and empty for some time as I continue to possess her again and again growing huge on her distress that excites me in increasing rhythm and re-creates my shape and my obsession with her aching my desire. Despite the increasing rhythm however or because of I need the rest-periods to withdraw my atoms after detumescence before gathering them up into the neuroblasts that will formulate me anew within her brain along the spinothalamic tract and the efferent fibres and she opens meanwhile the small exercise book and in thin impersonal Biro strokes she writes the words she hears like white sun swamping all other receptors in the brain so that the white page slowly engraves itself with the victim to be haunted is female. And beautiful. This makes a difference. She has the habit of confidence, but also a greater adjustment to achieve while I slumber rest in my detumescence. She betrays me.

She isn't thinking of a love-story spy-thriller although she loves me spies on me through the symptoms cherished nor a novel no Proust she à la recherche du pied perdu I also like my little joke I can make cleverer ones than Mr Poole but she starts humbly with a short story that says the victim is female and very beautiful as she knows very well with open eyes that can bring beauty alive with awareness of pain terror despair or anger, not to mention desire and liquid tenderness or even the alluring invitation down the pathways of pain swamped by the white sun of the words she hears, their nuclear cells radiating from the cochlear ganglion of the interior ear in the temporal lobe and round the cerebral cortex to the visual centre in the occipital lobe where the optic chiasm turns me and her whole body upside down until relayed into the parietal lobe and ending in the thalamus where contact pain heat cold localization discrimination recognition of posture merge with the power of responding to different intensities of stimuli so that I drown in merely abstract existence feel knocked out in percussion and bombarded till my imitation unmyelated nerve-fibres degenerate curl up and die.

It is a proven scientific fact that women have a higher pain threshold than men. Which makes the task more difficult but interesting. All right, let her continue I can bide my time in detumescence until she exhausts herself and begs me to return or re-creates me anew out of the tension from fatigue and emptiness. For even within that distinction the threshold varies from subject to subject and from time to time and there is rhythm in the haunting game as in any other according to stress drugs distraction violent activity including sex and literary creation as with a soldier in combat all senses occupied unaware of wound until his wild ferocity is abated. For there are ways to re-create distress. The electroencephalic treatment she has now prescribed herself may merely alter the nature of the pain and the position of the phantom limb. What fools they are. Variety of position is the spice of intimacy. I find it very exciting. Despite the annihilation through merely abstract existence on the rapidly neuroblasted paper there are still ways of lowering the threshold. Severe mental deprivation for example raise it and the highly intelligent undoubtedly suffer more than the plethoric unimaginative which she certainly is not being at the moment. She thinks about me, thus creating my shape her phantom foot, visually, aurally in words and sensuously in bones flesh skin and neuroblasts that dance along the axis cylinders within the myelin-sheathed fibres of the foot that isn't there except on paper to be read by careless unsuffering millions vicariously and thus dispersed.

I had existed so strong so hypertrophied and so cellurlarly detailed that her abstract creation will be the death of me unless the electroencephalic treatment she has prescribed herself merely alters my nature my position more or less distant from the stump as a projection of the central body-image in the higher sensory centres in excitatory state galvanizing my impulses into the free nerve-terminations of her pain fibres that tingle afferent propioceptive and the imitation neurones I am recomposed of agitate their dendrites like mad ganglia arborizing the system as the cell-bodies dance along the fibres of the foot that isn't there, move backwards now, tugging away from the interlaced antennae as if trying to wrench themselves off some submicroscopic umbilical tie anchored into soft tissue, caught in bone, straining to freedom birth and terror of time and space as the neuroblasts race down the fibrils and create me, shape me and I ache strongly I swell to huge existence that possesses her wholly and loves her loves her loves and hurts her unendurably until she moans and pants like an animal or a woman in joy ineffable and the cortical areas respond by switching off the supply of blood along the nerves leaving the spinal cord and out she passes out.

She looks so beautiful, so white and ashen pale in all that ashen hair like dead nerve-fibres that conduct no pain but sheath the white face peaceful now with conjugate upward gaze vanished beyond the slit eyelids to face the darker phantoms of the womb the tomb the cavern the ebb and flow of internuncial pools linked to the chasm of death and timelessness that draws her like a magnet from the moment of the first fall wrench of umbilical muscle rough manhandling tumbling lying in soft tissue sucking at heaven severed weight of body on crumbling legs and fall through days and minutes. Eyes open can bring archetypes alive and love that draws me like a magnet from the moment of my rebirth in desire to re-create my shape her phantom foot and devastate her beauty with my aching hugeness as an intractable phantom pain.

Yes, there are ways to re-create distress, less often perhaps, which is the way of intimacy and even haunting has its rhythm decreasing increasing according to stress fatigue drugs general constitution previous equilibrium distraction violent activity including sex and writing. I shall learn to be more discreet, play hard to get perhaps but only play. I cannot live without her and I know her weakness now, I know she needs my love my presence my shape her slim long phantom foot with its concomitant hugeness as a phantom pain.

She cries quietly now. I find this very exciting.

MY MAN CLOSTERS

by Anthony Rye

When one of those she preferred not to think of as customers
made an inquiry, Millie Consadine would say: 'Certainly. I'll send
my man Closters round with it directly.' And then Closters, in his
dignified way, would go out and slaughter a duck or a fowl—
though he hated doing it, really—and in due time deliver it,
plucked and prepared, on his bicycle.

They had always preserved the proper distance. And should one
of her 'summer guests', as she called them, though some stayed all
the year round, delicately hint surprise at a man so obviously
trained in a great establishment being content with hers, Millie
would say: 'Yes, isn't it wonderful. I could never manage without
him.' And no truer words ever were spoken. Millie was an excellent plain cook, and charming and easy-going, but she was not
very practical. Still, you could say that they were complementary
and reciprocal in gaining for Trivets its modest success. 'He was
Harry's batman, you know,' she might explain further, 'against
those Boers. He couldn't face indoor work after the Veldt.' Here
he worked both indoors and out.

She might have added that Harry hadn't been able to settle
either. He was, or you might say he had been her husband, known
always as the Captain, though his commission had been temporary,
and it was an open secret that he had left her. In a rash moment he
had told her to choose between her pets and himself and in con-
sequence had departed. For ever. Ah—he had liked a gay life, had
never cared for the country. They had had no children and it was
mean of him to take against her pets, if they were rather many.
Besides, it had left her almost penniless, in a house belonging to
his sisters, and had it not been that these, surprisingly, angry with
their brother and full of *noblesse oblige*, had come to her rescue,
reducing the rent to a minimum and prevailing on Closters to stay
and see her through, she really would not have had an idea what to

do. However she had not grown bitter. And thus it was that she found herself sitting with a trio of guests, agreeable though not of her own choosing—but you would never have supposed that—on the veranda of Trivets, on a fine summer evening, her innumerable cats and dogs around her, and her parrot, Feste, swinging in his cage which hung from the ceiling above them.

They had just finished a delicious meal. Closters had killed the ducklings which Millie had perfectly cooked. As soon as a dinner was ready she would dash to her room, leaving it to him to serve while she changed, which meant putting on a rusty black silk skirt and slinging a bedraggled tippet over her plump pink shoulders. Tonight she had added a turban from which her hair strayed soft and squirrel-red, and pieces of crude, cheap jewelry— green ear-rings, obviously paste, and a matching 'emerald' ring. With her feet bulged over evening shoes of soiled white buckskin she looked, as often, grotesque. But it was a measure of her character that usually this went unnoticed or it added mysteriously to her charm.

'You're looking smart tonight,' said Tom Longworth, critical once fed.

'Particularly smart,' corrected Dr Prewitt.

Having been a medical student hadn't made Tom too delicate in the first place, and some years as a writer of crime fiction had left him unimproved. Still he was a good fellow. Old Oswald Prewitt, LL.D., was a retired barrister. He had recently come to look Mrs Consadine up, having known her years before in India, and was staying on. Very young William Bankes had known her and her home for years, having been brought to stay in the neighbourhood as a child. He was a writer of sorts too: under cover of writing a serious novel he was attempting verse.

'Am I smart?' Millie preened herself in the male regard as though before a mirror. 'I wanted to look nice,' she said. She did not, open as she was, tell them that this was the anniversary of her desertion—the twentieth, as it happened—and that she had done it to boost her morale.

The moon was up. Scents arose from the tobacco plants, on which dogs were lying, against the house wall still reflecting the heat. All the cats were off somewhere hunting, or indoors curled up asleep. All the poultry were housed, and the goats—by Closters, of course, who was washing up. It was an almost perfectly peaceful scene, marred only by a rather dubious smell caused by an activity of Closters which, out of pure good-nature, he had first undertaken in the days of shortage at the end of the First World War. He supplied many locally with meat for their pets, cycling off to obtain sheep's heads, horse-flesh and other offal, which he carried in a large basket attached to his handle-bars. These, in a far-off tangled quarter of the demesne called by Willie Golgotha, he would boil and scrape and cut up small, afterwards burning the smaller bones and refuse, which had caused the annoyance which everyone got used to in time. It was an enterprise which appreciably helped the exchequer.

'Let's have some light,' said Millie. 'And I must take off these shoes.'

The conversation, so cosy in this setting, had been about Crippen, what was to be said of him for or against, and had gradually died down. All agreed that it was funny how you could not talk when you couldn't see each others' faces. Closters was by now in bed. Millie heaved herself upright and went indoors, coming back soon in roomier slippers and with an oil-lamp which shed its soft warm glow upon them. But the conversation was not resumed; rather they seemed content to enjoy the coolness in a silence only broken by the creaking of deep wicker chairs and the slight tick and twang of Feste, as he levered himself about his cage with beak and claw.

'Time that bird was taken indoors,' observed Millie, making no move. As though her remark had been a signal the dogs now became restive, scuffling and snapping among themselves.

'Oh, now, stop it, you!' exclaimed Millie. 'Sam! Tessa!— They're ruining the plants!' An enormous black cat leaped on to the stage and into old Prewitt's lap. 'Titus!' she cried. 'Push him off, Oswald, don't have him. Pfff! Get away—get off!'

But all the time she was laughing quietly, for she loved her pets and treasured each for its idiosyncrasies.

The hubbub was quelled. The animals, still a little restless, came in and stood or sat near their mistress. Feste suddenly gave one of his piercing screams.

'That parrot,' said Dr Prewitt. 'It doesn't seem to talk much, does it?' He had no great love for the breed.

Millie gave one of her richest chuckles. 'No,' she said, 'he doesn't talk at all. He used to, beautifully, but he hasn't said a word since Harry left me.'

At that instant, as if on purpose to belie her, Feste spoke.

'Holly! Holly! Holly!' called the parrot: 'Vic! Vic! Come on. Come on. Come here.'

'Why, that *is* Harry!' Millie started up in astonishment. 'Of all the extraordinary things. . . .'

It was a man's voice, certainly, clear and strong, an unpleasant stridency in the tones, but for all that just the voice of a man calling his dogs in, late on a summer night. 'Why, those were dogs we had when we first came here,' said Millie. All four stared into the night from which ventriloquially the words had seemed to come, while the present dogs barked like fury, and Titus, fur on end, bolted indoors. Nothing was to be seen, of course. Then an apparition far more extraordinary than any they could have expected arrived. Closters, in night attire, a night-shirt stuffed inconclusively into trousers from which the braces dangled, had come among them from the unprecedented direction of the hall. And he stood and glared at Feste as if in a world gone mad.

*

'I've never been so astonished,' said Willie Bankes later to Tom Longworth. They were sitting in Willie's room having a nightcap.

'What, at a parrot talking?'

'Of course not. At Closters. You know, he simply isn't obtrusive. Why, he even gets into his bedroom through the window, so as not to disturb us; and, as you know, rather than pass in front of the house when we're there he always takes the lower terrace. What he'd do if it wasn't a bungalow built on a steep I can't think. And then to come bursting in on us like that, through the hall . . . It's incredible.'

'I suppose it might be pretty eerie, hearing your master's voice after so long. You've known him for ages, haven't you?'

'Oh, ages. He was a sort of uncle to me when I was a child. Used to show me birds' nests and wildflowers and things. He's a thorough countryman. Do you know he can even hear bats on the wing. He loves animals. That's one of the reasons they get on so well, I think. Of course, he doesn't like greenfly; and I remember him saying once that he didn't care for foxes; said they made him uneasy yapping around in hard weather. The poultry, I suppose. He looked absolutely aghast, didn't he ?'

Tom Longworth, yawning, agreed.

The next morning Closters came late with the tea, murmuring apology. 'Too much excitement last night ?' asked Tom, strolling in to get his cup.

'Excitement, sir ? Oh! Ah! Very strange occurrence, sir, yes.' But Closters seemed disinclined to chat about it.

'He looks rotten,' said Tom, 'and I don't wonder. He's had a bad night. Several times I heard him stirring, and he talked to himself a bit too.'

'Talked ? What about ?'

'Well at times it sounded as if he was praying,' said Tom. But once—I was sitting at the open window and I suppose he was doing the same at his—I distinctly heard him say: "It couldn't have been! It couldn't have been!" And a little while after, "It was a signal." Just that.'

'What could he have meant ?'

'I don't know. It's interesting, isn't it ?'

'Blast that Feste!' said Willie. 'I wish to goodness he'd kept his beak shut. It's spoilt our atmosphere.'

*

And that night Feste did keep his beak shut, and the next night, and the next. Nor was he heard to utter in the daytime. But on the following evening, a Saturday, with Closters, as was his custom, up at the British Legion Club helping at the bar (he never drank himself), when they were again sitting on the veranda, the parrot broke out once more, much more spectacularly:

'Go and get it! Go and get it!' screamed Feste. 'Get it! Get it! Get it!'

'Well, in heaven's name!' cried Millie. 'What was that about ?'

'It would appear to be the same voice that was imitated,' said old Prewitt, cautiously.

'Oh, it's Harry all right. Absolutely marvellous. But . . .'

'Go and get it! Get it! *Get* it!' demanded Feste.

'Get what, you silly old fool?' stormed Millie. 'Don't keep on at it.'

'Did your husband often use this tone?' inquired Tom, delicate as usual.

'Well, yes, he might if he'd had too much, but I don't think he had, had he? You all heard it.' Everyone solemnly vouched for Feste's sobriety. 'I shall ask Closters when he comes in. Perhaps he can throw some light on it.'

*

Next morning old Prewitt came to breakfast in his bedroom slippers, holding extended a pair of lady's walking shoes.

'Ah!' said Millie. 'You'll find yours outside my door, I fancy. I do hope,' she went on, meditatively, 'that Closters isn't going to be ill again.'

'Again?' said Tom Longworth. 'He's always seemed so strong. Must be, with all he does.'

'Oh, yes, he was quite ill once—let me see, when was it—about the last year of the war: yes, in '18, it was. Went off his food, and fussed and fretted. I never did know why. Took to praying at odd moments. Of course you know he's a religious man? Will you pass me the mustard, please, Oswald?' Millie took a great mouthful of ham.

'So long ago as that?' said old Prewitt, admiring her.

'Yes,' Millie sighed. 'Yes, it must have been then, for it was just after I'd come back from visiting my poor sister at Mopporth, in Yorkshire, where we come from. They call it Mopporth, you know, though its spelt Mopworth. The only time, I think, I've ever been away.'

'And has he never been ill since?'

'No. It was a sort of religious mania, I think: crying in the night, and all that. It was distressing, but he got over it quite soon. But this hearing Harry again does seem thoroughly to have upset him. Upset me, too. He was even more shaken last night, when I told him, than the first time.'

'And could he throw any light on what the words meant?' asked old Prewitt. 'None whatever,' sighed Millie.

'He certainly seems in rather an abstracted state,' said Tom. 'There was a goat in my room this morning.'

'Oh, dear!—a goat! Oh, I'm so sorry. How did it get in?'

'Through the window, I believe. I was out at the time.'

'Closters must have left the gate unlatched, or made the collar too loose, or something. I thought I heard a commotion.' And Millie laughed. 'I do hope it did no harm.'

Tom laughed too. 'It's a critic, that goat. It ate two pages of my story.'

'Oh, too bad! Were they—I mean—?'

'Important? No, fortunately. If it had been Willie's now. . . .'

'Just as well. Probably have poisoned it,' said Willie. And on this happy note they left the breakfast table. But outside, Tom whispered to Willie: 'Closters *was* crying last night. And Willie, look at this.' He brought out of his pocket a small object. 'Down at Golgotha,' he said. Willie stared. 'No!' he breathed out at last, 'it's not possible.'

Not only had the atmosphere at Trivets altered, the whole structure and fabric of their happy life was threatened. And all the time the parrot ticked and twanged and hung upside down against the bars, and scattered seeds that rapped like sleet on the polished floor, and eyed them coldly. Willie had meant to put in some solid reading that Sunday morning, but instead wandered about. Tom was hard at his writing, whatever the day. There went Closters on his way to church, in his black best. The sturdy upright form Willie knew, so handsome in its melancholy brooding way, was dreadfully changed, somehow shrunken. . . .

A further confidence from Tom came at the end of the afternoon. After tea, thoroughly disturbed, it was almost with the idea of avoiding his friend that Willie proposed to himself a solitary walk. He wanted badly to think things over. As he was about to descend the steps from the terrace to the grassed-over drive which in turn led down to the lane, old Prewitt asked if he might accompany him. He was a decent old boy, with his large square head, and, though rather prim and cautious of manner, very sociable and kind, Willie thought. Fatherly. They went down the steps together, slowly. Bell-flowers and foxgloves obstructed them.

Upon the order of this large and well laid-out garden negligence seemed to have been imposed creatively.

Old Prewitt poked and peered along the bank. 'Ah! Here they are,' he said, pointing to the little wild cyclamen in the shadow of a bush. 'Closters showed me them, but I thought I had lost them.'

'Yes, aren't they beautiful? He planted them there, you know. And all the bulbs—daffodils, narcissus: you should see it in the spring.'

'I mean to,' said old Prewitt. 'I envy you your knowledge of this place. Perhaps you knew that I'd been acquainted with Mrs Consadine and her husband in the early part of my life? Did you ever see him?'

'Only once or twice when I was very small. I remember him as a disgruntled figure among goats.'

'Between ourselves,' said old Prewitt, 'she was well rid of him. One was very unfavourably impressed by his behaviour to Mrs Consadine, even in those days.'

'They are rather wonderful, don't you think?—she and Closters,' Willie broke out.

'Oh, decidedly: unique, delightful.'

'Dr Prewitt,' went on Willie, impulsively, 'you are our legal representative: could—could a parrot's words be used in evidence?'

Old Prewitt's shaven cheek rippled slightly. 'I beg your pardon?'

'I mean, could anything a parrot said be evidence?'

'No,' said old Prewitt. 'Shall we sit down?' He indicated a rustic seat which Closters had constructed in a grassy circle at the head of the drive, where once carriages could turn. 'I am not much of a legal anything nowadays, Willie, and my practice led me away from advocacy, you may know. However, if "what the soldier said" is not evidence, then how much less so a parrot. No. Except, of course, in ancient ballads,' he added, smiling. 'But why did you ask?'

'Well, why should Closters have been so disturbed—terrified you'd say, really? And now—well you seem to spot him about, at least just sliding off, while before he was always so out of the way until needed. I think he listens. Not that he'd need to be

very near, because he hears bats, you know. And then Tom
Longworth has heard him praying, or something—and last
night, he says, crying—and pacing about. And *I* saw him sitting
in his wheel-barrow early this morning, with his head in his
hands, and his shoulders shook. And then. . . .'

'Well?' said old Prewitt, gravely.

'Tom. He found a tooth down near the rubbish heap. Oh, I
know there are hundreds of them, and the pies and jackies pick
them up and drop them about; but this wasn't a sheep's tooth, it
was a—'

'I don't think,' said old Prewitt deliberately, 'that I want to
hear any more.'

'No, but Tom did leave that tooth on his window-sill, and it's
gone. And he says since that he found Closters "tidying up",
as he put it, down by the rubbish heap—on a Sunday. . . .'

Frowning slightly, old Prewitt took out his watch. 'Tom
Longworth is a somewhat rash young man—a writer of detective
fiction. And I seem to remember that there have been complaints
made about Closter's rather excessive tidiness before.' He rose.
'I must be getting back to the house. And, Willie, I should forget
all this. I shouldn't worry.' Turning away, old Prewitt began to
climb the steps with firm but cautious tread.

*

'Forget.' But it might not be so easy. Willie confided to Tom
as they sat on the veranda before dinner that he was not looking
forward to Feste's next performance. 'It's getting to be a regular
séance,' he said. Tom agreed. But he, on the contrary, found
things getting more and more interesting. 'Closters is on the
break. Quite plainly. I saw him coming back from church—Poor
fellow!—his eyes were glazed and set—he looked ghastly. He
gave a sort of sob when I asked how the service had gone—and
usually so communicative! If ever I saw guilt, Willie. . . .'

There was a slight noise from the other end of the veranda,
where old Prewitt had been apparently absorbed in his book.

'Mr Longworth,' he said, 'I could not help overhearing. I
would advise you to guard your words.' He made a warning
gesture with his head in the direction of the hall. 'We do not wish,

I imagine, to alarm anybody. I take it that we want above all to prevent any worsening of Closters's state—any recurrence of nervous breakdown. For Millicent—Mrs Consadine's sake we must do all we can to preserve the *status quo*.' And old Prewitt left the veranda.

'That's all very well,' grumbled Tom. 'If what I think is true—and everything seems to point to it—we may all be very much surprised by what Feste next reveals.'

'You don't really think—' faltered Willie.

'Oh, but I do. I expect a confession. The man's demoralized. Look: he knows that old Prewitt's an LL.D.—a legal eagle; he hears me displaying intimate surgical knowledge the other night, over Crippen, finds I take the *Lancet*, too. Probably he thinks of me as a doctor, and it wouldn't surprise me either if he thinks a writer of detective stories is a detective too. He suspects that he has been rumbled, I'm certain of it.'

Miserably it seemed to Willie that there might be truth in what Tom said. He had observed Closters in the past few days making up little bundles of kindling to store in the woodshed, as though, typically, fearful that in his absence there might not be enough to last. And the idea of Closters's absence was stupefying. The buddleias were in bloom and the air was full of their honey. No less than three humming-bird hawk moths were that moment circling and swooping and backing among the long mauve spears. A thrush sang, and up from the tangled slope drifted the scattered notes of blackcap and garden warbler. Closters somehow stood for all these things.

'Blast Feste!' Willie said again.

Sunday night's cold meat was followed by an exquisite caramel custard, and then there were cherries and red and white currants. 'Let's take them on to the veranda,' said Millie.

Closters had definitely fumbled the dishes during the meal, and had previously even broken a plate simply on hearing a routine squark of Feste's. Willie felt on edge: 'Wouldn't it be an idea to put that parrot to bed early?'

'Oh, Willie!' reproved Millie, ' "that parrot"!—and you've known him so long. I've had Feste from a chick,' she explained. 'When he came he had his fledgling down still on him.' Willie was shame-faced. Feste of course must stay. When Closters brought the coffee tray his hands shook so that there was a sound among the cups like a fairy orchestra.

'How are you feeling, Closters ?' asked Millie. 'You don't look very well. You look tired.'

'I am quite well, thank you, madam.'

'All the same I'm worried,' said she, when he had gone 'I think he needs a thorough change, but how is it to be done ?'

Willie thought Closters was getting rather too much of a change already, and that he, Willie, could do with something of the kind himself. The thing was one way and another plainly on all their minds, with the possible exception of old Prewitt's. He was looking out over the valley, where heat mists were dissolving in curls and streaks.

It was again a lovely evening. There were so many in that summer of '34. Everything had suddenly grown very still. Only the dogs seemed restless, as on the first occasion of Feste's speaking. An Irish terrier bitch called Lady kept up a continuous low growling, under its breath. Feste, after ruffling up his feathers to a prodigious degree, sat at the centre of his perch letting them slowly subside.

'Be quiet, Lady.' Millie stooped a hand to stroke the dog. 'I don't know what's come over her,' she said. She was just launching into an account of Lady's provenance—Lady was a stray like so many of her pets—when for the third time Feste spoke.

'You would, would you! You would, would you!' The now familiar voice was hoarse with passion. And then as if at a change of gear, horribly, swiftly, on an ascending scale: 'Get back! Take your hands off me! Take your hands—take your hands—your hands . . .' The scalding, scraping voice was quenched in an astonishing counterfeit of choking babble and rattle.

Instantly from the depth within came a stumbling inarticulate clamour. Running footsteps, the slamming of a door. Then more footsteps, rapidly receding. There followed dim-heard crashes, as if the slope was being descended in wild leaps.

Millie was the first to grasp the significance of these sounds, the rest being so concentrated on the parrot's words. 'Oh, the poor fellow!' she wailed. 'He *has*—he's got it—he's off again! Go after him, won't you, someone? Don't let him come to harm.' She collapsed in tears, her fingers groping convulsively in the fur of her pet's neck. Tom Longworth vaulted over the low balustrade and made off after Closters in the gloom. Willie saw old Prewitt, palish but still collected, lean across and say something to Millie, his hand on her arm as if to soothe her. After a moment's hesitation he followed Tom.

*

He found them at the bottom of the drive; Closters huddled against the bank, Tom, with his arm about his shoulders, trying to get him to rise.

'What's happened,' said Willie, 'has he broken something?' You cannot rush headlong down such a steep as Trivets is built on without risk, even in daylight. 'No,' said Tom. 'He's had a shock, that's all.'

'Oh, sir,' moaned Closters. He rocked himself to and fro. 'Oh, sir! Oh, sir!'

'Come, brace up, Closters. We must get you back to the house, there's nothing wrong. You've had a bad fall, you're shocked.'

'Oh, no, sir. No. No. No.' And Closters to their distress broke into passionate weeping. Seizing hold of his hair, he shook his head from side to side. 'Oh, no, no, no.' He seemed trying to bury himself in the earth of the bank.

'Let him go on,' said Tom, quietly.

They waited in the deep shade there, out of the moonlight; the cool keen smell of crushed grasses, the night-freshness of trampled earth in their nostrils. After many paroxysms calmness began to return to Closters, and they could distinguish words, the voice still broken, but distinct and quiet. 'I beg your pardon, young gentlemen,' said Closters, tremulously, 'I—I'm not myself.'

'Oh, oh,' he went on, doubling over once more: 'Myself!— if only I wasn't!' And he began to cry again, and all they could hear was: 'It's all over. I can't. I can't—never—go back again.'

'Oh, nonsense,' said Tom. But Closters, reared half upright,

almost leaned against him. 'I can't face it, sir. I can't indeed.'
And he fell back down on to the bank.

'Willie,' said Tom, 'run up and see if you can get some brandy
—whisky would do. And fetch old Prewitt, perhaps it'd be as
well.' 'There's someone coming now,' said Willie. Old Prewitt's
sturdy form, dimly discerned, came bearing slowly down on
them. 'I thought I'd located you,' he announced placidly, 'and
I've come prepared. Not badly hurt, I trust?' He bent over
Closters. He had a flask in his hand.

'Now, Closters, my friend, drink some of this and you'll feel
better.'

'Oh, sir! Oh, dear! Oh, sir!' Closters looked up at old Prewitt
like a hungry dog. He took the flask and drank a little, coughed,
spluttered and shuddered. 'Excuse me, sir. I'm not myself, as
you see.'

'I certainly do see,' said old Prewitt. 'Now, we will go up to
the seat you so thoughtfully built at the top there, and sit down,
and you shall tell me all about it, and we'll see what if anything
is to be done.' He spoke calmly and kindly, but with such
authority that the others were amazed to see the abject form
straighten itself and get up. Soberly they went up the drive, Tom
steadying Closters with a hand under the elbow. When they were
seated, old Prewitt again presented his flask. Closters drank—a
longer pull this time. 'Proceed, Closters,' said old Prewitt, 'of
course at your convenience.'

'Hadn't one of us better run up and see how Mrs Consadine
is?' asked Willie Bankes. He dreaded what might be to come.

'Oh, I hardly think it necessary. I left her quite composed and
about to make a cup of tea. She said she would then go to bed.'

Closters gave a long hollow groan.

'But he—you—mightn't he prefer to talk with you alone?'

'No, I think it as well we should remain together. Closters
knows we are all his friends, don't you, Closters?'

'Oh, yes, sir, yes: you are so very kind, but . . .'

'I think I know,' said old Prewitt. 'Don't worry. Just tell us
all about it. Say why you have been so upset by a parrot speaking
out of the long past.'

Closters stared at him, and his voice was hoarse: 'But it wasn't the parrot said it, sir. It wasn't that bird at all.'

They saw, in the moonlight, old Prewitt cautioning them to be silent over Closters's bowed back. 'Could you make that a little clearer?' he said gently.

Once launched, Closters went on rapidly if not very coherently. 'I had to do it, sir. You do see that? I swore to them I'd look after her. Captain Consadine, he'd never treated Madam right. "You'll look after her," they said, "for she's deserved better than this, and we'll make it up to you," they said. But I wanted no reward for what I done for Madam.'

'We know that,' said old Prewitt.

'Well then he come back, sir—which he could easy do, quartered at Wallerdown. Came over the top, sir, at dusk. Nobody seen him come. He used to hit her about, sir, as I knew by signs.'

There was a pause. 'Go on,' said old Prewitt.

'Madam was asleep, sir. Gone to bed with one of her heads. She'd taken her sedative, what the doctor had ordered. I brought him whisky to the veranda. There with the house door shut I thought I might buy him off, as before I'd done—I had a little by me, sir—without Madam's knowing. But it was the ring he was after this time, and he kept on and on.'

'The ring!' gasped Willie, despite himself.

'Oh, yes, sir. Madam's heirloom, sir. It's a very valuable ring, and was our stand-by, if you understand, if things got bad; and they was. He ordered me to get it, sir, as you heard.'

'And then I suppose he was going to get it himself?' said old Prewitt. 'Go on.'

'I didn't intend it, sir. And it can't be murder, can it—not if you don't mean it? He was in a bad way already, sir; fattish; a big man, and strong, but he hadn't been working like I had. I just grabbed him, sir, and hung on. I only wanted him not to go in. I really don't know how it happened, sir, but all of a sudden he went limp, like. Went dead. The poor man, sir—the Captain—he was dead. . . .

'I had to protect her, hadn't I?'

Out of the moon-filled dusk around came their various murmurs of assent.

'And Madam hadn't woken. And next day, by God's providence, she went away. The only time, sir!—think of that! So what was I to do? I put him in the woodshed that night, and next day, when she'd gone off, I dragged him down to the other by the rubbish heap. And afterwards . . . But that was easy, sir, after all. . . . But it took me all of ten days, sir. But our dogs never had none of it, sir, that I promise you. But the other, sir: that was a different thing. I thought and thought: wasn't there another way? I thought, could I exchange him?—too risky, sir. Couldn't get far enough, not to leave the place empty and that to do. So I had to do it, sir. I had to. What he heard, that was bound to come out. Such a beautiful talker! So I took the money I had, sir, and went along down to Pompey and bought this one. They're much alike. And I dare say you've noticed, sir, that Madam is very short-sighted. And—well, that's all there is, sir. And so you see, I can't never go back.'

'Thank you, Closters,' said old Prewitt. 'But—well, no. I do not see that, quite. Nor am I perfectly clear as to the conclusion of your narrative. But I am clear as to the fact of the Captain's demise—if it is a fact: that it was not of your seeking and only partially of your doing; and that you acted in your Mistress's interest throughout, and with devotion. If what you had later to do is unpleasant to contemplate—and it is—well then, in palliation, you had a special facility; and this too was done to save her, for you would have been removed. It would be no doubt premature to decide, but I suggest at least a good night's rest. There seems really nothing to prevent us repairing to the house.'

'But I *can't* go, sir! Don't you see I can't?'

'Well, I don't see what is worrying you either,' put in Tom, impatiently. 'We accept your story. We sympathize. And it's all years ago. And what harm can come from a parrot's talk anyway?'

'I entirely agree,' said old Prewitt. 'Closters, don't you understand; we want you back serving and fending for your Mistress without delay.'

Closters looked round on them all with bewilderment. 'How *can* I go back, sir, now that Madam knows? It'll have broke her heart, sir, that I fairly tell you.'

'What will? What does she know?' said Tom.

'But didn't you understand, sir—what the parrot said? I took and strangled him, with my own hands.'

'The parrot! What the parrot said?' It was their turn now to look bewilderment.

'Yes, sir, the parrot, like I said. Not this one, sir, the other. Well, he was only a parrot, sir, but he made it plain as plain . . .

'I see I haven't made my meaning clear, sir. Who was it you thought it was spoke?'

'The Captain was, I think, the prevailing belief,' murmured old Prewitt.

'The Captain!—never, sir. He was dead by then. All I done with the Captain, sir, was to hang on.' Closters's voice sank to an awe-struck whisper: 'No, that was Feste, sir, as he never would forgive. And no more will Madam, sir, as well he must have known.'

There followed a long silence. Tom lit a pipe and Willie could be heard stifling a mild hysteria with only partial success. Then old Prewitt, summoning his resources, spoke out level as ever: 'I see. Well, I think this much simplifies matters. For I assure you, Closters, your Mistress doesn't know, doesn't remotely suspect such a thing. She will be content, I promise you, to marvel at what she regards as Feste's remarkable recovery of speech. You have nothing to fear, either from her or us. I faithfully promise you she shall not know.'

If no summer dawn of relief was perceptible on Closters's face by moonlight it was in his voice and manner as he gazed from one to the other and spoke: 'Would you, sir? Would you all? . . . Oh, I beg you gentlemen's pardon for suggesting it, but—would you go so far as to swear to that on the Bible?'

Old Prewitt got up from the seat and the others followed.

'We would,' he loudly said, seeking and gaining what could only be interpreted as assent. 'Lead on, Closters. To the house, where I know your Bible is available.'

Closters drew from his pocket and laid on the palm of his extended hand a small dark volume. 'I always carry it, sir,' he said. 'It will be safer down here.'

Everyone duly swore.

A TALE IN A CLUB

by William Kean Seymour

The February morning dawned reluctantly through a blanket of grey mist. Above the fog, doubtless, was blue sky, but in this densely built-up area of Central London all was dark and very cold. I shivered as I peered at the narrow wedge of sky squeezed between two neighbouring buildings. The bedroom was one of the club's best, but I felt hemmed in, bitterly regretting the circumstances that had obliged me to forsake my Hampshire home, even for one night. As I drank a second cup of morning tea I determined to get away again as soon as possible after breakfast. The hour was absurdly early, but I rejected the temptation to turn over for another hour's sleep.

The convivial atmosphere of a man's club dissolves at midnight, leaving a stale aftermath of pipe and cigar smoke; and whenever I stay at mine overnight and meet other members on the staircase or in the lift I get the impression that we are survivors of an affront which none of us will admit.

I bought a paper before going in to breakfast, and then, because the head waiter explained that service hadn't yet begun, I retreated into the smoking-room feeling unreasonably disconcerted. My family engagement the previous evening had left me dissatisfied and rather sad, and as I entered the large empty room I welcomed the solitude.

But here I was to be frustrated. Someone was already there, sunk deep in an armchair at one side of the great fireplace. An uplifted newspaper descended with a rustle to reveal George Beauworth, a bachelor of about seventy who lived at the club all the year round and was generally regarded as a mild and inoffensive bore. His hobby was observing the flora and fauna of the London parks and writing stray articles about them. Remembering how he had once pinned me down for half an hour with a monologue about London's starlings, I gave a hasty nod and took a chair at the other side of the room, settling myself determinedly behind the Births, Marriages and Deaths. But not for long: George had scrambled to his feet and hurried across the room to greet me.

'Hel-*lo*, hello! Cowden, old chap! What a bit of luck! I've been wanting to ask your advice . . .' and he squared up a chair without more ado.

Beauworth's idea of consultation is to talk non-stop, with concertina-like movements of his hands which have a mildly hypnotic effect in deflecting attention and preventing judgment. This one was no exception, and as I recoiled from the blast of his egotism I marvelled that one apparently so sensitive to the silent beauty of plant-life should have so little awareness of his own noisy and bludgeoning effect on other people.

Then I received an unexpected reprieve; suddenly his frail body was convulsed by an explosion of sneezes. I clutched my *Times* protectively as his contorted face rose and descended while he fumbled for first one then a second handkerchief. Swivelling my chair to avoid his germs, I took the opportunity to glance at the front page of my paper. An inconspicuous paragraph drew my attention. It stated baldly that preparations were going forward in England and Ireland for celebrating the birth-tercentenary of the famous satirist and churchman, Jonathan Swift, born 30 November 1667. This I knew already.

'Just imagine,' I exclaimed, hoping to stop the further disclosure of George's private affairs—which had something to do with taxation and the possibility of settling in the Channel Islands— 'it's nearly three hundred years since the birth of Dean Swift. What a difference between his world and ours! What kind of man would he have been in London today?'

'Hm!' George said between diminishing sneezes, 'what does it matter? Who wants to know about a writer's personal life, after or before he's dead? It's his books that matter—if they do matter— and I'm not so sure about his, though I only read one, when I was at school.'

Gulliver's Travels, I thought, and then only the First Book. Inwardly I groaned. I was only too well aware of his attitude, having heard him inveigh on a club committee against 'muck-raking biographers'.

'I don't agree,' I said. 'If we knew more about the private lives of famous writers of the past that would explain much in their books that leaves us guessing. Heaven knows, some *have* been over-investigated; but wouldn't you like to know more about Shakespeare, for instance, or Fielding, or Thackeray—so lonely in his over-social and overworked life? Swift's the most fascinating enigma of them all.'

I pulled myself up, conscious of the folly of riding a hobby-horse at that time of the morning. George, I could see, was only interested in his own taxation problems.

'Hm! Well, I suppose it's different for chaps like you who dabble in such things. Now, for my part . . .'

I cut in quickly. 'You mean research? But that's what you do, if you take your flora and fauna seriously. Every time you go peeping and botanizing you try to uncover nature's secrets.'

'But that's different.'

'Tell that to Darwin, or Julian Huxley, or Harry Wheatcroft,' I said. 'Take Swift: to know more about him we must study his heredity and environment, the circumstances of his private as well as his public life, what made him tick, his emotions, relationships and associations; try to discover the complex thoughts and impulses that shaped his character and directed his actions. We have to search for clues in the letters he wrote and received—and conjecture the contents of those he destroyed. We have to uncover, if we can, some of his elaborate coverings-up. Very difficult, but extremely fascinating.'

'Evidently,' George said, 'but after three centuries surely there's a limit to what can be known about the man.'

'There's always the possibility of new facts coming to light. How about that wonderful find of Boswell's manuscripts at Malahide? Suppose Swift *didn't* destroy all Stella's letters? Suppose a parcel of them turned up one day in an Irish attic?'

I realized that 'Stella' meant nothing to Beauworth, but I went on: 'Such things seldom happen, I agree. Only, as you know, amazing discoveries are made from time to time in the dusty files of the Record Office. And now we're moving into an age of extra-sensory perception—a kind of ethereal "bugging". Wouldn't it be strange if someone a couple of centuries hence was able to tune in to our particular conversation this morning?'

George laughed derisively. 'We're safe from that, anyhow. But you're getting away from the point, the secrets of the dead. That's what I mean: we can't uncover the past, thank God! It would be intolerable if we could. A man writes what he wants to say, no more than that. His private life is his own affair.'

'To some extent, generally, I agree. But genius carries eternal responsibilities. We can never know too much about the life of a genius. What would we not give to know more about the man Jesus. . . . A far cry from the man Swift.'

'I'm glad you admit that,' George said. 'Don't bring religion into it. Anyway, as I say, we can't uncover the past.'

I was beginning to enjoy myself. 'Unless,' I suggested thoughtfully, 'one stumbles upon a truth, a moment of time, revealed by supernatural means.'

'What on earth do you mean?'

I pointed to the paragraph in *The Times* referring to the Swift Tercentenary. 'Let me put it like this. Would it surprise you very much to know that I had an "experience", many years ago, about this man Jonathan Swift—a manifestation which did just that? I mean, it answered at least one question about an aspect of his amazing personal life.'

'You're joking, of course?' The glance he gave me was decidedly uneasy.

'No, I'm completely serious.' The strange experience of a February evening in 1928, nearly forty years ago, surged back compulsively. I had never discussed it in all those years, yet now, having embarked on a train of recollection, I felt impelled to disclose it, even to this least sympathetic of listeners.

At that moment the head waiter entered to tell me that breakfast was being served in the dining-room. As I rose to go in, Beauworth explained that he never took breakfast; he usually went out for coffee and toast at about eleven o'clock, and that kept him going until the evening. 'But I'm all agog, mind you,' he added, and 'I'll wait for you here.'

*

'It's a simple story really,' I began when I rejoined Beauworth

'I was a very earnest youth at the time—nineteen: that betwixt-and-between age—with a passion for reading all the books I could lay hands on, and with some vague aspirations to authorship. For that reason my father, a doctor with a comfortable suburban practice, had procured for me—with many misgivings —a kind of apprenticeship in an old-established firm of general publishers. I started in the basement, among the stock, listing and compiling records of editions and sales. In my spare time, there at home and travelling to and from my work, I read omnivorously. My father called me a bookworm, and my mother defended me. Fortunately I soon tired of browsing over the vast field of good and bad literature which I borrowed from the local library and began to concentrate on the standard English authors which the firm published. From their works to their "lives" was a short step and soon I became absorbed particularly in the seventeenth- and eighteenth-century giants, especially in Jonathan Swift, Pope, Goldsmith and Sterne. Swift's life-story intrigued me more than any other.

'His early biographers had given contradictory accounts of his birth and parentage. The suggestion was made that he was a natural son of Sir William Temple, the statesman and diplomat—'

'Who wrote the *Essay on Gardens*,' George eagerly interjected. 'And was he?'

'No, modern research rejects that, but his paternity remains a mystery. Sir William was almost certainly the father of Swift's friend Esther Johnson—the Stella I mentioned earlier. I'm afraid she means nothing to you, George; but take it from me that her relationship with the Dean is one of the great unsolved romantic stories of all time. You've heard of Swift's *Journal to Stella*?'

'I'm afraid not.'

'It doesn't matter,' I said, 'but it would take too long to go into that. Any "Life" of Swift would enlighten you. The point I was making was that the supernatural experience I spoke of related to these two people, Swift and Stella—Esther Johnson: "Stella" was the name he gave her round about the time suggested in the vision.'

I felt bewildered by the necessity of repeating myself.

'The *vision*? What happened? Were you at a séance or something?'

'Good lord, no! I've never attended one. At the time I was on a cycling holiday.'

'In February?'

'Yes. It was a mixed month; I remember some pleasant, almost spring-like days in the second half that year. As a very junior member of the staff, you see, I was at the bottom of the holidays list; I had to take my fortnight's leave either early or late in the year; and in 1928 the last fortnight in February fell to my lot. Tentatively, my father had hinted that he might pay for a hotel holiday at Torquay or the Isle of Wight, but I preferred to try my luck on a cycling tour. And so, I set off gaily on a Sunday morning, rather overweighted by a huge canvas knapsack.

'My plan was to make a kind of peripatetic literary pilgrimage. My itinerary took in Putney Hill, where Swinburne had lived at The Pines; Cobham, where Matthew Arnold spent his last years; Chessington (for Fanny Burney); Mickleham, Burford Bridge, Box Hill and Dorking (Keats, Stevenson, Gissing and Meredith), and so on. It all comes back to me very clearly. I walked or dawdled around these places, pushing or propping my bike while I explored. Usually I contrived to get into a C.T.C. cottage by four o'clock in the afternoon, and after a high tea settled down in the long evenings reading and making notes. I often wish I had kept them. . . . At Guildford I tried to imagine the steep town as Malory's Astolat, but then I pushed over the Hog's Back towards Farnham, spending a very cold and wet night at a place called Seale. At Farnham I skirted Moor Park and rode along the side of the River Wey towards Waverley Abbey. It was at Moor Park that Swift met Stella, when she was eight years old. The place fascinated me and I explored the whole neighbourhood in the best part of two days. As a botanist, George, I'm sure you'd be interested in the flora in the grounds of Moor Park. You should go there one day.'

'I'm too old. I can't tackle more than London parks nowadays.'

'Well, perhaps not. But for me, with all these Swift associations, visiting Moor Park was like refuelling an engine; I felt keyed up. Even with the little knowledge I had of him then I was more excited than at any time before or since.

'When I left Farnham I was two days into my second week. I intended going to Winchester and decided to make a detour to start with, through villages in the wooded parts lying behind the main road. It was because I did just that, instead of striking straight for Alton, that I chanced upon a hamlet of four or five cottages three or four miles west of a place called Froyle. I didn't note its name, but I remember that it was islanded in densely wooded country, most of the trees leafless and blackened with winter rains and frosts. I arrived there under a lowering sky on the Tuesday afternoon and stopped to pass the time of day with a woodcutter who was carrying faggots of tinder-wood to his cottage. A couple of his children came out to join us on the wide grassy verge, and when I mentioned my hope of getting a cup of tea somewhere he called his wife and soon we sat talking in their cosy kitchen while she poured tea.

'I asked about the neighbourhood and its associations, but this nonplussed them. When I opened my map the man asked what I was looking for. I said, "Old names and old places," and mentioned that I had just spent two days in the Moor Park area, where Swift lived as a young man. The man looked at his wife and said, "Maybe that's the one they used to say had something to do with the Lodge yonder." "*Jonathan* Swift?" I prompted. "Aye, that's right—*Jonathan*—that's the name he went by, so I've heard tell, like David and Jonathan. But not in our time; not in my grandfather's, nor his, so I've always understood. But it must have been him or somebody gave his name to the place. He's said to have written a book—Gallopers something or other." This was incredible. "*Gulliver's Travels*," I suggested, but the couple looked blank.

'The woodcutter told me the house wasn't much of a place. It was in a tumble-down state; about three hundred years old; the lodge of a manor house which had long since disappeared. A maiden lady had dwelt there as long as living memory, but she had died several years ago and her sole relative, a brother in Australia, was too old to do anything about it. Apparently, this man had got in touch with an old gardener through the Vicar and had arranged to send him five pounds every quarter to keep the garden roughly in order, and he was to have the benefit of the produce. The arangement had already lasted five or six years, but the caretaker, I gathered, was nearing eighty and the acre of garden was getting too much for him.

'When I left, the woodcutter indicated a rough woodland track which would lead me to the Lodge, about a quarter of a mile away. I followed it and shortly came to a clearance and the house. It was the end of nowhere and I could scarcely curb my excitement as I approached the high straggling hedge which almost hid the Lodge from view.'

George's interest was thoroughly aroused; there was no doubt about that, but I took the opportunity of asking whether I should go on. 'Oh, my dear fellow, do please. I'm eager to know what happened—this "experience" you had. Do go on!'

I continued. 'There was a wicket-gate in a sad state of disrepair: one of the Victorian kind with spindles, several of which had been knocked out. The bottom hinge had parted from a mouldering post, and to enter I had to lift the gate clear of the rusted latch. The porch was about thirty feet in front of me, a tangled mass of briar and creeper supported by lattice work and squared posts. The house itself seemed, at first glance, to be of any period, so covered was it by creeper and briar; but my eyes took in a window on each side of the front door and two equal-spaced above flanked by beams set in plaster. The path from the wicket-gate was narrow and edged with box.

'I stood irresolutely gazing at the house until a man advanced from behind a privet hedge. "Good-afternoon," I said, and he responded indistinctly. He was short and very old, wearing an untidy overcoat, muddy boots and a soiled cap. I asked if the house was Swift's Lodge and told him the woodcutter had directed me. "That's right," he said, "that be Jim Thaxton." He waited for me to speak, and I said, "And you're the caretaker?" He coughed. "You might call it that: I do a bit o' tidying and keep the vegetables going, at the back." He led the way around the house and I saw that a sizeable plot was planted and in good winter order, with a flint-edged path between. Beyond were dilapidated fruit cages. "I expect you want to see the place?" he said, not needing an answer. "It's just as the old lady left it five years ago, nearer six." He looked up at the darkening sky. "I was just going home. There's nowt doing here, not till Easter." I explained my interest in the place and asked if he knew why it was called Swift's Lodge. "No more than anyone else, I reckon," he said. "There's a tale going that a man of that name used to gallop over here in bygone days. I've heard my grandfather say it, and he had it from his'n. The old lady used to talk about him, this Swift, though the Vicar said she had nothing to go on save legend and hearsay. She kind of made a hobby of him, if you know what I mean."

'I nodded encouragement. "What was her name?" I asked. "Mansell; Miss Stella Mansell she called herself, and everyone knew her as such; but when she came to be buried—she was eighty-three when she died—the Vicar found out her real name was Sarah, and that's the name on her grave. But, as I say, she'd always called herself Stella, since she came to live at the lodge when she was about thirty." "A long time ago," I commented, "nearly sixty years." The old man agreed. "I wonder why she called herself Stella?" I asked, and he responded eagerly. "Ah, now you mention it, the Vicar thought it must be something to do with this Swift, though I can't think why, for they say he died a couple of hundred years ago. The Vicar took a great interest in the old lady. Just before she came here, he once told me, she was plighted to marry a clergyman, but he'd died of consumption. I suppose that gave her and the Vicar something to talk about when he came to tea."

'The old man saw me gazing at a weather-worn elm board fixed on the front of porch. The carved letters, SWIFT'S LODGE, were just visible. "Ah, Miss Mansell got my father to make it when she came to live here. It hadn't a name on it before but everyone knew Swift's Lodge."

'The rain which had been threatening suddenly thrashed down in a deluge. "You'd best come in," he said, "though there's nowt to be seen." He reached up to the back of the name-board and produced a large old-fashioned key. As he let us in he chuckled, "Now you'll know where to find it! Better bring your bike in."

'The room we entered was moderately large, empty save for a

dirty deal table and a wickerwork armchair with a torn cushion-seat. The old fireplace had been partly bricked up and a Victorian grate fitted, but an ancient bread-oven had been left at one side of the blackened brickwork. There was a scuttering sound in the chimney, followed by a fall of rain and mortar. "Birds!" he grumbled, "they'm had it their own way too long. Look at they windows." Several of the diamond panes were broken and the lead-work bent. "They fly in and out as they please; no one to stop 'em—and the same with the mice. Can't be wondered at."

'At the back of the room I saw a doorway to the scullery and kitchen, and to the right of it a latched door. Intercepting my glance the old man said, "The stairs. I'll show you up above when you've seen the back." There was a rusty cooking grate in the kitchen; two or three open cupboards and a fitted dresser. In the scullery was a primitive earthenware sink served by a hand-pump; shelves and a broken mangle. In a covered entrance from the back garden an old zinc bath hung from a wooden hook; and I suspected that the shut door led to a bucket-closet. I thought of Swift and what one latter-day critic has called his "excremental vision".

'Evening was coming on. The gathering gloom was suddenly pierced with lightning. Rain was deluging down, and the reverberating thunder shook the house. "I'd be home now, having tea by the fire, if you hadn't come," the old man grumbled. "What about you, sir?" I assured him I was all right, that I'd wait, if he'd let me, until the storm passed, and then be on my way. He warned me it would be getting dark, but I told him I had an acetylene lamp and would find my way easily once I passed the woodman's cottage. "Then I'll show you upstairs," he said. The staircase was narrow and shut in, but led to a landing and two good rooms, one on each side, each with windows front and back, with the landing separating them. Remembering the downstairs plan I tried to account for the extra space above. I put the point to the old man, "I saw a window on each side of the front, but only one room." "Ah,—but the stable's built into the house, you see, and a window serves it. The door's at the side. It's not been used in my time. The Vicar used to say it would make another room, but no one will want it now: the whole place is falling to bits."

' "Which was Stella's—Miss Mansell's—bedroom?" I asked, and he indicated the left-hand one, above the sitting-room. The wallpaper had a flowered pattern, soiled and stained by time and damp. A broken wooden chair stood by the small high grate. Where a double-bed had rested the wide oak floorboards were deeply dented. A strip of faded carpet was rumpled diagonally on the floor. Two oil-lamp brackets testified to primitive illumination. From the back window I looked down at a small neglected lawn and, beyond, three well-tended fruit trees, apple, plum and pear. The gardener caught my eye, "And how Miss Mansell loved the blossom: it did me good to hear her getting excited about it in the spring!"

' "What became of her furniture?" I asked. "Did she live as simply as this?" He grinned, "No, I wouldn't say that. She had everything she wanted. My missus used to come in, and looked after her when she was took ill with rheumatism. More than twenty years ago. She left everything to her brother, and he told the Vicar to sell what he could for the church and give the rest to me and my wife. She had some nice bits and pieces, a four-poster, carpets and plenty of silver, and they fetched a tidy sum for repairing the church roof. She was always very good to us."

'The storm still raged in a pandemonium of rain, thunder and lightning. "How far have you to go?" I asked. "Not far, but I'll wait till the lightning stops; I don't fancy being struck in yon wood, like happened to one of my nephews, only just married and fresh back from the war." That must have been the Great War.

'Downstairs, we made desultory conversation. There was nothing further he could tell me about the place or any association it could have had with Jonathan Swift. He looked bewildered when I said I'd like to stay there awhile to "feel" the atmosphere of the place where Swift had lived. He took me up on that. "I've never heard exactly as he *lived* here; I only know what my grandfather said, and he had it from his'n, that this Swift used to gallop over to see—" "Stella?" I prompted, "The name Miss Mansell adopted when she came to live here? I wonder why she did that?" I shot the questions at the old man who looked puzzled and confused. "I can't tell you no more," he protested; "I never heard no more except what Vicar said about this Swift being a parson, like himself and Miss Mansell's young man."

'The rain had stopped. Only distant rumblings of thunder reached us. "I'll be off then. Missus'll be worriting. But you can stay as long as you like; you're young, and no one will mind, if *you* don't. You know where the key goes." He crossed to the fireplace and took a candle and a cracked saucer from the hole which had been the bread-oven. "In case you get skeered when the dark comes down," he said as he placed them on the table beside the key. Pressing half a crown into his hand, I thanked him and told him I'd be on my way in a few minutes.

'I watched him hurrying along a puddled path to the wood in the deepening dusk. Even the far-off sounds of the storm had ceased, and as I closed the door behind me and climbed the steep staircase I had misgivings about staying in the house any longer. An eerie silence pervaded the place, broken only by a creaking stairboard and a fluttering sound which I thought came from the chimney. Had I really come to a house once used by Swift and his friends; and was one of them Stella? I went into the bedrooms and tried to bend my thoughts to the possibilities conjured up by the comments made first by the woodman and then by the old gardener. Could this room, or the one opposite, have been occupied by Stella or Rebecca Dingley or both? What would they be doing here, only a few miles from Moor Park? And where would Swift come into the picture, and when?

'Outside the darkness spread deep folds over the garden and the woods beyond. My head throbbed with conjecture as I came out on the landing and descended the narrow stairs. I lit the half-candle and watched the small area of light reach to the polished handle-bars and lamp of the bicycle leaning against the wall. I counted on the lamp for my woodland ride to Alton, and so I busied myself checking the apparatus and satisfying myself that the tyre pressures were right. These were remote unlighted parts and I could take no chances.

'Yet I was reluctant to forgo the opportunity of absorbing the atmosphere of this derelict house which two conversations had invested with such unexpected significance. For more than a year I had studied Swift and his period; I knew his life-dates and the periods he spent in Moor Park, Dublin, London and other places. Yet common sense told me that if I stayed in the empty lodge all night the vigil would yield nothing but further guesswork. Also, I felt tired and chilled, and the thought of arriving somewhere safely for the night and retiring early after a good meal in a cheerful inn had become suddenly very alluring.

'I was about to light the cycle-lamp and leave the place when the storm recommenced with spectacular fury. Lightning flashed about the room, rain drove in through the broken window panes, and a thunderous blast of wind shook the house. I began to count the flashes and the peals of thunder, until suddenly a deafening crash was followed by a rending sound and a length of guttering thudded on the ground outside and lurched through the casement. The effect of shattered glass was terrifying. My whole body shook as the storm raged with increasing intensity.

'I gave up any thought of leaving. Gathering my coat about me I sank into the wickerwork chair, wrapping the cycle cape closely about my legs. There was another frightening display of lightning and thunder. But I was beyond caring.

'What followed is as intense an experience now, in recollection, as it was forty years ago. The room, which had been empty and cheerless, was suddenly transformed. It was furnished simply but with good furniture of a long-past period. Candlelight shone from branching silver candlesticks placed on the gleaming walnut table and on the mantelpiece. A fire of coal and logs blazed on the open hearth. And where I had been sitting, or so near that my mind raised no question, a young woman, dressed neatly in a silver grey gown, sat needle-working. Her pale countenance and raven-black hair harmonized with her gown. She was completely unaware of my presence, and I—an observing but unseen participant in the scene—accepted hers quite naturally. She wore, I noticed, a white camellia at her bosom and I caught myself wondering what gardening skill had produced it. The open door at the rear of the room showed a glimmer of light from the domestic quarters. There were vague sounds, as of preparation for a meal. I looked at my watch but could not read the hands: all my attention was riveted on the scene before me. While I gazed, the young woman laid aside her needlework and crossed to a corner cupboard from which she took a decanter of wine and three glasses. From a side-table she selected a tray to carry them, and then, smiling with secret satisfaction, she placed it on the table within my reach.

'Light-heartedly she sang a snatch of a song, and this elicited a response from her companion, a woman of about forty, who entered the room from the kitchen.

' "You're mighty happy, Hetty. You look like a queen with that camellia."

'The younger woman replied, "Happy, oh I am, I am! Jonathan's coming, my Jonathan—Jonathan Swift, the Vicar of Laracor and Prebendary of St Patrick's, who'll soon be made a bishop, and I'm to be his wife." She laughed delightedly. "Is all ready for his lordship, Becky?" I realized then the identity of the two characters,—Hetty, Esther Johnson, or Stella and Rebecca Dingley, her close companion.

' "Not *too* ready," the older woman answered. "Better keep him waiting than spoil the dinner. He hasn't come yet. I've made the sauce for the carp, a fine fat fish from the manor ponds." She bent anxiously to Stella. "I hope you haven't tired your eyes with that needlework." The other waved the question aside: "I sit dreaming half the time, twiddling my fingers." Dingley insisted: "Put it away then, dear. You know how vexatious he finds your poor sight. Last week he spoke of getting spectacles for you in London."

*

George, I realized, had been staring fixedly at me during this ghostly dialogue. He broke into my story now with feeble urgency: 'I don't wish to interrupt you, Cowden, old man—please believe that. I'm most interested of course, naturally, but, are you actually telling me that you not only *saw* these people moving about in the room, but clearly heard their conversation so that you remember it to this day?—forty years later, mind you?'

'Yes,' I said, 'that's what happened. I'm just as surprised as you must be, but you must understand that my mind was young and receptive at that time. The strange experience left an indelible impression. Also, before I returned home that week I wrote several pages about it in my diary. I've long since destroyed the actual jottings I made of the tour, mileages etcetera, but this diary entry remains in a small octavo book. I've often referred to it and am always amazed that what I saw and heard in that woodland lodge fits in so well with what I've since gleaned about Swift's life. If I'm right in thinking that the ghostly vision was a re-enactment of a scene which took place on a night in February 1708, that supplies all the confirmation I need. Swift—who was Vicar of Laracor at the time—had been in London since the end of November the previous year, pressing claims on behalf of the Church of Ireland and angling for a high position for himself in the English Church, a bishopric or at least a deanery. The two ladies had followed him there a month or so later, on a holiday visit, and the understanding was that the three would return to Ireland together in the spring. Stella was about twenty-seven at the time, and Dingley was her companion and chaperone. Seven years earlier they had left Moor Park for Dublin, so as to live near Swift—and obviously with his active encouragement. The details of Swift's life are too complicated to go into now, but you can always fall back on the club library. . . . I mustn't run on.'

'Oh, but you must, my dear Cowden; I shall be deeply disappointed if you stop now. I won't interrupt again. I think I see the picture. Do go on.'

'There isn't really much more to tell,' I said, 'yet it's the most important part. We left the two ladies discussing dinner preparations; and I remember Stella gathering up her needlework and hurrying upstairs. I had an impulse to speak to Rebecca Dingley, but of course no words came and I watched spellbound as she laid fresh logs on the fire and then stood with her back to it, bending forward like some old clubman and warming her bottom. I was convulsed with inward laughter as she rubbed her hands together.

'Suddenly she straightened up, frowned, and then crossed to the staircase, calling up to Stella, "And when you're the wife of the right reverend the lord bishop and inhabiting a fine palace, what becomes of Dingley?" The reply came, instant and silvery, "Silly, silly Becky, how often must I tell you? Where we go, you go too; you are one of the family." Dingley's face lit up as she called back, "I know, I know; but I never tire of hearing it: it is what His Honour would have wished. All the same, the sooner we get away from this place the better. London wasn't too bad, though we saw little enough of Jonathan; but here there's nothing but dripping trees. And only a few miles from Moor Park, and nobody knows we're here—not even your mother. I don't know what His Honour would have said." Stella's reply was almost inaudible, but the burden of it was that they had been there only two weeks and at any moment Jonathan would be arriving with joyful news. At the time, Dingley's references to "His Honour" baffled me, but later study of Swift's life reminded me that during his residence at Moor Park as Sir William Temple's secretary that was the form of address used to the master of the house. This clue, more than any other, convinced me of the authenticity of the manifestation.

'At that moment an onslaught of hail smote the house. I watched, fascinated, as Dingley grasped one of the candlesticks from the table and carried it to the window. Holding it high and steady she stood like a statue while, outside, the hail swept the panes. She had chosen the time well, for soon, beyond the rattling din, came the thud of galloping hooves as if a horseman was charging at the house. A pause followed, and then the sound of stable doors opening and shutting.

'Dingley opened the huge door as Stella descended to greet the rain-soaked traveller. I had a confused impression of both women being held at arm's-length, being given hurried kisses and then brushed away like over-eager puppies. I had no difficulty in recognizing Swift as they fussed solicitously about his substantial figure. He cast a dripping semi-clerical hat on the floor and shook the rain from his shoulders while they danced about him with screams of mock dismay. He was wigless, revealing a high forehead with dark receding hair. He wore a frocked brown riding-coat, full-fashioned to protect his breeches from wind and rain; and black thigh boots fitted with ball spurs. Coat, hat and boots were soon collected by the devoted pair, and all the time the three clamoured greetings and inquiries. I heard him rally them with quips such as "Saucy rogues!" "Insolent sluts!" "Naughty brats!" "Silly baggages!" which evidently delighted them. It was clear that they were his devoted slaves; and when Dingley retreated to the kitchen with the wet garments, Stella pressed him downwards by his shoulders into the large fireside chair, kneeling before him and easing his feet into a pair of buckled shoes which had been warming near the hearth. She rose and went to the table, filling two glasses with wine, and then, handing him one and placing the other on the hearth, she sank to the floor. "Dearest Jonathan!" she murmured, "Lover and lord! I'm so happy you've come. Soon we shall be together all the time." She bowed her head to his knees, seizing his disengaged hand and kissing it passionately. Her attitude was one of adoration and complete humility. She only edged closer as he withdrew his hand and rested it on her head. He observed her gravely as he drank the wine and persuaded her to take her glass and drink with him. She obeyed, barely sipping the wine before putting the glass by and again covering his hand and knees with kisses.

'During these voiceless protestations and endearments Swift smoothed Stella's raven-black hair with one finger while holding his empty glass. He was staring sideways across the room past where I sat. In a sudden wavering illumination by the candles I saw his eyes darken. Years afterwards I read that they were intensely blue. There was reproof in his voice when he said: "Foolish Stellakins! I fear you do not understand. I came to London, as you know so well, charged with an errand—to solicit the Queen to extend her Bounty to the Church of Ireland. For nigh three months I have laboured unceasingly, waiting on ministers and grandees, pleading and exhorting, enduring suffocating ante-rooms, dinners and receptions, often far into the night. My hours have been governed by my mission: First Fruits and Tenths; the Queen and her placemen; the Church and the Test Act; writing and pleading; hopes rising and falling; sometimes encouraged, more often rebuffed. What do you know of these things, Stella poppet? You ask that we shall be together all the time. You ask the impossible. Pembroke and all these London schemers control my days. And always the Queen, thirstily licking up gossip in the Bedchamber. And in Dublin our good Archbishop hungry for results. Poor Presto! Poor Sluttikins! Try to understand."

'At a sign from Swift, Stella rose and refilled his glass. He drank greedily and made her share his glass. Over the rim as she drank, the look she gave him was one of disappointment and unutterable need. I heard her say, "But if the Queen is married, why should not I be married too?" For all answer he leaned towards her and thrust his free hand behind the camellia into her bosom. "The warmest place in the world, save one," he said, lightly touching her forehead with his lips. Her eyes closed with ecstasy as she gripped his hand deeper and closer to her heart. "Dear foolish pretty rogue!" he murmured caressingly, and then, withdrawing his hand and moving her gently away, he rose to his feet and strode towards the kitchen.

'A couple of minutes later he returned with Dingley. He poured wine for her and himself, and then, bowing deeply to Stella who was still seated on the floor, he commanded her to rise and take up her glass. She did so, looking flushed and discomposed, and I noticed that she again only sipped the wine when he drank to the "health of the Ladies of Laracor".

'The two women exchanged glances. "When shall we return to London, Presto?" Swift looked grieved. "But are my little sirrahs not contented here?" Dingley replied firmly, "Could anyone be? Dear Presto, you sent us here two weeks ago, to this bleak wintry place in the woods where we know nobody—while you stayed in Chelsea." And Stella added, "We came to London to join you, and for a holiday, and we find ourselves in this bog."

' "Because I had important business to transact. *I* was not on holiday, to show you rogues the Town week after week." He turned to Dingley, "Already I have explained to this naughty Sluttikins how it is with me in London. I am not my own master; I am a man entrusted with a mission. Life for me is all contriving and scheming, from dawn till midnight." He opened and closed his arms expressively. "Doors are shut on me, or opened just so far. My mission does not prosper; but I shall prevail." His eyes flashed imperiously.

' "And Laracor?" Stella asked quietly. "You called us the Ladies of Laracor, where we only visit. What becomes of Laracor? The canal you have made? The willows you have planted."

' "Laracor must wait! I have other fish to fry!"

'Dingley chimed in. "Ah, at last! He's been teasing you, Stella. Do you hear what he says?—other fish, bigger fish! Canterbury? Westminster? So we shall be together in England, you, Stella and little Dingley; at the seat of power, as you've so often said."

'Swift frowned uneasily. "Do not mind all I say, young women. Dreams seldom become realities. Let us have more wine!" He refilled his glass, while the ladies declined. Dingley spoke placatingly. "*Your* dreams will, Presto, and ours with them. But I must leave you; I have a carp cooking—from your friends at the Manor House. And did you see the camellia the gardener gave to Hetty—with his lady's compliments to Dr Swift?"

' "Faith, she was kind; I cannot think why. I do not know the woman. Her husband I've met once, at the Smyrna Coffee House; and then he lent me this lodge, for the convenience of friends on holiday from Dublin." He addressed Stella, "Do not speak of me to them—I've no liking for the town's tittle-tattle. The gardener grows fine camellias. The flower suits your complexion, but you must turn it into a rose, a blush rose."

'Dingley was moving towards the passage, but I noticed that she waited to hear any rejoinder that Stella might make. Stella smiled faintly, glancing down at the flower. "This one is fading. It recalls one you gave me at Farnham, Jonathan, that July when you came back from Hart Hall, a Master of Arts of Oxford University. How pleased you were! I was eleven. You kissed me on the forehead, and then we danced and sang all the way to Mother Ludwell's Cave. I thought you were the most wonderful man in the world."

'And Dingley, as she moved away, called back, "And she still thinks so."

'When they were alone, Swift took Stella in his arms in a protective hug. "Why did you speak of Laracor?" he asked, and she, meeting his gaze with mock defiance, replied, "Because I thought you loved your garden there—*our* garden, you said when we planted the willows. But now you say you have other fish to fry. Will you leave Ireland, Jonathan? Has any promise been made?"

' "If so, I would have told you."

' "So we shall be going back home soon? Neither your mission nor your hope of preferment has succeeded?"

'Swift released his hold. "You speak like a lawyer, Stella."

' "Am I not near twenty years your pupil? You taught my love to march with my mind. That is what it does now. Oh, my dear, you would be happier at Laracor, away from the plotting and scheming. Shall we not be going back there? I would make you happy, a thousand times more than we dreamed when you brought us to Dublin seven years ago."

'It was an impassioned plea, to which Swift listened intently; but when he replied there was a note of decision and finality in his voice which chilled even me, an immature and unsophisticated youngster of nineteen who could only guess at the complexities of their relationship. "Did I not say I'll not give up? London is my oyster and I must open it. I will not admit defeat." His tone softened as he continued, "Lele sele Stellakins—do you know me so little, to think I should be satisfied to remain an Irish country parson, as poor as a church mouse? Would you, my friend and companion, wish to marry a failure? Could I ask you to?"

'She made as though to speak but he stopped her with a gesture. "But I shall not fail: be assured of that. Time is my lever, and with it I shall open destiny—mine and yours. But you must be patient. You and Dingley must return to Dublin, to Laracor if you wish. Parsivol, my agent, is at your bidding; my curates serve me well. Do you still not understand? The time is not propitious for preferment. The Queen's ear has been poisoned against me; she dislikes the smell of my *Tale of a Tub* and her duchesses fan her swelling prejudice with whispers and malice. She will hold me back if she can; even refuse this act of justice to the Church of Ireland. The court and the ministries are filled with intriguing placemen, but I have set my course. I shall not be baulked; I am what I am."

'There was terrible conviction in his rising voice, and I saw Stella visibly yielding, yet making one last despairing effort. Her voice trembled with emotion as she renewed her plea for complete identification with his life and work. "We came to London, Becky and I, for a holiday, the only one we've had for seven years. I believed that a blessed miracle would happen while we were here. I told myself that the time had come for our marriage; I should be your wife in the eyes of all men as you have so often told me I am in the eyes of God."

' "And so you may be, one day," he said uneasily, "but not yet. The Vicar of Laracor is a poor man; I have to be careful at all times. Need I remind you?"

' "But there is my income to reckon with," Stella said eagerly. "Together we could manage well." She hesitated, reaching a hand forward in tender entreaty. "And Jonathan, dearest—I should give you children."

'He drew away, avoiding her eyes. "I could not support them," he said coldly, "besides, the thought is not one that lures me. The trick is as old as Lilith. You must not press me."

'Stella, I realized, was at the breaking-point. As she faced him, compelling his attention, her stature seemed to increase as her cheeks went ashen pale and her eyes welled with tears. Despairingly she tore the camellia from her bosom and flung it into the fire. "It is not *I* who press you, Jonathan," she sobbed, "it is life, the force you have in such abundance and yet deny. Can't you see what it is doing to me?"

' "If you mean you are giving way to your emotions, yes, I see that,—it is the way of your sex. But it is not important. Life is not only love, Stella. Love is a part, not the whole. Life is a process which, to be sure, has given you beauty. The process, we must hope, will continue. But meanwhile we must face realities. When the Queen ceases to listen to my traducers, when her ministers persuade her to give my intellect its just rewards, my domestic condition may be safely changed. We must pray that these things will happen. I must remind you that, years ago, when we left Moor Park, I told you of two of my decisions concerning matrimony: one, that I would not marry till I possessed a sufficient fortune; and the other, that, if and when I did, it should be at a time of life which gave a prospect of seeing my children properly settled in the world. At the moment there seems scant likelihood of either the one condition or the other being fulfilled. I am forty; I have no fortune, and will not be beholden to yours. . . . No, my pretty, you must not press me. Go back to Dublin,—you have been absent too long, two months, dangling in London with Dingley, both of you spending too much money. I shall return when circumstances permit."

' "And that will be ?" she sobbed.

' "I know no more than you. I shall do what seems right or expedient. It may be weeks, it may be months. You must have faith in Presto—who loves you dearly."

'Stella swayed towards Swift, swooning. It was a tense moment as he caught her under the arms and helped her into the fireside chair. He called loudly to Dingley who came running into the room as the tableau dissolved as suddenly as it had appeared. I was conscious of writhing in my seat, struggling to rise and confront the apparitions, but nothing happened save the onrush of a heavy atmosphere of desolation and grief. Out of the darkness I heard voices faint and disembodied—Dingley's protesting, "What have you done, oh, what have you done ?", and Swift's explaining the heat of the fire, that Stella had been too long away from home and that they should return with him to London next day where he would put them on the next coach to Chester and Holyhead.'

*

'And what,' George Beauworth asked, 'do you—er—*think* happened then ?'

I started as violently as though someone had exploded a paper bag close to my ear. The thin, matter-of-fact tone of his voice brought me suddenly and uncomfortably back to my surroundings—the dreary early-morning aspect of an almost totally deserted club smoking-room. Through the glass doors I could see women cleaners dusting the corridor, a waiter passing with used breakfast trays. I could have wished the transition had been more gradual.

'Well,' I replied lightly, only too well aware that I had allowed myself to be completely carried away by my narrative, 'it's a long time ago. So far as I remember, the storm cleared quite suddenly —the way it does so often in winter. The sky was clear, and I left with my bike to push on to Alton.'

'*I see.*' There was a wealth of meaning underlining the two words, and I glanced at him sharply. Quickly he evaded my gaze, although he had been watching me intently. 'D'you know, Cowden, old chap,' he went on, after an awkward pause, 'I wouldn't tell that story if I were you. People might think it odd, particularly if you suggest you're serious about it—that you think it really happened.'

'But it *did* happen.' I felt completely bewildered by his abrupt change of manner. Whereas half an hour before he had been my willing, even eager listener, he seemed now to be observing me warily and his tone was admonitory.

'Only in your imagination,' he assured me dryly, 'that's perfectly clear to me. Look here, Cowden, you admit that you were an impressionable, bookish youth, desperately anxious to catch up on literary matters. It's quite obvious: your mind was over-stimulated by all you'd read, that's all.'

'Well, if that's your opinion . . .' I spoke coldly, while realizing that I had only myself to blame for unburdening myself of a strange happening which in forty years I'd not mentioned to a living soul.

'It is.' He spoke firmly, even pityingly. 'You writing chaps get some queer notions; probably you don't really know where half your ideas come from. After all, there must have been plenty written about these people by that time.'

Before I could inform him that much of the information which enabled me to identify the circumstances and allusions had not been available in Swiftian scholarship an amazing thing happened. Beauworth rose from his chair to take leave of me. In twenty years of club acquaintanceship I had never terminated a conversation with him save after elaborate manoeuvring on my part.

'Well, so long,' he said, 'I must write a few letters for the early post,' and then, ambling back from the doorway, he paused to regard me quizzically. 'Don't overwork, old man. Keep cheerful. You ought to get out and about more. You know, imagination is a fine thing, but it's got to be kept in bounds. That place you say you called at all those years ago—it wouldn't surprise me if it never existed. You should look around for it sometime: I bet you wouldn't find a trace of it. So long!'

He did not, I told myself, intend to be provocative, but I felt annoyed as I watched him move off towards the writing-room. At that moment a woman entered and began to work a vacuum-cleaner. Perforce I moved to the window. Outside the fog was lifting slowly. I felt unaccountably depressed, for I realized that it would be difficult meeting Beauworth again, also that he might 'talk' about me in the club, as one given to 'queer' ideas.

Yet, in a way, I was relieved that he had rejected my story so uncompromisingly, for it remained still wholly my own. I was thankful, too, that I had not, in a further burst of indiscretion, confided to him a queer half-confirmation I had received the previous day when, prompted by a completely unaccountable impulse, I had made a detour from the direct road to London in an attempt to identify and rediscover that remote woodland glade. Eventually, after many inquiries, I had found it. The area had largely been deforested, drained and dried, and where there had been a muddy woodland track leading directly to my objective of forty years ago, I drove up a well-kept tarmac road. There was no lodge or cottage; only a trim enclave of semi-bungalows, each with a tidy strip of sward separated by white-painted chains, and the whole approached through a communal entrance, gateless between two substantial brick plinths. On the left-hand plinth the name was painted in vivid yellow on white, SWIFT'S CLOSE.

ARE YOU THERE?

by Jean Stubbs

The room was large and comfortably carpeted, with dusty plants and faded velvet curtains; like a Victorian hotel which had once been opulent and much admired. And though she had never intended coming here, nor passing through the heavy glass swing doors, she walked automatically to the reception desk and sat in a chair indicated to her.

'Good evening,' said the lady behind the desk, who was very marcel-waved in the style of the 30s. 'Delighted to meet you. Now, dear, if you can just give me a few particulars we'll make out your card.'

And she selected a white pasteboard square, and picked up her pen.

'Name, please?'

'Madame Benito.'

'Real name, dear.'

'Ada Norton.'

'Age and occupation?'

'Spiritualist—and fortune-telling by cards, crystal, hand and teacup. Large or small groups taken, by private arrangement. Fee conditional. Fifty-four years of age.'

'Married?'

'Widowed.'

A small woman who was knitting in one corner of an old plush sofa, and appeared to be waiting for someone or something, tittered and shook her head. The marcelled receptionist was also amused.

'Have I said anything funny?' demanded Ada stiffly.

'Oh, you weren't to know, dear. It was probably very sudden. Where were you B.D.?'

'I beg your pardon?'

'B.D.? Before Death!'

Ada stared at the grey hair, at the gleaming pebble glasses, at the mouth permitting itself a small prim smile.

'Miss Trellis, dear,' said the receptionist, turning to the small woman who was convulsed, 'I think this lady could do with a nice cup of tea. Your call isn't due until 9.30. Could you oblige, dear?'

The small woman dropped her knitting and scurried away.

'Before Death?' said Ada, and felt her arms and head to make sure they were still there. 'Am I dead, then?'

The receptionist laid down her pen.

'Feeling a bit trembly about the knees, dear? Well, as I said, it was probably sudden. Some ladies, half-expecting it as it were, are delighted to get here after the journey. You must have flown, in a manner of speaking!'

And she permitted herself another smile.

'I was took!' said Ada. 'Took! And in the middle of Mrs Dowson's séance, too!'

'A very professional exit, too. Quite a touch of the theatre about it, dear. Ah, Miss Trellis, thank you. This lady has had a bit of a shock.'

The telephone rang and she answered it briefly.

'Clacton this evening, Miss Trellis. A small group of six. Nothing much doing. Just the usual messages, dear. Off you go.'

Ada unwound her black chiffon scarf, which gave her such an air, which *had* given her such an air, at the séances.

'But how can I drink tea if I'm dead?' she said.

'Of course, it isn't exactly the same, one can't expect that. But you'll find all the usual home comforts here. We like to treat our ladies well.'

Ada felt her capacious bosom bulging beneath the black crêpe, checked on her rings and bracelets, stuck out a stout black shoe.

'I'm all here,' she said aggressively. 'Are you having me on?'

Then something else struck her.

'Where *is* this?' she demanded. 'Hell?'

And her jaw dropped at the thought.

'Certainly not!'

'Heaven, perhaps?' said Ada hopefully, but had her doubts.

'Well, not exactly, dear. What religious denomination were you?'

'Church of England.'

'Ah, good. A broad canopy, as you might say. Some of the R.C.

ladies get quite upset and start talking about Purgatory. I had quite a bit of trouble with one R.C. lady about half an hour ago.'

'Well, what do *you* call it ?' asked Ada with considerable asperity.

'Just drink your tea dear, while I explain,' and she folded her hands as though she were a lady story-teller before an audience of well-bred children. 'We're betwixt and between, as you might say. Now dear, like most of us, you haven't been very bad and you haven't been very good. You've been Human. That's what I tell our ladies. We're all Human. So consequently, you wouldn't feel very homey in either of the other places. One's a bit on the dull side, and other's a shade too saucy. What *we* are, dear, is a Spiritual Working Section. And you'll find us very much in your old line of business. We are the Communicating Line between the living and the departed, one foot on earth and the other in here. You'll have your own room for privacy, and the common room for little get-togethers, and of course you'll be fully occupied with the Beginner's Training Course.'

While she spoke she had been looking at information on Madame Benito alias Ada Norton, and tapped the notes lightly as she spoke.

'I can see that you've had quite a broad experience. It shouldn't be long before you're fully employed.'

But Ada had been simmering beneath the carefully chosen words.

'Am I to understand,' she demanded, in the tone of one whose fee has been questioned, 'that after a lifetime of hard work I'm not going to get a bit of well-earned P and Q ?'

'I'm afraid not, dear. Peace and Quiet is for Heaven. But, on the other hand, neither are you going to be driven to distraction twenty-four hours a day like they do in the Opposite Place. No, dear, as I keep saying, we're all Human here. You'll find Death here pretty much the same as Life. In fact, dear, barring that your appearance is in the Spirit rather than in the Flesh, you'll find very little difference!'

Ada, like her whereabouts, was neither satisfied nor dissatisfied. She recognized, too, that her tone had been abrupt.

'No offence meant, I'm sure,' she said contritely.

'And none taken, dear. Your reactions are quite normal, quite

Human. I've been here since 1932 and everyone asks exactly the same questions. I've got used to it, dear.'

'Am I to understand that I'll be employed as a Spiritualist, then?' she asked, and contemplated the notion of a fresh costume for her new role.

Something white and diaphanous, with sequins, she thought.

'Not exactly. A Spiritualist's *Guide* would be more the thing. But the work will be familiar. The essential fact about Our Place is that everything is pretty much the same.'

'Then I might just as well have not died at all!'

'I'm afraid, dear, we don't have a choice.'

Ada adjusted her bracelets, and then said in her most social tone:

'Is there anyone here I know?'

'I doubt it, dear.'

'Oh?' said Ada, bridling.

'You see, dear, those that come to Our Place haven't really communicated with anybody in life, if you follow me. Not that they've *harmed* anybody, either, or they'd be Elsewhere. And acquaintances don't count. You wouldn't even recognize the oldest acquaintance if you fell across her, here.'

'I suppose it could be worse?'

'Oh yes, indeed, dear.'

'Only, somehow, I'd expected a Reward.'

The receptionist gathered Ada's papers together, clipped her admission card to the top sheet, and filed everything. She rang a bell.

'I expect you'd like some time to yourself,' she said. 'The maid will show you to your room.'

*

'Now ladies,' said the lecturer, pointing to the diagram on his blackboard, 'the main difference between Life and Death, in Our Place, is that though *we* know about *them,* they *don't* know about *us.* So their little notions must be humoured.'

He surveyed the group of middle-aged and elderly women before him, each trying to look more important than the rest. The first lecture was the most difficult. After a while they softened up and tried to look part of an important group. Neither effort succeeded.

'The fashion for the past years has been Indian Guides, usually of the male species, and you ladies will all understand that, though the name your medium may give you is not your own, it must be answered.'

A soft murmur of rage and outrage silenced him at the usual point. The usual protestor stood up.

'May I say,' and she looked round for confirmation of her attitude, 'on behalf of us all,' nods of agreement, 'that this is a most humiliating and unprofessional procedure? Are you suggesting that our own Spirit Guides—mine for many years was Red Eagle of the Sioux Indians, who died in the eighteenth century—are merely Spurious Creatures of Fancy?'

'Certainly not, madam.'

Ada signalled him with one stout arm and cried, 'Mine wasn't an Indian. Mine was Japanese. Peach Blossom, eighth daughter of the Emperor of Japan.'

'Exactly so,' said the lecturer. 'Ladies, please. Your attention, please. Ladies.' And to their sullen faces he cried soothingly, 'Not all ladies are possessed of your natural talents, and many ladies require assistance from such good people as yourselves. I am simply asking for your help with those less fortunate than you undoubtedly were in Life.'

Mollified, both women sat down, and whispered with their neighbours.

'Now let us pass on to Stage Two,' said the lecturer. 'Having established yourselves as a Spirit Guide—be it by Any Name or Race—you are required to attend whenever needed. In order to prevent unpleasantness, and to give the maximum comfort to those who seek contact with their dear ones, we issue each of you ladies with two sets of cards. Upon one are written broad questions which will establish identity, such as *Have you an elderly relative in mind? Was there some illness in the upper part of the body?* and *You are grieving for some close friend who has passed over, I believe?* Having then drawn the correct picture you turn to the other cards on which are written standard messages of comfort. *Father says Thank you Ethel, you have done well,* or *The pain has gone and I've never been happier,* or *The friend says you will find someone to take his place*. Permit me to explain!' he shouted, over the clamour. 'Ladies, please!'

As they subsided he switched on a television set.

'Now at the moment our Miss Trellis is waiting on a Hammersmith medium. Just a small group. I will point out the main features as we go along.'

On the screen appeared a shrouded suburban front room. And round the polished table sat six ladies with their hands clasped and eyes closed.

'Observe Miss Trellis's ear trumpet and speaking horn,' said the lecturer in quiet triumph. 'Her medium finds communication particularly difficult. The trumpet enables Miss Trellis to hear what the medium is saying, and the speaking horn enables the medium to hear what Miss Trellis is saying. Thus communication is established between the two.'

Miss Trellis looked distinctly harassed. Two sets of cards floated in the air before her, to refresh her memory.

'Four of these ladies are regulars, and the fifth is the only new member,' said the lecturer, 'so Miss Trellis's task is not difficult. You will find that she establishes the new member's confidence by drawing out familiar experiences from the regulars. Then her task will be made easier, and she can find out who the new member is calling. Ah, yes, here we go. Two mothers, a guardian uncle, and a child who died young, are being sought.'

Miss Trellis bawled the appropriate messages, and her medium relayed them in a high thin voice.

'Most impressive,' said the lecturer, ignoring the uncomfortable shiftings of his audience, 'and now observe how Miss Trellis deals with the new member. This takes skill, ladies, great skill.'

'*I feel a stranger present*,' said the medium in her false voice.

This was not surprising, since they had been introduced only half an hour before the meeting, but a dowdy little woman ducked her head reverently and blushed.

Miss Trellis fixed a floating card with her eye and spoke through the medium.

'*Does she seek a near relative?*'

A murmur of 'yes'.

'*An aged or young relative?*'

'Old.'

'*A Mother or Father.*'

The dowdy woman, overcome at this perception, wiped her eyes and amended the question.

'Mother-in-law.'

Miss Trellis crossed over to the second set of cards.

'*She is well,*' cried the medium, '*very well and very happy. She says, "Smile, Alice. Dry your eyes. I'm well and happy now."* '

'Further information is sought,' said the lecturer, arms folded, eyes beaming at the screen.

'*Did your mother-in-law have trouble with her legs?*'

The dowdy woman was puzzled.

'Lungs!' shouted Miss Trellis. 'Lungs, you fool, lungs!'

'We all lose our tempers at times,' said the lecturer soothingly, 'but this medium is a great tryer, a great tryer. Observe.'

'*I find it difficult to breathe,*' said the medium, and gasped, and placed one white hand upon her velvet chest.

'She died of pneumonia,' said the dowdy woman, awed.

'*Ah yes. The air is clearing now. I see her. She is smiling and happy.*'

'Why, that's my daughter-in-law,' said Ada's neighbour, suddenly aware.

'Hush, please,' said the lecturer, not hearing what was said.

Miss Trellis bawled her message.

'*She says, "You were good to me, Alice."* '

'She was not,' whispered Ada's neighbour fiercely. 'The little bitch. Left me to die of pneumonia and never came near. How she's got the Face . . .'

'Ladies! Please!'

'Ask her,' said Alice, 'what it's like over there.'

'*Lovely, Alice, lovely! It's all one heavenly garden. I'll be waiting for you, dear.*'

'Heavenly garden, indeed,' cried the lady sitting next to Ada, and she cast a scathing glance at the shabby lecture hall.

Had it been possible to have died of an apoplexy she would have done so.

'And I'll be waiting, will I?' she continued, in a fine rage. 'With my umbrella I'll be waiting.'

'That lady over there,' cried the lecturer, 'will she please refrain from interrupting?'

Ada's neighbour leaped from her seat, and shouted at the top of her voice, 'But it's ME they're talking about. It's ME. I'M Alice's mother-in-law!'

'Well, well, I think we have the general idea,' said the lecturer, switching off the séance in mid-message. 'No need for questions I expect.'

'But they were talking about ME. And it was all LIES.'

Two ushers escorted her, voluble, hysterical, through the doorway.

'A slight technical hitch,' said the lecturer, gathering up his notes. 'Same time tomorrow, ladies, for ectoplasm. Rather more difficult but highly fascinating. Good day, ladies, good day.'

*

As Ada passed him on her way out she saw him lift the telephone receiver on his desk, heard him cry in exasperation, 'Continuity? Give me Continuity!'

And then, sharper, 'Continuity? What the Our Place are you playing at?'

*

Ada sat in her best black crêpe and chiffon outfit in the Director's Office.

'Madame Benito? Ah, yes. A very adaptable pupil, Madame. May I congratulate you on your particularly rapid and excellent comprehension of our course?'

He said this to everyone, on principle.

Ada inclined her head, dignified and meritorious.

'I have here a lady from Blackburn who feels the Call, and needs some assistance. You know, of course, that our earthly friends have difficulty in seeing and hearing us? So please put aside your natural feelings and assume what guise she offers. Just a brief first appearance is necessary. She is quite alone at the moment. Present yourself to her Inner Vision, as instructed.'

Ada assumed her most magnificent attitude of repose, and the Director lifted the telephone.

'Put Mrs Bagshaw through, will you?' he asked.

And quite clearly, Ada saw a rasp of a woman in a print overall, sitting at her kitchen table, eyes squeezed tight shut. Ada loomed.

'Sitting Bull!' cried Mrs Bagshaw. 'I hear you, Sitting Bull!' It was a good thing she did not.

'These respectable ladies!' said the Director, as Ada was escorted out, still breathing metaphorical fire, 'where *do* they learn such language?'

*

Mrs Bagshaw was a worker. She had worked her children out of the home, her husband into his grave, and herself into the profession of medium. Now she worked Ada, alias Sitting Bull, without respite. Like many mediums she was hard of hearing, and what with bawling through a megaphone and standing for hours while Mrs Bagshaw 'got through', Ada's patience evaporated. The inmates of Our Place had their own, similar, problems, so Ada's voice and feet suffered unregarded. No complaints were received at the Reception Desk.

'Well, if I'm on my own I'll *be* on my own,' said Ada to herself. She saw the diligent Mrs Bagshaw concentrating, toothbrush in hand, in her faded blue dressing-gown.

'Slee-eep,' said Ada, fixing her. 'Slee-eep. Sitting Bull says Slee-eep.'

'The Vibrations aren't coming through so well tonight,' said Mrs Bagshaw.

'Oh go to bed, for Our Place's Sake, you old faggot. We've been at it all day!' cried Ada, exasperated.

Mrs Bagshaw looked puzzled. Ada picked up the megaphone wearily and rammed it home.

'Sitting Bull say Slee-eep.'

Mrs. Bagshaw's face relaxed. She cleaned her teeth quite girlishly, clutched her hot-water bottle to her chest, and crept between the sheets.

'Oh, Sitting Bull,' she said, 'whatever would I do without you?'

I'm getting too old for this game, thought Ada, leaning against the wall of her room and kicking off her shoes. Then realized with horror that this would never be possible.

Rarely did the inmates meet. The Common Room was a polite fiction. But one evening, some time later, a Miss Chick received a late call from her medium in Birmingham. Hurrying to Reception Desk for details she collided with a tired, middle-aged woman, shoes in hand, making her way down the corridor.

'Evening,' said Miss Chick.

'Evening,' said Ada, and with a quirk of old humour added, 'Sitting Bull he say Slee-eep!'

Miss Chick giggled, comprehending.

'Oh, I *know*!' she said. 'Isn't it *awful*? Never mind, dear. No medium lasts for ever. I had an old terror for twenty-six blooming years. Called me *Peach Blossom*, if you please. But we change when they change, dear. Duty calling, as it were, *Little Eagle* says "How".'

Ada's shoes fell from her hands. For some minutes she stood still in revelation, then picked them up again and went on. The night trolley passed her. She accepted powdery cocoa and thick biscuits. The food was as institutional as the Place. Undressed, she sat on the side of her bed, curled her aching toes, sipped and thought. For the first time in many years she looked in the glass, and face to face.

'I'm no better than them,' she said.

She thought of Mrs Bagshaw.

'No better than her, neither.'

'I don't know nothink,' she thought.

'I *am* nothink.'

She put the empty mug and plate outside her door, switched off the light, lay down.

'It don't do me no *good*,' she shouted into the darkness, 'to put me in here with a lot of phoneys. I shan't learn nothink *that* way, I can tell you.'

She did not dare think to whom she was shouting, but knew it was someone more powerful than ever reigned in Our Place.

'If I was You,' she said into her pillow, 'I'd Improve people, not let them be laughed at and foxed silly.'

She was struck by her own counsel.

'I would,' she said, softer, and slept.

*

'And now ladies,' said Mrs Hurst, chairman of the local Heart and Mind Group, 'we are gathered together this evening to meet Mrs Bagshaw, whose own gifts have enabled her to pierce that wonderful veil between ourselves and Those Who Have Passed Over. She will tell us, first of all, about her own experiences, when the spirit of an ancient Indian Chieftain called Sitting Bull communicated with her. And then she will bring us messages from our own Dear Departed. Ladies, Mrs Bagshaw.'

Ada dozed through the travesty of Mrs Bagshaw's Experiences, and then, mindful that she was to be televised that afternoon for a class of beginners at Our Place, arranged both sets of cards in the air and adjusted her megaphone. She had waited for this supreme moment, when more than one or two persons might be enlightened. Mrs Bagshaw was in full spate, arranging that the Mayoress should sit next to her, fussing over the seating arrangements of the other six ladies. But at last she settled down, lay back in her chair, and emitted deep snoring noises.

'I think she's Going,' said the Mayoress in a deep voice.

The stagey tones of Mrs Bagshaw brought Ada to attention.

'Are you with us, Sitting Bull ?' she demanded.

'I am,' shouted Ada down the megaphone.

'Have you messages for us this afternoon ?'

'I have.'

Ada moved nearer and nearer. She put the megaphone down. She concentrated.

'I feel a Great Power possessing me,' cried Mrs Bagshaw, and there was genuine awe, even terror, in her tone.

A general gasping and clutching of hands in the circle.

'I have a message for everyone present,' cried Mrs Bagshaw in exultation.

It had happened at last. For months she had worried and fretted over the unsatisfactory nature of her relationship with Sitting Bull. At times he was far from clear, and his words seemed rather stereotyped. At others, usually late at night, she had had an impression of downright bad temper. Once she thought he had told her to shut up, but put away the thought as disrespectful. Now she knew that he would speak, and she be simply the receptacle of his wisdom. Her limbs felt heavy, as though bound with iron, her tongue was numb, her eyes tight shut. She struggled a little, and spoke.

'Now ladies,' said a very different voice, the rough down-to-earth voice of an uncultured but forthright woman, 'I want you all to be very quiet and listen to me, because I am going to tell you the truth. And when I say the truth I mean the truth, which is what Jesus Christ said when he brought Christianity to this world. He said, "I bring you not Peace but a Sword." And I'm not bringing a sword to this meeting out of ill will, neither. I'm bringing it out of good will so that none of you lands up where I've landed up, because it isn't flowers at all, nor angels, nor haloes, nor any of that. It's a Place full of what my grandmother would have called the Scum of the Earth.

'All of you, sitting round this table this afternoon, have probably come for comfort. You might be feeling a bit lonely. You might feel that the only person who ever loved you can come back and speak to you. And you'll go away feeling satisfied for a bit if you're told that Father sends his love, or Mum says Well Done, Ethel, or Uncle George hasn't forgotten. But you'd be a lot better off doing the ironing, because what you're getting here isn't the real thing.

'You can't know what it's like on the Other Side because you haven't the brain for it. That's not your fault. You're Living and they're Dead. Why not leave them that way? It's like a son leaving home,' said Ada, and her voice shook a little as she remembered, 'and you've skimped and saved for years to put him through college and give him a good education. And when he comes back he isn't the lad that went off. He knows things you'll never know in a hundred years, because you haven't the brain for it, and however much you both want to understand and love each other you can't do it. He's gone where you can't follow, and where he can't turn back from, and you'd both be wrong to try. Well, that's what you're doing. You're trying to bring them back, and you won't do it. The only sort you'll bring back are the in-between sort like me, the ones that can't cross over proper, the ones that haven't done well enough in life to be able to die proper. And I can't tell you nothink. I don't *know* nothink.'

She heard a terrifying click and knew that the television had been turned off in the lecture hall at Our Place. She remembered that she had never seen Miss Trellis since that first episode, and trembled.

No good hanging for a lamb instead of a sheep, thought Ada. I'll talk till they take me off.

'Now go on home,' she said strongly, 'and never mind the dead. Somebody'll take care of them. Living's what you're supposed to do. Go home and get them a good tea. You'll all be gone in a hundred years' time, and no tea to be got then. And if you haven't anybody to make tea for, ask somebody in. Don't be one of them that's so busy thinking about yourself you can't spare a thought for someone else. And make friends. If you've only got *one* friend to care about you won't have lived in vain. . . .'

The circle was breaking with shock. The Mayoress was crying '*Mrs* Bagshaw! Mrs *Bagshaw*!' over and over again. And the medium herself was struggling against Ada, struggling out of a sense of self-preservation.

'You don't want to *know*, do you?' cried Ada, in sadness. 'You'd rather pretend, wouldn't you? It's easier, isn't it? It's easier.'

'Mrs Bagshaw you are unwell!' shouted the Mayoress, and shook the little woman right off her chair.

'Oh, Sitting Bull,' sobbed the medium, 'how *could* you? Sitting Bull! Sitting Bu-ull!'

On a long wail of regret Ada was wafted back to Our Place, unrepentant and afraid. Outside the glass doors she adjusted her chiffon scarf before going in.

The usual receptionist was not there. Another woman sat in her chair and motioned Ada to sit down.

'Well?' said Ada, 'what happens now?'

'What would you think?' said the receptionist, conversationally.

'Prison?' Ada suggested, out of her meagre experience.

'What would you suggest?'

All the fight left Ada. She slumped in the chair, tired, middle-aged and ignorant.

'Eh, *I* don't know,' she said wearily. 'I don't know nothink.'

'Good,' said the receptionist briskly. 'You place yourself entirely in our hands, then?'

A flash of anger brought Ada to her feet. In the dark, after her cocoa, on the evening when she met Miss Chick *alias* Peach Blossom, she had struck a core of truth.

'Yes,' she said emphatically, 'since I've got no choice. But let me tell you this, you young madam, I wouldn't sit and torment *nobody*. And if I see'd anybody torment anybody I'd stop them. So that makes me a lot better than any I've known round here, doesn't it?'

'Indeed it does,' said the receptionist, 'which is why I am instructed to send you on to Our Place Two.'

'And what happens there?'

'It's one step up the ladder of self-knowledge.'

Ada eased off her right shoe, which pinched the hardest. She paused. It was after all a stroke of pure good fortune that she had met Peach Blossom.

'Nothing,' said the receptionist, reading her thought, 'happens by chance. Good evening, Mrs Norton. First on your right, through the glass doors. You'll find things more comfortable there I think.'

'How many steps to the top?' asked Ada hopefully.

'I'm afraid we are not allowed to divulge information of that kind.'

Ada eased her shoe on again, and took the pasteboard full of her particulars.

'I'd be glad of a spot of P and Q,' she said, wistfully.

On her way out she passed a fussy woman in full evening dress, and knew instinctively that this was another new recruit. She caught at the woman's arm.

'Here,' she said, out of compassion, 'don't fret. It'll all be all right in the end.'

But the woman passed straight through her, without noticing anything.

'Over here, Mrs Norton,' cried a doorkeeper she had never seen before. 'It's not a bit of use talking to the new ones,' and he gave her a wink. 'They're a bit hard of hearing, you see.'

THE BRIDGE

by *Paul Tabori*

1

Rusty iron stairs led to my bridge—but the bridge led nowhere. It ran parallel with the river, spanning some derelict railway tracks. It was illuminated by a gas-lamp whose cobwebby glass was never cleaned.

2

Last night when I climbed the stairs I found someone standing under the gas-lamp. His red hair was matted with rain, his fierce red beard glittered with the drops of water. As I watched him for a moment, uncertain whether to stay or go, he spat over the railings and turned his clear blue eyes on me.

'You wouldn't have a fag, would you?' he asked. His voice was deep and pleasant. It belonged to the beard, it was part of the jutting chin, the large red nose and the millions of tiny wrinkles criss-crossing his cheeks. 'No, I didn't think you would,' he answered himself.

He reached into the pocket of his greenish-black frock coat, making elaborate wriggles to get at his treasure trove, and produced the stub of a cigar. He scraped a match against his trouser seat and lit up.

'Dead end', he said, with a sweeping gesture intended to take in the bridge, the alley, the river, perhaps the whole universe. 'Whatever you come here for?'

'I like this place,' I answered, clearing my throat first. My voice sounded rusty and defiant. 'I come here almost every night. It's private.'

'I can go,' he said, but did not move. The cigar had an evil smell; with a crooked forefinger he knocked off the ash; a strange, dandified gesture.

'It doesn't belong to me,' I replied. I was curious. His striped shirt, his trousers tied with string at the bottom, his enormous boots, one with a flapping sole—the whole get-up had an air of debonair freedom. No dead ends for him, obviously, even if he had temporarily landed here.

'My name's Peter Rags,' he said and added belligerently: 'I ain't made it up. It's what I was born with.'

I smiled. 'I think it's a nice name,' I said. 'Short and unusual. I don't see anything wrong with it.'

'Well,' he paused, considering my statement, 'I've got to live with it so I made up my mind not to pay any attention to the ragging. It used to be something fierce at first.'

He sucked at his cigar in silence and we both stared at the river. The mist swirled on the far shore, sending its grey-pink tentacles up the slopes of the hills, curling round the steeples and putting a ragged halo around the Castle and the Observatory Tower. A tug hooted querulously. Across the down-stream bridge a late bus rolled with an asthmatic rattle. But the noises were only commas in the unbroken sentence of silence.

'You gotta keep moving,' Peter Rags said suddenly. 'That stands to reason. It's life as I see it.'

'All the time?'

He nodded. 'All the time. Otherwise they'll catch you. Sit down and peel the potatoes. Sit down and mind where you put your muddy boots. Sit down and give me a hug. It's sickening.'

'But don't you ever want to sit down?'

'Sure—where and when I please myself. See, you're a toff. You've got a job, you've got a girl, it's obvious. You press your pants, and if you don't shave one morning, you feel as if you'd committed the original sin. And where did it get you?'

Ah, my friend, I thought, that would be telling. Where did it get me? I felt a vague uneasiness as if I were approaching the crossroads, getting nearer some crisis. I stared at my hands, clutching the railing. White and almost transparent, they seemed to belong more to the mist than to my own body.

'You mustn't mind me,' the red-haired tramp continued. 'I always say what I think even if it ain't pretty or polite. And you didn't look too happy.'

'It's not much use discussing that,' I said and even while I spoke the words I felt that I would like to discuss it. But how could I tell him? How could I tell anybody? It was too late for remembering, too late for curse or prayer. I pulled at my long Puritan nose and felt my long Puritan face becoming even longer and more lugubrious. And yet this man was full of hidden laughter, the fat, vulgar laughter of ripe life, homely wisdom and the utter lack of conventions.

'No, perhaps not,' he agreed, a little too easily for my liking. 'Though mind you, it's just as easy to become unhappy as to finish a bottle or fall into a canal. And sometimes it happens when you think you're all set for happiness. For instance,' and he threw away the cigar stub in a grand, spendthrift gesture, 'I almost got caught once myself. In Germany it was, just after the last war. A farmer's widow, her husband was killed in front of Verdun, she said, though a fat lot I cared as long as she gave me a square meal and let me sleep near the big tiled stove in her kitchen. Only soon I saw it wouldn't be the kitchen. She'd been lonely with the big farm and not even a brat to keep her thoughts on mother's sweet duties.'

He laughed, a lazy and tolerant sound that was snapped up by the mist and the night. 'I thought I'd let her do the asking, the wooing, play the whole infernal game. I was younger, of course, but I'd been on the move since the age of fourteen. You got to be on the move, all the time. Still, I had no objection to a little rest, a little cozening and coaxing. She did that part all right. Cooked the biggest and tastiest suppers I've ever had in my life. Her sweet pudding, now, it was a dream. I can still taste it on my tongue. It melted and it filled your mouth with soft sweetness, lingering and delectable. Sometimes, it's funny, I still dream of that pudding. I took three helpings. She watched me, her fat red elbows on the table, her bosom shaking with satisfied vanity. There's nothing that flatters women more than seeing a man stuffing himself with their cooking. At least, not the sensible sort of women to whom the mirror is no longer kind. I ate and drank and made love to her and she began to take things for granted. Oh, it was gradual-like, just as a spider working at its web. About a week later we had pudding again for dinner. Just the way I liked it. The young wench who worked about the house— thin she was and moon-eyed—put some on my plate. The woman snapped at her: that's a bird's peck, give him a man-size helping, you know how he dotes on it. That night I left. Why? Because I was becoming a habit. And the pudding was becoming a habit too. She had sized me up, she had me pigeon-holed, dead on a pin. It was cold in the woods that winter but there was no damn woman to tell me how big helpings I was to have—of pudding or of life.'

He fell silent and scratched his hairy chest meditatively.

'You must keep moving,' he murmured a little later. 'There's nothing you can't leave behind. That's the only thing: to keep your own sweet will. It's a tough life—sure. But I like it.'

He swung his bundle over his shoulder.

'Not for you, of course,' he added as he shuffled towards the stairs. 'You can't let go. It's too bad.'

The shuffling steps passed behind me. He was gone before I thought of the questions I wanted to ask. But I was again alone and no one could answer the questions.

3

The rain stopped suddenly as I turned into the blind alley. Only a moment ago the tiny wet needles had pricked my skin like soda water on the palate. It was a sprinkler turned off at the main; the clouds still hesitated, uncertain whether they would be called for an encore.

Water gossiped in the gutters; big fat drops fell singly, bent on making the most of the trip from eaves to cobblestones. The rain had stopped but its echoes went on unceasingly. I turned up my collar and put my hands in my pockets. I was cold, always cold, and did not trust this sudden armistice with the weather.

The iron steps gleamed as I climbed them to the bridge. Moisture clung to the glass of the gas-lamp; everything was damp to the touch, and I could not find my gloves. As I leant against the railing and looked at the river, its belly swollen with too much drink, I felt a shiver running down my spine. As if my bones had taken on the texture of damp metal, rusty and creaking; as if I could never unbend once I had fixed myself in a certain position.

The boy's voice came from the bottom of the stairs, fresh and clear, an undertone of impatience and weariness unable to spoil the bell-like clarity:

'Oh, get on, Tim. Whatever are you waiting for ?'

A short yapping was the answer followed by a snuffing and sighing.

'All right, all right, I know that you love me. But get up. One would think you've never climbed stairs. Oh, all right, if that's the way you want it. But I am not going to carry you all the way.'

As I turned round, the head of a small smooth-haired terrier appeared on top of the stairs. Two warm brown eyes regarded me with suspicion. Then a white body followed, flecked with soft black markings, and the dog ran towards me in a happy expectation of a romp. It stopped dead a yard from the toe of my boot and began to retreat, whining and clawing at the iron sheets as if it wanted to dig itself in.

The boy who followed the terrier was coatless and hatless; raindrops glittered in his short fuzzy hair. He was eleven or twelve; hard to judge age at this indeterminate period when a human pup begins to emerge from grubbiness and shrillness into the tortuous maze of adolescence.

'Evening,' he said, and crouched down near the dog. 'Silly,' he scolded. 'Silly monstrosity, you! Get up! Your tummy will get all wet! Haven't you had enough ?'

He looked up and smiled. A front tooth was missing and it gave him a quick, flashing, funny smile. The tender furrow in his nape was glinting with golden hairs. I wished I could touch it with a gentle finger, following it to his shoulders.

'He's not a dog,' he explained. 'He's a duck. Rolls in every puddle.'

The dog gave a short bark and licked the boy's face in ecstasy. The boy fended him off, cradling him in his arm.

'We ran away from home,' he announced, still squatting on his heels. 'Yes, sir, we simply ran away.'

'Why ?' I asked, foolishly, for want of something better to say.

'It was dull. And she always scolded Tim. Grudged him his horseflesh and his biscuits. She gorges herself.'

'Your mother ?'

'Auntie. She keeps house for Father and me. But she doesn't

really want us, does she, Tim?'

The terrier wagged his tail, caught my eye and immediately became a cringing, spotted mass of terror.

'What's the matter, Tim?' inquired the boy. 'He's always friendly,' he said apologetically; 'perhaps it's this rain and wind that have confused him. He'd go away with any stranger, he's that trusting. Sit up, and show your tricks, Tim,' he told the dog. 'Come on, sit up, sir!'

The dog sat up, lifting a paw half-heartedly. 'Now beg,' commanded his master. But Tim wouldn't. He retreated to the corner farthest from me. I felt that I ought to touch it but I stayed where I was.

The boy found the tender spot behind the terrier's floppy ear and started to scratch it absent-mindedly.

'I had a dream,' he announced just as suddenly as he had spoken about running away from home.

'Yes?'

'I thought I'd better tell somebody. Dad has no time and Auntie thinks I'm foolish.'

'I'm sure you are not foolish,' I said politely. 'And I'd love to hear your dream.'

The dog was giving little snorts and barks of ecstatic delight. But one brown eye still watched me, warily, suspiciously.

'It was . . . terrible,' the boy started, drawing the words reluctantly from his memory. 'You see, I was dead and I was to be judged. Judged for ever and ever. And suddenly I stood in a long corridor with many doors on both sides. And I walked along, all the doors were closed, and I thought I ought to knock at one of them and find out what was behind it. . . . But someone opened a door. It was a man with a naked torso, a hairy chest. His face was broad and his two eyes were . . . full of poison. . . . As soon as I saw him I thought: this is Judas Iscariot!'

'But why? Why did you think that?' I asked.

He shook his head slowly. 'I don't know. You remember, how it is with dreams—you haven't time to stop and think. You just know. Well, he said he was St Peter and welcome home. And would I come in, the Lord was waiting for me right inside. So he opened another door—and there sat God. But, of course, I realized at once that it wasn't the true God, not the real One, I mean. He had a bald head and wore a red velvet coat. It was a shabby coat, even patched here and there and you could see where the colours didn't match. And the carpet in the room, that was quite shabby and worn, too, as if millions of people had walked over it. . . . And this fake God smoked cigarettes, he smoked all the time; a little devil stood at his side and struck one match after the other, so that he shouldn't have to wait for the light. And when he looked at me I knew that I was going to hell. I felt so frightened . . . I never felt so bad in my life. Can you imagine it? Do you know what it means? I knew well enough that I had done nothing wrong—but I also knew that it would make no difference, that nothing could help me. Judas grinned and gave God a slate and he started to chalk up figures and dates. On one side he wrote all my sins—on the other all my good deeds. You know, just to strike a balance. I could clearly see every figure and letter and you can believe me—the good deeds were a good many, far more than the sins. But when he started to add it all up, he made a mistake. Many mistakes. On purpose, too; I could see that from the glance he gave me. And when he had added and substracted, there were many more sins and he said to Judas: take him to hell!'

'But . . . you dreamt all this?'

The boy gave me a quick, hurt glance. He stopped scratching the dog and it reached out a reproachful paw.

'Why should I make it up?' the boy asked. 'If I wanted to make up things, they would be pleasant and amusing—not this . . . not this. . . .'

'I am sorry,' I said. 'Go on please. I want to hear everything.'

'I got frightened—even worse. Judas took me back into the corridor and led me to another room. It was bare with a stone floor. And on the floor there were children lying, stretched out on the stone. That was their punishment, they had to lie there, on the stone, in the cold. And an old woman sat in one corner and watched them. She was the Devil's grandmother, you know. And all the time she was cutting up wood, splitting it into thin slivers to make matches. . . .'

He looked at me again, quickly, defiantly.

'Perhaps you think it wasn't so awful. But it was terrible, I tell you. Nothing I have seen, nothing I have dreamt, could be worse. When I saw the room, I tore myself away from Judas and rushed back to the false God, to the fake Lord. I wanted to beg him to add up the columns again, to make a fresh calculation, because it just couldn't be right the way it came out. Then . . .'

He looked at me. His eyes pleaded: help me. But how could I? I didn't know what was coming. Perhaps I didn't want to know.

He took a deep breath.

'I saw heaven, standing open. It was a big red curtain someone had drawn back, and there was a big staircase rising up like a big tremendous tree. Angels stood on the stairs and far, far away there sat the true God. And the true St Peter came walking down the stairs. He carried a big iron key. He rushed towards the false Lord and started to hit him with his key. I wanted . . . I felt like crying in my happiness when Judas grabbed me and said: it is too late for you, too late, too late. He pushed me back into hell and then I woke up. . . .'

The terrier got to his feet and shook himself. Little drops of rain scattered around it, gleaming in the gaslight. It nudged the boy's shoulder but he was still lost in the memory of the dream.

'But I keep on thinking . . . about the room in which the false Lord sat and made up his sums. It was just like a church—exactly like in a church, but if you looked closer, everything changed. There were pictures on the walls—you know, showing Jesus when he said, let the little children come to me. . . . But the children had horrible, devilish faces and long nails and their hair was full of worms and Jesus wasn't Jesus at all. Oh, I really remember how terrible it all was. . . .'

He fell silent, hunching his shoulders. The dog sniffed at his right ear and gave it a quick lick.

'It was only a dream,' I said.

'If I could be sure,' the boy replied. 'If I could be sure. . . .'

He got to his feet and stood scowling, his hands in his pockets. The dog, thinking that they were about to go, danced around his legs, uttering foolish barks. The boy patted him once and then turned to me.

I felt then that I wanted to touch him; the memory of the

tender furrow in his nape was in my fingertips, unfulfilled. But before I could move, he touched my hand. The contact lasted only a moment. He stepped back a single pace and looked at me.

'You're cold,' he whispered. 'Cold . . . cold. . . .'

He turned tail then. It wasn't a flight; his small back was square with the dignity that despises fear. The dog kept to his heels and started to bark only when they were half-way down the stairs. I watched them across the small bay of the dirty square, watched them along the bleak factory wall with the broken glass on top. After fifty yards the boy began to run and the dog jumped joyously around his feet so that he stumbled and almost fell. He cried out and in his voice there was wonder and relief. Then the twisting alley hid them and I was alone once more.

4

The icy tenuous fingers reached up from the river, clawed at the railings of the old, forgotten bridge. As the mist thickened, it wove a curtain, separating the water and my high perch. Gradually the curtain became a wall that enclosed me completely; me and the dusty gaslight, the few feet of the iron platform. I felt secure and proud in this airy cabin; as the mist melted into my bones and I melted into the mist I lost all sense of time and space.

The voices that came through the whirling, swirling mist were muffled at first. And as the constantly shifting vapoury whiteness now and then showed clear patches, moving and drifting, through which the cold stars sent a momentary gleam and the sluggish river became visible for a fleeting second, the voices, too, gained in intensity or faded away. Sight became sound and sound was interchangeable for shadow and light. It was an evil night.

'No!' cried the woman's voice. 'Leave me alone!' And, with a small, dry sobbing noise: 'Why can't you leave me alone?'

The man's voice was a murmur, hot and intimate, heavy with desire:

'Because . . . you're all I want. Darling, because of your skin and hair, your mouth and your arms. Don't you know what you have? Do you never look in the mirror?'

There was a peeping hole in the mist now: a small, ragged

oblong. I saw his head. Young, a shock of dark hair lightly powdered with the glittering drops of moisture, his face eager and naked. Of her I could only see the line of the cheek. It was tender and soft, but she was older than the man. Older and wiser, but why so angry? He was searching for her lips, but she turned her face to him, avoiding his hungry mouth.

'Mirrors!' she laughed bitterly as the white, soft curtain closed in again and they were lost in its folds. 'What good is it to look into mirrors? That won't make me any happier.'

'But it is so easy,' he said, trying to argue with her, trying to keep the trembling impatience out of his voice. I am sure he had forgotten that she had a mind, too, of whatever quality and texture; all he thought of was her body in the circle of his arms, and yet miles away. I could not see her but I knew that her back was rigid, that she tried to keep the final inch away lest his fire burn her and sweep her into something she feared. 'So easy,' he repeated. 'Don't fight against it. For six months now you have been fighting. Whenever I came near you . . .'

'Too near for my liking,' she said, and her voice was a little shriller, more laden with panic. 'If I let myself go . . . where would we end up? In a furnished room, with me darning your socks and a squalling brat in a cradle you made out of an old soap box. No, thank you. I've had that once before and I want no part of it.'

'That's not true!' he protested. 'If two people want each other, what else matters?'

She mimicked his voice savagely. 'If two people want each other! You think the landlord or the butcher is interested in that? You think because two people go to bed together, there are no more bills to be paid? Can you eat love? Oh, you make me sick . . . .'

The curtain was drawn aside again and this time it was a full-length picture. He had released her and faced her, a strip of wet stones between them. His hands were clenched. The fury of desire had changed to the fury of resentment.

'Money!' he said, and the single word held a dozen long sentences. 'Is it my fault if I can't get a better job? Can I juggle the stock-markets or change the tariffs? Can I go to the board of directors and tell them that a store-keeper ought to be better paid? What do you think, how many are there waiting for me to make a single slip so that they can cut my throat and take my place? Of course, you can do better. There are plenty of fat crooks who'll buy you fur coats, with whom you can swill champagne! But you picked me out of a million. Seven months ago, in that café you looked at me and . . .'

'I was lonely! Bored! And you stared at me with those calf's eyes of yours as if you'd like to swallow me, feather-boa and all. How was I to know. . . ?'

I shifted my place on the bridge. The woman looked up. She stopped talking suddenly, stared. Her eyes swivelled to the man who hadn't noticed anything.

'What was that noise?' she asked.

'What noise?' He was disconcerted by the commonplace question; all he wanted was to get on with the grand scene, to bring it to the only essential finish. 'A cat or something. Listen, honey. . . .'

'It wasn't a cat,' the woman said.

'What does it matter? The mist's that thick, no one could see us.'

'There's someone up there,' she persisted. 'Listening to us. Watching us. Let's go. This place gives me the creeps.'

'Nonsense, you're just imagining things. You've been jumpy ever since we came out of the cinema. Let me explain, Helen. Let me prove to you . . .'

'You can't,' I said suddenly, surprising myself because I hadn't really planned to speak. 'It's no use. You'll only go on hurting each other.'

There was a little silence. I regretted having spoken but it was too late. What was the sense of offering people advice which you had rejected yourself?

The man spoke again; his voice harsh with anger.

'Who are you?' he cried. 'What do you mean, prying into private affairs?'

'I was here before you,' I answered. 'I didn't ask you to come here and have this argument. . . .'

'Let's go, Martin,' the woman said. Once again the mist

swirled aside. She was tugging at his sleeve; but he had turned his back to her and stood now facing the bridge, facing me.

He shook her off. He was the protective male now, the cock, the bull, the stag—only a little puzzled, because his enemy was not at striking distance.

'Where are you?' he shouted. 'Come down here and stand up to me like a man.'

'Would that solve anything?' I asked. 'If you knocked me out, would she be kinder to you? Would you get a better job?'

'He's right,' she whispered. 'Come on, Martin. I am cold.'

'I meant no harm,' I tried to conciliate him. 'Only I couldn't help hearing you both. Forgive me for eavesdropping. But I've had . . . I've had experience.'

'Well, keep it to yourself,' he grunted, little mollified.

'That's what we all do,' I laughed. 'But sometimes it spills over. Now you love her, don't you?'

'That's none of your blasted business,' he cried. 'Leave us alone. Can't a man have a little peace and privacy? If I could only make her see. . . .'

'He doesn't mean it,' the woman apologized. 'Only he gets into a fever so easily. He's highly strung, that's the matter with him. And I . . . can't keep up with his ideas most of the time. He thinks I am a queen or something silly. I am just a woman. I only want what any woman expects to have. I haven't had an easy time either. . . .'

'Don't try too hard,' I said. 'You'd be both better off if you went your separate ways. . . .'

'That's what I keep telling him. . . .'

'I've had enough of this,' the man cried. 'If you won't come down, I'll come up there and knock your silly head off. Encouraging her in her silly ideas! Interfering with . . .'

He made half a dozen steps towards the stairway of the bridge. Again the mist closed down, a billowing, almost tangible fabric that shut us off from each other.

'Come down here!' I heard him shout. 'Come down where I can see you.'

I did not speak. The woman called him back, with frantic anxiety in her voice. She did not like to be left alone in that grey-white swirling mist. But he paid no attention to her. I heard his steps, mounting the stairs and waited.

His head appeared first, then his shoulders; his hair was tumbling into his forehead and he held his arm stiff, his hands clenched. I did not move. He looked at me. His eyes seemed to be wide open, yet there was blind puzzlement in them.

'Come on,' he said, 'come out of there.'

I did not speak.

He lifted his hands and started to hit out at the empty air. Then he stumbled and saved himself from a fall by clutching at the railing. He straightened, turned tail and clattered down the stairs. I heard his voice, talking to the woman.

'He's bolted,' he said. 'The yellow-livered rat. Talking big and then running away.'

From my perch under the gas-lamp I looked after them as they walked down the alley. He put his arm around her waist and after a few steps she let her body sag close to him. Then the mist swept in again and there was no sound, no sign of them.

5

It was a clear frosty night; a thin film of frozen snow covered the iron platform of the bridge. The cold seeped up under my clothes, twined around my legs and arms until I became part of it, a Laocoön made of snow, struggling with the invisible serpents. As I stood there, in my usual corner, turning my back to the alley and the little square, I heard heavy breathing. Someone was climbing the stairs, coughing and panting; heavy boots clanked against the iron steps. I did not turn round at first. I thought that if the visitor, whoever he was, should see my unfriendly back he might retreat. But this was really a forlorn hope; who would take the trouble of coming to this god-forsaken place unless he had some definite purpose in his mind?

I stared across the river; it was almost completely frozen, only along the banks was there a narrow black ribbon of open water. The snow-powdered hills looked like the mountains of the moon or a futuristic setting for some atonal opera. I could see no human beings; even the beggars were driven indoors. The frost had lasted for a fortnight and there was little prospect of milder weather.

Behind me the man who had climbed the stairs cleared his throat and blew his nose. It sounded like the trumpet of Gabriel; not a single corpse could remain unaffected by it. I craned my neck, looking back over my shoulder.

It was an elederly man, his grey hair straggling unsteadily from under his hat, a curious combination of bowler and topper, long hair reaching well down over his collar. He was swollen with many layers of clothing and I could see little of his face as he wore a muffler over the lower part of it. His hands were mittened; he carried a black bag which he now set down with exaggerated care. But with one hand he held fast to the railing, as if afraid of losing his footing on the slippery iron platform, as he well might have done. Only the beak of a nose and a few square inches of mottled skin showed. His eyes were blue and full of innocent wonder, half the age of his body.

I turned round completely and give him a little bow. The cold grew more intense; one could almost hear the mercury going down in the thermometers of the city.

Again the stranger cleared his throat. Then he said:

'Of course, you don't exist.'

I thought he was drunk or mad; certainly a queer remark to address to a perfect stranger on a night like this. He might have referred to the weather, its inclemency and the possibility of a thaw; he could have invited me for a drink to the little pub on the corner; he might have introduced himself. But what could you expect from a man who wore such a hat? He was fumbling in his pockets now, embarrassed by his mittens until he pulled off one with his teeth and produced a small black notebook and a pencil. I watched him, puzzled.

'Hallucinations,' he muttered, while he made a note in his little black book. 'The clearest possible case.'

'Can I help you?' I asked politely, as I saw him once again diving into his pocket, trying to reach some hidden receptacle way under his layers of clothing.

'The time,' he murmured, 'I must have the exact time. . . .'

'Half-past twelve,' I said. 'Or near enough. You can see the

clock of the Garrison Church perfectly easily from here. It's
illuminated, too.'

'Half-past twelve,' he repeated, and wrote again in his notebook. Then his hand stood suddenly still. 'Did you speak to me?'
he asked.

'I hope you don't mind,' I said. 'But you seemed to be in
distress. Always glad to oblige. . . .'

'Not only visual but aural as well,' he said, which sounded
most irrelevant to me. But perhaps that was how his mind
worked—tortuous and unnecessarily complicated. 'But how does
that fit in with McDougall's definition—to think of remote
objects with sensory vividness?'

'I wouldn't know,' I said. 'But if I can do anything . . .'

This seemed to irritate him. 'I wish you wouldn't interfere,'
he said testily. 'I've told you, you don't exist. A figment. Of
course, hallucination may or may not be accompanied by delusion,
by belief in the physical reality and presence of the object halluci-
nated. . . . Do I believe in you?'

He peered at me near-sightedly; the muffler became undone
and now his whole face was exposed: clean-shaven, ponderous
jowls, his lips shadowed by that predatory beak.

'I really wouldn't know,' I said, but a slight irritation kept
nagging at me. It happens to you sometimes when you aren't
quite fluent in a language and someone's talking to you too fast;
you catch a word here and there that you understand, but you
still can't get the hang of it.

'Of course,' he continued, licking his pencil, which made me
slightly sick, 'probably most normal persons occasionally have
hallucinations; but it's a different matter if it's persistent hallucination. Now that's really serious. One of the most common
symptoms of mental disorder.'

There was nothing I could say to that nor did he expect me to
say anything. He peered at me suspiciously and stabbed suddenly
with a nicotine-stained finger at my midriff. For some reason or
other he did not quite reach me; at least I felt nothing. Of course,
I wasn't lightly dressed myself; still, it was queer.

He nodded, as if in satisfaction.

'I thought I shouldn't listen to a silly servant girl. Talking about seeing things. Hysterical. Probably in a hypnoid condition. I ought to write to Dr Morton Prince. And Professor Freud might like to hear about it, too.'

He pulled off his second mitten and felt his own pulse. His antics ceased to amuse me; I was about to turn my back on him when he fired another question at me:

'Do you come here often?'

'On and off.'

'No particular reason.'

'Are you certain? You know . . . it's quite possible that you may have seen it without realizing. . . .'

'Seen what?'

'The apparition, the Thing, whatever you want to call it. Now it may be a hallucination that you are standing there near the railing. Visibility is fairly good, my pulse is normal and I feel no vertigo, no headache. All that is subjectively stated but can be transferred to objective observation. I mean, I should be able to decide whether this is a question of reproductive, constructive or creative hallucination. In the case of the first group . . .'

'Stop!' I said.

He stopped and stared at me.

'My dear Professor Whatsisname,' I said and moved a little closer, 'have you read Shakespeare?'

'Of course I have, what a silly question,' he wheezed. 'But what has an irresponsible author got to do with the theories of visual hallucinations, worked out so carefully by Dr Prince?'

'Stop!' I shouted again and came even closer.

'But my dear man . . .'

'Do you remember Hamlet's speech to Horatio?'

'But surely you don't expect me to . . .'

'You'd better.'

He started to cram his apparatus into his pocket and sidled towards the black bag.

'This is a public bridge, anybody can stay here,' he grumbled. 'And laymen should not interfere with serious psychical research. I'd have you know that I have received degrees and testimonials from . . .'

'Shut up!' I roared, now thoroughly roused. 'You blinking,

blithering idiot! You and your hallucinations!'

He bent down to snatch up the black bag but I was quicker. The bag seemed to be suspended between us as if held there by our angry eyes. I opened it. Inside there was a camera and a flash-bulb.

'Don't touch that,' he whined. 'It's my property. I forbid you. . . .'

I lifted the bulb and focused the camera.

'No,' he protested in crude, shivering terror, 'no, for heaven's sake! I can't stand it. I won't! I won't!'

The universe exploded in a burst of violet light. It seemed that even the iron would melt. But it only lasted a second and the blinding flash left an even deeper darkness. I saw Professor Whatsisname flying wildly, flying for life.

I bent over the railing of the bridge.

'Catch!' I called and swung the black bag, with camera and flashlight inside, after him. He caught it with his fingertips but lost his hat in the process. Laughter bubbled out of me, irresistible, cruel and happy laughter. It pursued him down the street and the ice seemed to splinter on the river, the icicles shivered under the eaves. But silence came again, silence and darkness and the eternal solitude that no one could ever escape.

6

Something has happened tonight that makes it different from all the nights, endless and countless, I have spent here on this narrow iron platform, every inch of which I know. The air is in constant motion, the wind constantly assails the houses and the very cobblestones; it hurls itself against the wall of the factory beyond which the machines whine and groan in protest. There are shapes in the air, indistinct, ever-changing shapes that hide the lights of the distant shore, the outline of the mountains. Sometimes I reach for them but they are never there.

I am restless myself with the restlessness of spring and the uneasiness of my solitude. Something must happen to break it, someone must come. Perhaps Pete Rags with his red beard and his curious ideas that a man must keep moving. Perhaps the child who dreamt of the false heaven. Or the lovers who tore each other to shreds because they could not let go and could not stay together. Or even the professor with his notebook. If only someone would come. Someone to talk to.

And suddenly I have left the bridge, I am running down the alley. I hammer at the door of the cheap drinking shop. I can see the silhouettes of people inside, drawn sharply against the pink packing paper; I can even hear voices. But however I strike with my fists against the door, it does not open. I know it never will.

As I turn back, a woman's shape emerges from the shadows, singing softly. It is one of the whores frequenting the alley. I hurry to her—cheap and tawdry, she could still give me a moment or two when this aloneness would be deadened if not killed. I reach into my pocket to pull out some money, all I have on me— but she passes by, shaking her hips a little, a cigarette between her lips, humming the cloying-sweet tune. I stretch out my hand to arrest her and the movement dies half-way because I cannot reach across those inches; they have grown suddenly to a distance of light-years.

Something drives me back to the bridge, I mount the stairs, feeling them slightly slippery under my soles. The dancing air still shakes her thousand veils in front of my eyes. And I cry out: Julie!

The echo is in the wind, torn and useless. I repeat my cry and from the misty dance the figures emerge. First my father, with his tobacco-coloured moustache, his quick, shy smile. Then my mother, her hands fussing with a lace handkerchief, puzzled distaste on her face. Then—Bob, my best friend and worst enemy. Tall and handsome and full of vigour. Nothing happened to him that he could not endure. And at the end of the brief procession, set apart from the others: Julie, my love. Julie as she was in the summer nights, Julie of the silver key that opened our secret hide-out and of the greedy desire for life. Julie whose body I knew like the palm of my hand.

And as I plunge forward with a hoarse cry, they pass beyond reach, all of them. The wall of air, the wall of restless wind is between us. Here is the bridge where I stood watching the city; here is the bridge where I stood before I dived into the black, swirling water. Here is the bridge where . . .

And than as a retching sob burst from me, I knew that I was a ghost myself, a wraith, a poor thing of no substance, fading away even from the only place I was allowed to haunt. I knew that even my death had not ended my loneliness. I knew that I was dead and alone and that my solitude was final and infinite.

THE GHOSTESS WITH THE MOSTEST

by Fred Urquhart

The black ghost chuckled venomously and vanished. It was shortly after dawn. The gardener who had come into the kitchen, carrying two trugs of vegetables, had stared when he saw the large fat black woman in the old-fashioned clothes. And when she stuck out her tongue, chuckled and dissolved, he had let out a yell, dropped the trugs and fled.

'A pox on you, Lilywhite,' the Countess said. 'You've scared the poor fool out of his wits, you black cow.'

'He got no wits to scare, missy.'

Lilywhite clucked irritably as she examined the scattered vegetables. 'This cabbage full of slugs. This marrow not fit for pigs. I'd whip that gardener's bum good and hard.'

'I see no reason why you needed to manifest,' the Countess said.

'Just felt like it, missy. Lilywhite don' see why she shoulden manifest if she want to. It's a free country.'

'Too free. Like your tongue,' the Countess said. 'You need your own bum whipped.'

'Don' forget, missy, what happen the last time you try that caper,' Lilywhite said, glowering.

*

At the beginning of the eighteenth century the Countess of Torryburn was the mistress of huge estates in her native Scotland as well as in the Midlands and Sussex. In London she was one of the great hostesses and, being an intimate friend of Sarah Churchill, Duchess of Marlborough, she was often at the court of Queen Anne. But she really preferred the country, and her favourite home was Ardmore Manor in Sussex. Usually she stayed there from May until September, and during these months hardly a week passed without her giving a large dinner party or a ball. No sooner had her servants cleared up after one party than they were ordered to make preparations for another. The Lady Margaret Campbell, Countess of Torryburn, a widow for ten years, had no children and she had nothing else to take up her attention.

Although there were many servants at Ardmore, this constant entertaining irked the ones who found they always had to do most of the work. There were constant dark murmurs and occasional flarings up of temper, especially among the kitchen staff, the grooms who baulked at having to look after the horses of the guests, and the gardeners who resented their fine vegetables being eaten by silly Sassenachs and their flowers being used for floral decorations that were thrown out next day. Whenever there was a flare up of temper, the Countess always outdid it with a flare up of her own. She would scream and swish her riding-crop and threaten to whip whoever dared complain. To the men she always cried: 'Drop your breeks, you insolent rogue, and bend over,' and to the women: 'Put your skirts over your head, you brazen besom, and kneel down.' But her threats were never allowed to go beyond words. The maids would counter-threaten to leave, the grooms would grin and the boldest would seize the whip and boast that he'd use it on herself first, and the gardeners, most of whom were old men from her Highland estate, would say: 'Dinna you threaten me, my lady. Many's the time I've skelped yer ain doup when ye were a bairn, and I'm ower auld now to be bothered wi' yer tantrums. If ye want to use yer bit whip, why no' try it on that impudent nigger wench o' yours ?'

The nigger wench was Lilywhite, who had been given to the Lady Margaret as a wedding present by her husband. Lilywhite, six years older than the Countess, had been brought to England when she was a baby. Ever since she was twenty-two she had been at Margaret's beck and call, looking after her clothes, listening to her complaints and cajoleries, cooking special dishes to tempt her delicate appetite, and ministering to every capricious whim. But although often threatened with the lash, Lilywhite had her own methods of quelling her mistress's temper, and she never felt it until the Baron Charles de Riveaux came to Ardmore Manor.

After the battle of Blenheim in August 1704, a number of important French prisoners were brought to England and lodged in honourable captivity in various country houses. The Countess of Torryburn was asked by Sarah Churchill to be the jailer of Baron de Riveaux, a handsome young cavalry captain. De Riveaux arrived at Ardmore with his arm in a sling but with his sexual blandishments unimpaired. He was twenty-five, twelve years younger than Margaret Torryburn, but the discrepancy in ages was as unimportant to her as last year's ball gown or last week's dinner menus, and it made little difference to him whether he rode an old mare or a young one so long as she was mettlesome. When he swaggered out of the coach at the Countess's front door and saw her red hair and the dark, hungry eyes in her thin face, he knew that here was a frisky filly who'd canter at his slightest touch; and as he bent his blonde head over her hand and kissed it, Margaret's heart dropped as low as her curtsy.

He came to her bedroom that night. Margaret could not do enough for her lover, and in the following weeks she entertained even more lavishly than ever, if that were possible, to help amuse him and to make him forget each fresh piece of news of Marlborough's victorious campaign. At the end of September she usually went to London for the winter season, but this year she put off her journey to the middle of October. This caused great mutterings among her servants; those who came from London wanted to get back there before the cold Sussex winter started, and those who always enjoyed a peaceful winter at Ardmore wanted to get rid of her, her lover, the other servants and the constant entertaining. And then when the chosen day of departure came and she announced that she'd decided to remain for another month and give a great dinner and ball for the opening of the hunting season, because the Baron wished to hunt with the local foxhounds, there was such an uproar in the kitchen quarters that Lilywhite said: 'White slaveys say they goin' to walk out, missy, if you have this ball.'

'What insolence!' the Countess screamed. 'I'll soon settle their hash. I'll have them all sent to the treadmill.'

'You be quiet, missy,' Lilywhite said. 'Slaveys is mutinous. No knowin' what they might do.'

'How dare you talk to your mistress like that,' said the Baron. '*Cette bête noire* needs a whipping, *madame*, I will do it for you with pleasure.'

'As much pleasure you got when you try to pull me in your bed, eh?' Lilywhite cried. 'This bad man, missy. He chase white maids too.'

'Enough! Enough!' screamed the Countess. 'You hold her, Charles. I'll whip the slut myself.'

Lilywhite was almost as tall as the Baron and almost as hefty, but she was much older and less supple; he reached down, grasped her skirts and pulled them over her head, using them to restrain her flaying arms and to throw her to the floor, where he sat on her head and shoulders while the Countess thrashed her naked bottom with her riding-crop.

The whipping of Lilywhite frightened the other servants and, although they muttered among themselves, they began to prepare for the Hunt dinner and ball. For days Lilywhite went about with a sullen face, speaking to nobody. The Countess had regretted her impulsive action almost before it was finished, mainly because she suspected that what Lilywhite had said was true, and now she did her best by cajoleries and small gifts to win back the allegiance of the sulky slave. But Lilywhite was unresponsive. She did everything asked of her, she accepted the gifts, but she did not respond to her mistress's smiles and shows of affection.

The day before the ball the Countess said: 'Lilywhite, will you be a love and make that delicious dish of mushrooms and trout that only you know the secret of, for tomorrow's dinner. The Baron dotes on it, and so do I, and I'm sure our guests will too. I know it means a deal of extra work for you, so I'm going to give you that blue brocaded gown you've always fancied. You'll like that, won't you?'

'Yes, missy,' Lilywhite said.

'Now don't be sulky, you black bitch,' the Countess said. 'After all, I didn't whip you too hard, did I?'

'No, missy.'

'And most slaves get whipped nearly every day,' the Countess said. 'So you're lucky. And the Baron's sorry about it, too. He told me to give you this gold piece. So now you've got that and the gown. What more can you ask for?'

Early next morning Lilywhite went into the great park to pick the mushrooms. She had refused the Countess's offer to send some other maids with her since many times the quantity she usually needed for a dish for two people would have to be picked. 'I manage by my own self, missy,' she said. 'White slaveys be better to prepare the trouts. Lilywhite don' like making her hands fishy.'

Amidst a clump of trees there grew a virulently poisonous variety of toadstools, and she picked them all; then she filled the rest of her huge basket with mushrooms. She prepared the dish in a small scullery off the kitchen and got rid of any maids who showed desire to help her. Not that many did, for they all kept running outside to watch the progress of the hunt and to shout 'Tallyho!' whenever they thought they saw a fox. Most of the toadstools went into a large dish, which Lilywhite had earmarked for her mistress and the Baron, and among them, for good measure, she put a quantity of deadly nightshade chopped up among herbs. The rest of the toadstools were distributed among the bulk of the mushrooms for the dishes that would be offered to the guests; there were not enough toadstools among them to do more than make the eaters ill. Lilywhite did not want to have too many deaths on her conscience.

There were twenty people at the dinner table. Lilywhite, dressed in her mistress's discarded blue brocaded gown, carried in the deadly dish and placed it in front of the Countess while the footmen and the white maids placed the other dishes in front of the guests. Then Lilywhite stood back, her arms folded across her great bosom, behind her mistress's chair, and watched every bite that she and her lover took.

As soon as the Countess began to moan and to clutch her stomach Lilywhite knew that the poison was taking effect, and when the Baron also went greenish-white and made gurgling noises, Lily-white screamed: 'Oh, my poor missy, she ill! Get the physician man!' And she rushed out, so that she would be well away when the Countess died, for she'd heard a footman shout 'The mush-rooms!' And she knew by the look he gave her that she could expect no help or sympathy from her fellow servants. She hid outside one of the long windows and watched the confusion, and she grinned when she saw footmen lift the Countess and her lover and carry them out. But she became alarmed when old Squire Huggett, who had been sitting at the Countess's other hand, went into convulsions and died. A few seconds later, old Lady Carstairs, who had not uttered a groan but remained patrician to the last, sagged in her chair.

Suddenly she realized what would happen if she remained; she clutched her throat, seeing herself being hoisted onto the platform of death by the hangman. And she ran madly across the park and threw herself into the river.

On the day after the funerals of the Countess of Torryburn and the Baron Charles de Riveaux, the drowned body of the black woman was taken from the river. It was driven in a cart to the village green, and there it was stripped naked by the hangman from the nearest town. It was then dragged at the cart's tail to the gibbet outside the village and hanged ceremoniously. The body mouldered on the gibbet for many weeks before somebody with a strong stomach took it down one night and buried it in a hole beside the river bank.

*

For over two hundred and fifty years the ghosts of Lilywhite, the Countess and the Baron had haunted Ardmore Manor. Although they also had died at Ardmore, the ghosts of Lady Carstairs and Squire Huggett were allowed by what was then the Council of Ghosts to stay at their own homes; and now Lady Carstairs spent all her time in the tower of ruined Carstairs Castle working endlessly on the tapestry the dish of toadstools had interrupted, while Squire Huggett lived in the church where once he'd been chief worshipper, making nightly forays into the churchyard to lift the mini-skirts of village maidens who had strayed into its dark corners with their boy friends. But once a year, on the anniversary of the dinner party and the ball that had never started, they and the ghosts of the other guests, most of whom had died peacefully enough in their beds, had to return to Ardmore and re-enact the fatal dinner party.

Throughout the centuries the trio at Ardmore had found plenty to interest and amuse themselves. Descendants of a branch of the Countess's family lived in the Manor for generations without worrying about the presence of the ghosts. Indeed, they were proud of them and always did their utmost to get them to emanate for the entertainment of guests. During the 1914–18 War, when it was turned into a hospital for officers, and again in the 1939–45 War, when it was a secret S.O.S. headquarters for training special agents, Lilywhite had a wonderful time moaning and rolling her large white eyeballs beside the beds of light sleepers. But those good times finished after the estate was sold in 1947 to pay heavy death duties, and it was broken up into building plots for bungalows and pseudo-Tudor cottages. Only the house and the ground immediately surrounding it was left untouched. The house was occupied at different times by branches of the civil service, local government departments and other peculiar administrative bodies. None of these officials and their clerks and typists were in the building at night, so the trio had nobody to frighten, and they grew lonely and had to fall back on each other for company. They tried to relieve the tedium of their ghosthood by materializing at odd moments in daylight, but the little officials and their satellites were so wrapped up in their own petty importance that they never even noticed them. 'You're wasting your energy, you silly black cow,' the Countess said after Lilywhite had spent a whole morning groaning and waving her arms at a typist, who had stared through her and gone on chain-smoking and lacquering her nails. 'They have no imagination whatsoever, and you'll just make yourself a nervous wreck if you keep on at them.'

But in 1961, when they received a special dispensation from what was now called the National Union of British Welfare State Ghosts to travel within a radius of fifty miles, the ghostly life began to brighten for them again. Every night, with secret glee and without telling Lilywhite where they were going, the Countess and the Baron galloped off on horseback, for there were still several ghostly horses in the ruined stables. Lilywhite was left alone to wander through the deserted mansion. At first she amused herself by mixing up the papers in the office files and shuffling through the ones in the trays on the desks, but as this never caused the expected commotion, she got tired and joined a course of evening classes to learn reading and writing at the Brighton Ghosts' Technical Institute. She had always been afraid of horses, so every night she stole a motor-scooter from a shed beside one of the bungalows and drove at full speed to the Prince Regent's favourite town. It was always a black night for her if she did not manage to cause at least one accident on the way. She learned quickly to write C A T and D O G but after she had graduated to four-letter words she became bored and dodged the classes. Instead, she took to gallivanting along the beach, frightening the lovers lying in dark corners by flashing her teeth and eyeballs at them. She even went as far as Hove, but one night after she'd made an old queen, who was teaching the facts of life to a delinquent youth, die of heart failure in the act, she never went back. Nor did she return to the evening classes. 'That ole nance tell me he tear my skeleton into little pieces if he ever catch me, missy,' she told the Countess. 'Though how he goin' to see my skeleton I don' know. It's black as the ace of spades. It's all nonsense that poem they teach us in evening class about the black man saying "But oh my soul is white." My soul is black and so's my bones.'

'Thank heavens, mine isn't,' Margaret Torryburn said.

'Don' boast, missy. Your soul is as black as mine. It only your bones that's white.'

The Countess said: 'Never mind. Charles and I'll take you with us to London tonight and then we'll see if your black skeleton frightens the blackamoors in Brixton and Notting Hill Gate as much as they frighten us.'

While Lilywhite had been enjoying her innocent pleasures in Brighton and Hove, the Countess and her paramour had been waging a campaign against the West Indians who had come to London in thousands, gone on National Assistance and bought up most of the old mansions that had housed the Victorian bourgeoisie, turning them into gambling clubs and brothels or partitioning the rooms and letting out the cubicles at huge rents to other immigrants who had followed them into the paradise of the whites' Welfare State.

That night when the Countess and the Baron were chalking 'Niggers Go Home' on doors and walls and pavements in Brixton,

Lilywhite rolled her eyes and flashed her teeth in the houses, but so many other black people were rolling their eyes and flashing their teeth that hers were not noticed, and when she moaned and screamed they could not hear her for the noise of their calypsos. Disgusted, she went back into the streets and watched the Baron chalking on the pavement. 'What for you do this, Charlie boy?' she asked. 'What them black people done to you?'

'It is not what they have done, it is what they will do,' the Baron said. 'Wait until the blacks rule the world and make the whites their slaves. The sjambok will swish again.' He wrote 'Angleterre Needs Apartheid' and said, 'I am enchanted I am dead and will never need to call a nigger "master".'

Lilywhite began to chalk four-letter words beneath the slogans written by her fellow spirits.

'Don' count your chickens, Charlie boy,' she muttered. 'You might get borned again next century. I hopes I see you jumpin' when yo' master crack the whip.'

When dawn came and they prepared to gallop off to Ardmore, Lilywhite grinned malevolently at the Baron's back and, before she leapt on her scooter, she chalked: 'Frenchy Go Hoem.'

For the next few months the ghosts went to London every night, and their slogans caused a number of race riots, many innocent people being blamed for racial discrimination and incitement because of them. The trio enjoyed themselves enormously. Lilywhite chalked her slogans with the greatest enthusiasm. 'All them niggers should go home, missy, and leave more room for you and me,' she said. 'All foreigners should go home and leave the world to the English.'

'But I'm Scottish,' the Countess said proudly.

'That what I mean, missy.'

And so not only the walls and pavements of Notting Hill Gate and Brixton but those in many other districts of London were treated to a deluge of slogans as Lilywhite raced around on her scooter, chalking 'Scots Go Hoem,' 'Yankees Go Hoem,' 'Jews Go Hoem,' and 'Poles Go Hoem.' But when she got a tin of red paint and splashed MPEES PIS OF HOEM on the Houses of Parliament, the Countess became alarmed at Lilywhite's scholastic progress.

At that moment—luckily or unluckily, Margaret Torryburn could not make up her mind which it was—Lilywhite's attention was diverted by a new development at Ardmore. The civil servants left; their files and papers were taken away. Gangs of workmen invaded the mansion and its remaining grounds. They tore down the old stables and erected a strange building in their place. The Baron, who affected to be knowledgeable about such things, said it was a Sauna Baths. Bulldozers dug a great crater in the park and a bathing pool was built. There was so much activity that the ghosts stopped their trips to London. Many of the workmen were Irish labourers, so Lilywhite plagued them by chalking 'Irish Go Hoem' all over the place. While this was going on, painters and decorators transformed the mansion. The walls, which had been drab olive and brown for many years, were repainted in garish colours, and every room was fitted with thick expensive carpets to match them. Electricians installed weird lights and heating appliances. Then rich silk curtains were draped at every window, and vanloads of peculiarly shaped Swedish furniture were carried in and arranged under the supervision of a chain-smoking woman with pink hair and a hard white face. And, at last, Ardmore began to resume a little of its former glory. 'Though it's different, of course,' the Countess said. 'It's in deplorable taste, and you couldn't say that about the place in my time.'

'It must have been bought by some important man, missy,' Lilywhite said. 'A duke maybe? Or some prince?'

'A film star, I should say. Whoever it is must be immensely rich.'

The Countess became so excited that she preened in front of all the new mirrors, wondering if by some wonderful means she could manage to persuade the National Union of British Ghosts to give her a special dispensation to renew her corporeal form for a period. She deserved it. She had put up with Charles for over two hundred and fifty years, so she was entitled to a bonus. After all, Madame Du Barry had been allowed to be reincarnated as Mata Hari in the days long before the Council of Ghosts had become a Welfare State Union with much greater powers. Of course, poor silly Du Barry had made the same mistakes as she'd made in her previous existence and had died unpleasantly a second time. But Margaret Torryburn was determined that she wouldn't give cause for any complaint. Perhaps that nice Mr Cameron, the head of the Union and a fellow Scot, might be wheedled into seeing reason. . . .

But the Countess's dreams and hopes were shattered when she saw an announcement in a copy of the local newspaper that a workman had thrown down. Ardmore was to be opened the following week as a Motel for Underprivileged Youth. It was a new scheme sponsored by many people who believed that 'the products of poor overcrowded homes should have a chance to expand their horizons by sampling gracious living in glorious surroundings'. These 'deprived underlings' were to be given this opportunity at Ardmore at a price—'since modern youth is independent and believes in paying its fair whack'. The newspaper reported that charges for a week's stay would be twenty-five to fifty guineas, though suites consisting of a bedroom, private bathroom and sitting-room would cost more.

*

The Ardmore Motel had been going now for nearly a year. It was efficiently run by the pink-haired woman, Mrs Courage, the Lady Supervisor, sycophantically addressed as 'Madam' by the staff, most of whom, male and female, looked as though they either had been or should be warders in prisons. The Countess often said: 'Seeing what they have to cope with, they need to be tough. They should have barbed wire whips to control their charges.' For, even yet, she and her fellow ghosts could not stop being surprised at the behaviour of the underprivileged visitors, whom everybody kowtowed to and respectfully called 'teenagers' as if they were a race apart.

Most of these teenagers spent their days sitting in front of the television sets, and their nights in racing around the countryside in fast cars or in smoking pot. Almost all were drug addicts of some sort. The more naïve took amphetamines and barbiturates, the more advanced got high on heroin. Some who came with purple hearts in their zip-bags had graduated to L.S.D. and cannabis by the time they left. Their favourite word was 'psychedelic'. One of them, Gary Greatheart, who had occupied the most expensive suite for months and now looked as though he'd become a fixture, tried everything from marijuana to hashish. When Gary came to Ardmore Lilywhite had taken a fancy to him; he was a pretty youth with a fine pair of legs. But after a few days Lilywhite's infatuation was flattened. 'You never guess what I see last night, missy,' she said. 'He in bed with two other boys, and you woulden believe the things they got up to.'

'Och, you're havering, woman,' the Countess said.

'It the Gospel truth. Cut my throat and hope to die if I tellin' lies. He what they call a pop singer, missy.'

'Ah, a strolling player,' the Countess said. 'With the manners of a barnyard rooster.'

'He a cockalorum all right,' Lilywhite giggled. 'I don' know about his heart bein' great, but somethin' else sure is. You should see what they was doin'. They a lot better than the telly.'

Lilywhite loved the television. There was a set in every room, even in the lavatories. Some of the swinging young would sit for hours on toilet seats, staring vacantly at the screen until Lilywhite either pinched their bottoms or switched the television to another channel. When she was at a loss for other diversions she rushed from room to room, playing havoc with the sets. Her pranks caused endless consternation, and the TV engineers were kept busy searching for faults on the sets and aerials. The Baron got his chief entertainment from watching the more athletic of the long-haired youths and girls being beaten by birch twigs in the Sauna Baths. But Margaret Torryburn, who loathed television and never had a bath if she could help it, had nothing to amuse her. 'Why'n't you frighten the knickers offen Ole Mother Courage, missy?' Lilywhite suggested.

'She doesn't wear any. I've tried my damnedest to scare her, but nothing'll shake her. She's got nerves like steel.'

The Countess had only the young to take up her attention, and by this time she was heartily tired of their antics and attitudes. 'They're such bores,' she said. 'I could forgive them for being almost anything but that. They never say anything worth while—a lot of them can hardly utter, they just grunt—and they keep doing the same stupid things day after day. They think they're trend-setters, but everything they do and say has been done and said a thousand times before—only much better. What's original about taking dope? My father smoked opium every night of his life. He kept ten mistresses at the same time and kept them all satisfied, but he didn't go around boasting about it and saying the world had never been so wonderful. There's nothing wonderful about it. It's dreary. Damned dreary.'

'They don' think that, missy,' the black ghost said. 'They say, like that ole Prime Minister, yo' fellow countryman, that we never had it so good.'

'I'm sick of them,' the Countess said. 'They must leave my house. We must get rid of them. *Canaille!*'

'Easier said than done, missy. And don' let them hear you usin' that nasty French word. Some of them not so stupid as they look. They got low cunning.'

'They must leave my house,' the Countess said. 'Immediately.'

A few days later she said: 'I've got a plan. I've put an idea into Old Mother Courage's thick skull. It was a job, but I managed at last to get my thought-waves to connect with hers. She has decided to have a fancy-dress ball on our anniversary night.'

'So what?' Lilywhite picked her nose as she watched an art student kneeling on the lawn, throwing bits of mud and grass at the canvas he had streaked with red and yellow paint.

'That night we'll all meet as usual. We spirits will have our ghostly dinner party while the peasants amuse themselves in their own way. But instead of preparing your usual dish of toad-stools, you will prepare one three or four times the size and put it where the mortals will eat it. And eat it they shall. I'm determined about that, even if I have to shove it down their throats. Nobody who once enters my house must leave it unnourished.'

'You nev' forget the times you was the hostess with the mostes', do you, missy? But you not that any longer, remember. You just the same as pore Lilywhite. A ghostie without two pennies to jingle on your tombstone.'

'Well, at least I've got a tombstone, and you haven't,' the Countess said.

'Don' boast, missy. You as bad as them teenagers—only you not so young and you got less excuse.'

Lilywhite stared again at the kneeling artist; then she leaned forward and kicked his bottom, making him fall on his face among the wet paint.

'I not goin' do it,' she said. 'Lilywhite don' want any more deaths on her conscience.'

'You'll do what I tell you, ye black besom,' the Countess cried.

'I won', you white besom. You only callin' the kettle black, missy.'

'If you don't do it, I'll send you back to Africa.'

'Lilywhite never been to Africa.'

'Well, I'll send you there anyway, to join the rest of your black brothers.'

'I got no brothers, missy. Lilywhite was borned in Constantinople and brung here when she was a babby. She as English as you.'

'You'll do what I tell you. Or to Africa you'll go. The Ghost Control Commission will fix it. I have influence with them.'

'I won' do it. I got no bone to pick with them trendies, except they make a lot of noise and take funny drugs.'

'Well, it's Africa and *Uhuru* for you—and see how you'll like that!'

'*Uhuru*? What that mean?'

'Freedom, you daft cow.'

'I still not do it, missy. You can ask till you as black in the face as me.'

Margaret Torryburn threatened, wept, pleaded and wheedled, but Lilywhite was adamant. Even when the Countess and the Baron wrote NIGGER GO HOME all over Ardmore, she refused to budge. 'If you don' like them teenagers in their funny clothes, missy, and if you can't stand their music and racket, why don' you go back to Scotland? You got plenty of big houses there,' she said. 'You could have a fine time scarin' the kilts off the Highlandmens.'

'My houses are all in ruins,' the Countess said, 'and the Highlanders don't wear the kilt any longer. Anyway, I died here, and here I'm going to stay.'

'I died here too, missy. I not goin' leave it either. Lilywhite like it here.'

Day after day went past and the anniversary dinner got nearer, and at last Margaret sent for her friend, Mr Cameron. He tried to bribe Lilywhite with a free trip to Constantinople, but she still refused. 'Lilywhite not goin' kill any more people,' she said. 'Plenty of ghosties in the world already.'

'Weel, weel, this is a bonnie kettle o' fish, is it no'?' Mr Cameron said. 'I doot, ma guid woman, that there's nothin' for it but to send ye back to Africy, like ma lady says. I'm thrang to dae it, ye understan', but I doot I'll ha'e to take off the velvet glove. One word frae me and the Immigration folk 'll be on yer track. Ye've nae right to be in this country.'

'Immigrations can't touch Lilywhite. She been here all her life.'

'Can ye prove that, ma bonnie hen? Whaur's yer papers?'

'What papers? Lilywhite never have no papers. She got nothin' but this ole frock she die in.'

'Oho, so ye havenie got a passport, ma wee black doo? If ye havenie, ye must ha'e made illegal entry into this country.'

'Lilywhite came here as a babby.'

'Ah, so ye were smuggled in? This looks bad for ye. I doot there's nothin' for it but to get the Immigration authorities to deport ye as an undesirable alien—unless, of course, ye change yer mind and gi'e thae folk the poisoned toadstools like her lady-ship says.'

'Lilywhite don' want to kill anybody.'

'Ah well, ye'll just have to take the consequences. We'll ha'e to get the Immigration folk to deport ye on the night o' yer anniversary. I'm sorry aboot this, but the law must be upheld.'

And Mr Cameron disappeared back to his London office with a whiff of brimstone.

It was only a week to the anniversary dinner and ball. The Baron gave up his amusements in the Sauna Baths to taunt Lilywhite with tales of prisons and concentration camps in Ghana and other parts of Africa. 'You know, of course,' he said, 'that under the Deportation Act you will resume your corporeal form as soon as you are taken into custody? So, after ten o'clock on Friday night, *ma belle sauvage*, you will not be able to get up to any more ghostly high-jinks. You will become a poor human again until you are lucky enough to die another time. I hope you'll have a very long and unhappy second existence. I wonder which part of Africa they'll send you to? South Africa perhaps? The Boers will have a lot of fun with you. You won't be able to write any of your filthy slogans there. But probably they'll send you to the Congo. *Ma foi*, I would not be in your shoes. I hear they have the best witch doctors in the world there. You will not be able to queen it among them and the ju-ju boys. They won't put up with any of your silly nonsense. Instead of you frightening them, they will frighten you. Some of the witch doctors are more ghoulish than any ghost. And I hear they have cannibals. I expect you'll end up in some pot and your black bones will be used as chopsticks by a witch doctor. But I hope it will be a long, long time before I can say with the playwright, "It was in another country, and the wench is dead." '

The Baron gloated over Lilywhite so much that even the Countess thought he went beyond the score. 'Och, leave the poor wretch alone,' she cried. 'How would you like it if I got Mr Cameron to deport you to Devil's Island?' And she said to Lilywhite: 'Why don't you change your mind, you thrawn bitch? After all, what's a few more deaths between friends?'

Lilywhite said nothing. She went about in a sullen state, impervious both to the Baron's taunts and the Countess's wheedlings. She did not even try to lighten her last days of freedom at Ardmore by terrorizing the staff and visitors.

But three days before she was due to be deported she rushed to the Countess, her eyeballs rolling with agitation, and screeched: 'Oh, missy, that ole nance here!'

'What old nance?'

'That ole queen I scared the living daylights out of on the beach at Hove. He've come to Ardmore.'

'However did he find out where you were?' the Countess said. 'Don't tell me there are snoopers in the Brighton Ghosts' Technical Institute?'

'No, he see one of Gary Greatheart's boy friends swaggering at being Mister Muscles on the beach and he take a fancy to him and follow him here. Now he in Gary's room watchin' him and his boys playing at being Roman slaves.'

'So what ?' the Countess said.

'I happen to go into the room and he get a shock.' Lilywhite wrung her hands with agitation. 'He pleased to see me, missy. He *delighted* to find pore Lilywhite. Such a pleasant surprise, he say, I been lookin' everywhere for you. Revenge is sweet, he say. And he say he follow me to Africa and haunt me for ever and ever.'

'We'll soon settle his hash,' the Countess said.

She thought a minute. 'We'd better give up this African idea,' she said. 'I'll go and see Mr Cameron at once and tell him to get the Immigration authorities to deport this old queen instead of you. He can spend the rest of eternity playing at being a white slave in Africa. But if I do this for you, you'll have to do something in return for me.'

'Anything you say, missy. Only don' let me be haunted by that ole nance.'

'You can get rid of the trend-setters and Old Mother Courage and her brood.'

'O.K.,' Lilywhite said.

★

On the day of the anniversary dinner and ball there was great activity at Ardmore. The young visitors started to dope themselves early so that they'd get into the proper 'groove' for the evening. Transistor wirelesses banged out pop music; the trendies rushed from room to room, showing each other the fancy dress they were going to wear; and Mrs Courage and her staff drank quantities of gin and whisky to get themselves as high as their charges. By mid-afternoon there was such pandemonium that the Countess, arraying herself in her ghostly finery, thought the ball had already started. 'Ah well,' she said, placing a beauty patch under her left eye, 'it'll all soon be over and Ardmore'll go back to its former peace and quietness. I must arrange with Mr Cameron to get Mother Courage and these trendies all sent back to their native places. We can't have their ghosts here to disturb our peace and quiet any longer.'

Early in the morning, as was customary, Lilywhite had gone out into what was left of the great park to gather the toadstools. By mid-afternoon there was no sign of her, but the Countess thought she was probably in the kitchen preparing the fatal dish.

About six o'clock the first of the pantheon of ghosts, Lady Carstairs and Squire Huggett, arrived. Lady Carstairs was horrified when she saw the television sets and the crowd of teenagers. 'My dear Margaret!' she cried. 'How can you possibly put up with the noise? I never realized it was as awful as this. I thought it was bad at the Castle when trippers come on Sundays and climb the ruins and yell and throw their sandwich papers around and spit into the moat, but it's nothing like this *bedlam*.'

'We won't have to thole it much longer,' the Countess said. 'Lilywhite is busy now, preparing to put an end to it all.'

'Hark! What's that?' Lady Carstairs cried.

'Sounds like the hunt,' Squire Huggett said. 'Here they come! Tallyho! Tallyho! They're after the fox.'

But it was not the fox. It was the ghost of the old queen screaming with terror as he was pursued by the Immigration authorities. They watched them disappear among the new bungalows and houses. 'I hope they get him on the plane for Lagos without too much trouble,' the Countess said. 'I told Mr Cameron to get them to give him a sedative before they grabbed him, but they don't seem to have managed.'

Some more ghosts arrived to watch the hunt when the old queen doubled back across the park, dodging here and there in frenzy as the Immigration men tried to lassoo him. 'I wonder what has happened to Lilywhite?' the Countess said. 'She should have been here by this time to help me with my ball gown—though there's little she can really do, the gown's got so tattered with all the wear and tear through the years.'

She went to the kitchen, but she found only the chef and Mrs Courage arguing about how much sherry he should put in a trifle while they toasted each other with champagne. 'This is most mysterious,' the Countess said, going back to her guests. 'I hope those stupid Immigration folk haven't grabbed her too. They're quite liable to make a mistake.'

'It is pleasant to think of Lilywhite and that depraved old man flying together in an aeroplane to Africa at this moment,' the Baron said, taking a pinch of snuff.

'For you, perhaps,' Margaret said acidly. 'But not for me. I must get rid of this *canaille*.'

More ghosts arrived, and by half-past seven, the time when they should have been preparing to enter the dining-room for the fatal meal, they had all congregated except Lilywhite. The Countess was frantic. The human beings had already started their fancy-dress dance. Many of them were standing in the ballroom, twisting themselves into quaint shapes, facing each other but scarcely ever touching. Others were staring, with drugged looks, at the various television sets. A famous pop group with long hair, moronic faces, electric guitars and obscene gestures were posturing around a girl singer who was clutching a microphone and moaning strange, uncouth gibberish. Upstairs in his suite Gary Greatheart and his boy friends, doped into unconsciousness, were lying in abandoned states of nakedness. The staff had already started to eat the buffet supper that they knew none of the teenagers and their friends would probably want to eat. The pantheon of ghosts stood helplessly among the gyrating and comatose humans; they were behind schedule, and each was wondering whether the National Union of British Ghosts would blame them for the delay and exact some dire penalty.

At that moment Lilywhite whirled into the dining-room, screaming: 'Missy! Missy! What we goin' do, missy? There no toadstools left. I been hunting all over the great park. I been for miles, but all the toadstools gone. They been poisoned and killed by that new artificial manure they putting down everywhere. Lord have mercy on us all! What we goin' do now, missy?'

SHEPHERD, SHOW ME . . .

by Rosalind Wade

As I approached the house, my curiosity increased. In this
uncultivated landscape, punctuated only by derelict mineshafts
and an occasional slag-heap, it seemed impossible that any
habitation could be concealed. My impression was of the Atlantic
Ocean boiling up all around me like a vast cauldron, on the surface of which a couple of distant tramp steamers were no more
noticeable than match-heads.

I stopped the car, hoping that no unwieldy farm cart would
wish to pass, and studied my directions. Once the car was still the
full force of the gale sounded like giant hand-slappings. Even a
gull, irresolutely straying inland, barely maintained its poise.

The instructions were meticulously clear . . . 'Continue after
leaving St Huthy for two miles. At the first bend you will see a
farmhouse with the shutters painted bright yellow. I should warn
you, it's a one in four descent after that, but it leads you straight
to Lancevearn. . . .'

Very soon I identified that farmhouse—and why anyone should
have chosen such a bilious colour for the woodwork remained a
mystery. I skirted it with caution and changed gear, speculating
as to what manner of man had written that letter. '. . . I do indeed
hope you will forgive me for being so presumptuous as to trouble
you, a complete stranger . . .' it continued. 'My only excuse is
that a very old friend of yours, Miss Queenie Newton, has told
me of the wide experience you have in so many spheres, including
that unknown quantity, the power of mind over matter. I myself know virtually nothing about "spiritual" treatment and so I
am quite unable to cope with my present predicament which,
briefly, is that my wife is completely dominated by a couple of
faith-healers. And so, seeing that you are spending a few days in
the St Huthy neighbourhood . . .'

I began then to form a mental picture of him as a fussy,

precise person, practical enough when describing a route but a
crank and, even more deplorable, husband of another crank.
This could be a case of *folies à deux;* and it was more than ever
puzzling to know what I was expected to do about it.

Almost without warning I came upon a pair of elaborate stone
gate posts set in the high granite wall which enclosed the grounds
of Lancevearn. On one side the boundary sliced through a strip
of moorland; on the other, a narrow path led directly to the sea.
Within, a riot of escallonia. A young gardener was hacking away
apathetically at the overgrown plantation. The house appeared
to be of medium size and rather squat in appearance; the wonder
was that stone and timber had ever been transported to this
inaccessible spot.

An agreeable-looking maid opened the front door to me. She
was very dark, although her eyes were china blue, suggestive of a
lingering element of the Spaniards who, in remote times, had
invaded these shores and intermarried with the indigenous
Celts. She led the way across a large square hall to the drawing
room. The furniture was strangely heterogeneous and I paused
to inspect one of the most striking pieces. At that moment I
heard my name spoken and turned to greet my host. With
difficulty I concealed my astonishment. For here was no elderly
eccentric but an undeniably handsome young man.

'You *are* Mr Stephen Hallam?' I inquired unnecessarily.

He nodded. 'Let me say straight away how terribly grateful I
am to you for coming to the aid of a complete stranger. I was
feeling quite desperate when I wrote to you, but Queenie assured
me you wouldn't mind. I mean, you have so much experience. . . .'

I raised my hand to ward off the unwelcome and undeserved
compliment. 'Please, Mr Hallam, may I make this absolutely
clear? I am not an authority on faith-healing; nor, indeed, on
anything else. It's true I'm interested in a great many subjects,
but purely as an observer and, if you like, a commentator.'

'You're far too modest. Why, Queenie was telling me . . .'

Not for the first time I shook my fist, figuratively speaking, at
Queenie. Her interpretation of the obligations of our lifelong
friendship was to belittle such modest talents as I possess to my
face while recommending them fulsomely in other quarters.

'But how did you happen to discuss me with Queenie in the first place?' I asked. 'I haven't seen much of her since she became Matron at St Benyn's school, although we keep in touch in a vague kind of way.' Frankly, I could not see my garrulous, muddle-minded little friend in this man's orbit.

'We often have tea together in her sanctum; at the school, that is.'

'You're a schoolmaster, then?' I exclaimed.

'Does it astonish you so much? I should have mentioned in my letter that I'm on the staff of St Benyn's.'

'Forgive me,' I begged him, 'I didn't mean . . .'

'I don't look like a teacher?'

'Well, no. . . .'

'Then what do I look like?'

The question at first sounded a mere provocation until I realized that he was attaching a quite disproportionate importance to my reply. I inspected him covertly. His eyes were amber-coloured; his hair combed back to conceal an unobtrusive wave. And his voice, vibrant though unaffected, was rich with subtle cadences.

'An actor,' I replied impulsively.

'Well, that's exactly what I am—or was!'

The explanation proved simple. He had originally trained at a teacher's college and then gone on the stage, following a totally unexpected invitation from a West End manager who had seen him playing in an amateur production. But despite this promising start he ended up in a provincial repertory company and it was there that he met his wife, Mira. Alas, the strain of the life told on Mira and she suffered a complete breakdown after the loss of an eagerly awaited first child. And so it seemed wise to get right away from the theatre and fortunately he was able to return to his early profession in an ideal post at St Benyn's.

I listened attentively to this story, filling in the gaps, wondering whether the affinity between acting and teaching was sufficient to support his *amour propre*. And then I found myself voicing the inevitable query. What precisely was I expected to do about it?

'You've every right to ask that after listening to my tale of woe so patiently. Mira was much better by the time we came here but

she still wasn't off the sick-list. She injured her leg, you see, when
she collapsed during a performance.'

'She's not actually crippled, or lame?'

'No, no. Nothing like that. Her leg just needs massage or
"light" treatment. You know the kind of thing.'

'And she isn't getting it?'

'I'm afraid not. A few days after we came here—in January
that was—I registered with the local doctor, asking him to call on
Mira as soon as possible. For some reason he didn't come at once.
I was rather annoyed about it at the time. Anyway, when he
did appear at Lancevearn it was too late. By that time the faith-
healers had moved in on us and Mira was entirely satisfied with
them. In fact, she got furiously angry when I questioned their
qualifications. Since then the doctor has looked in several times
and been sent away by Mira—rather rudely, I'm afraid. Unfortunately, I was out each time. I should think it must have been about
mid-March that he telephoned me at school and put it pretty
clearly that there was nothing further he could do.'

'Well,' I suggested, 'is it possible that she really has recovered
from the breakdown and wants to establish the fact?'

'I'd like to think that. It did occur to me at first. But no, I
believe she really needs quite a bit of help. She still suffers from
insomnia. I see a light under her door all night. And there's the
leg. I'm sure she's in pain. Anyway, it's bad enough to keep her
in bed. She hasn't been downstairs for weeks now.'

'That's terribly frustrating for both of you.'

I found myself considering two kinds of faith-healer: one, a
visiting lay preacher conducting a service in the parish church
with people queueing up to receive his blessing without noticeable results; and the other, a frowsty spiritualist of the kind a
woman of my acquaintance consulted in a fit of emotional despair.
Into which category did the present practitioners fall?

His reply was surprising. 'I can't say. I've never seen them.
You see, week-ends and holidays when I'd be at home, they've
never shown up. They don't wish to meet me, obviously.'

'Then why don't you write or telephone them, forbidding them
to call here except by appointment with you personally?'

'That would be the obvious thing, of course, if I knew their names and where they come from. But Mira absolutely refuses to tell me. Naturally, I've asked her again and again.'

As though a curtain had been abruptly drawn back I witnessed the extent of his inner turmoil and deprivation. 'You could easily find out,' I answered gently. 'There can't be so many faith-healers in the St Huthy district! But, in any case, is it so import-ant? I expect she will come through, with or without a doctor.'

'Perhaps. But you see, it isn't only a matter of her health. In some strange way, these people have turned her against me. She hates me now. When she speaks to me, which isn't often, she's like a hostile stranger. The summer term starts tomorrow and they'll be back, for sure. That's really why I wrote to you, to ask you to talk to her for me, before it's too late.'

I refused unconditionally. As a stimulus to my creative imagination the complexities of the human predicament might have their uses; yet I shied away from actual participation in them. But he persisted. Just *because* I was a stranger I might break the impasse. . . . And in the end I capitulated, reflecting that I undertook very little of practical service to fellow humans less fortunate than myself.

He fetched a decanter and glasses and together we sat out in the conservatory. His hand trembled as he poured the wine. Tentatively, I sought to distract his attention. What chance had led him to settle in such an out-of-the-way place as Lancevearn?

'Oh, simply seeing an advertisement.'

He had rented the house furnished, for one year, at a surprisingly modest figure. Eventually, the place would be auctioned as part of a much larger estate. Lancevearn was built some seventy-five years earlier by a Cornishman who had spent most of his life in the United States and made a fortune there. Nearly all the furni-ture had been collected in the United States and shipped to England. Each piece was listed with the price paid and where purchased in a large leather-bound volume reposing on the hall table. We laughed a little at this evidence of Victorian precision.

But soon he was glancing at his watch. 'I have to go into St Huthy to fill up with petrol,' he explained. 'And I may need to have the engine looked at. After you've seen Mira, do you think you could wait for me until I get back? Our maid, Rhoda, would get you anything you wanted. And then, if these people should show up, you could cope with them for me; or, better still, persuade them to wait until I get back.' He assured me that he had already told Mira that a great friend of Queenie's would be calling and she had raised no objection. Presently I heard the engine of his car purring away up the track. For a full minute I waited on in the conservatory, gazing out at the incomparable view.

The surface of the hall floor shone like polished ebony. The carving of the balustrade struck me as unique. But it was the magnificently sited landing window which finally captured my attention. Set within a large recess, the alcove afforded the illusion of being built right out over the sea, with Godrevy, a gleaming platinum strip, just visible on the western horizon. There was some furniture, conveying the effect of a small extra room, a rocking-chair and a most unusual escritoire or 'lady's bureau'.

Of the six doors opening onto the landing all but one were closed. 'Is that my visitor?' a faint voice inquired and I braced myself for the ordeal, for the thought of the invalid, immured from the morning freshness, was repellent rather than pitiful.

I do not quite know what I expected her to look like, although names do conjure people and 'Mira' is the 'variable' star. At any rate, the person who greeted me from the vantage of an enormous four-poster bed was one of the most beautiful women I had ever seen and I thought what a striking pair the Hallams must have made at that Repertory theatre. But that she was genuinely ill I now had no doubt. There were about her mouth the traces of deep suffering. And as she shifted her position she winced involuntarily with pain.

'Come and sit down,' she invited, quickly mastering it. 'Stephen told me you were going to call this morning. You're a great friend of Queenie's, aren't you?'

'We were at school together,' I explained. 'I'm sorry you're ill. How very disappointing for you when you've just moved into this glorious place.'

She acknowledged my sympathy with a polite nod. 'Well, we've been here nearly four months now, you know. It might be disappointing if I didn't know for certain that I can be completely cured. In fact, I *am* cured, although that's rather a negative way of putting it because, actually, there never was anything the matter with me. It's just a matter of time until my own faith is strong enough to banish all these—illusions—of "evil". I have to fight all these wicked whisperings which try to tell me I'm an invalid, but also I have to stand up against—er—people who try to make me believe my body and my mind are still sick.'

She outlined her problem in a common-sense manner which would be hard to combat. She wore a lace-topped nightgown and through it her breasts showed firm and opaque. It was not difficult to imagine the emotional frustration which her husband suffered.

'All that might be so, in a general way,' I agreed cautiously. 'But does it apply to every kind of ailment? Haven't you hurt your leg? I think I noticed when I came in that it was paining you. A thing like that can do with some orthodox medical treatment, surely?' I was uncomfortably aware that I was catechizing her, and until this moment she had not appeared to resent it. But my last comment stung her to anger.

'You mean, by a doctor? I wouldn't have one inside the place. Don't you know that they are mere "purveyors of evil". "Confectioners of disease", someone once called them, and that describes them perfectly!' I saw then that her husband had not exaggerated. She spoke with such concentrated venom that the immediate effect was of an actress rehearsing an unpleasant part.

'Aren't you a bit hard on the profession?' I countered lightly. 'I feel sure your husband would be greatly relieved if you would agree to, say, a routine check-up?'

'Then I must resist him.' Her voice rose to a shout.

I was shocked and shaken: 'But you do have some advice, don't you, Mrs Hallam?' I cut in quickly, determined to keep control of the situation. 'What kind of people are they, these "faith-healers" of yours?'

'Oh. I see he *has* been complaining about them to you. I thought as much.' Her lips tightened into a thin vindictive line. 'Actually, they are two charming, very devout people, who certainly have my interests at heart!'

'I'm sure they have. Do they call regularly? Are they both women, by the way?'

'They come when they can. No, it's a man and a woman. *She* is quite elderly and rather delightfully old-fashioned. *He* is much younger, but not at all "modern" in the way he talks and dresses. I *think* they're married but I've never been quite sure. Anyway, they have a perfect mutual understanding,' she concluded rather wistfully.

'I can see they mean a great deal to you.' I stood up and held out my hand. 'I do hope you'll soon be up and about again.'

'Oh, but I *do* get up, nearly every afternoon. I sit in the window recess.' She spoke quite pleasantly as though unwilling to part on bad terms. Perhaps because of Queenie?

I responded in the same spirit: 'On the landing, you mean? It's lovely there at the moment.'

'Well, I may not trouble today.'

I paused at the alcove, thinking that the reclining chair and the low bureau might have been specially constructed for an invalid. Idly, I rested my hand on the leather-topped desk and as I did so I experienced the strangest sensation. It was as though an over-mastering personality took complete control of me. Darkness obscured my vision, while insistent voices reverberated in my head like a distorted radio. Involuntarily I took a step backwards; and stood very still, waiting for the attack to pass. Gradually, the scene lightened and silence reigned. Though still trembling, I began to feel normal again. By the time I reached the hall the odd, frightening indisposition might have happened only in my imagination.

On the table lay the leather-bound inventory Stephen had mentioned. I turned to the relevant entries. 'One lady's correspondence bureau, one reclining chair, Boston, Mass. (1911).' Also, from the same source, an umbrella-stand in the hall. I was quite amazed at the price paid for these three items. At that moment the telephone bell rang and the maid, Rhoda, came hurrying from the kitchen quarters to answer it.

The caller was Mr Hallam. The garage at St Huthy needed to keep the car for a couple of hours. Thus, he must not detain me if I wished to leave. 'In that case,' I said to Rhoda, 'I'll be getting along.' Through the open dining-room door I could see the table laid for one. 'I suppose Mrs Hallam won't be coming down for lunch?' I inquired.

'She has never done so since I've been working here,' Rhoda answered. 'When Mr Hallam is at school I take her up a tray and see she has everything she requires before I go home at two o'clock.'

'That's very helpful. I do hope she'll soon be better. I understand she is being treated by faith-healers,' I remarked with assumed detachment. 'Do they strike you as reliable people?'

Now her china-blue eyes were directed at me with merciless disapproval. If I had anticipated the co-operation of a garrulous Mrs Mop I was doomed to disappointment. 'I really couldn't say,' she replied coldly, 'I've not been here when they called.'

Outside, the sun's rays were quite scorching. I negotiated the track carefully, castigating myself for having handled a delicate situation so clumsily. By the time I reached the cross-roads I was still smarting from the rebuffs I had received. And who was responsible? Why, Queenie, with her inveterate passion for putting in her oar. On impulse, I decided to tell her so without waiting for our pre-arranged meeting three days hence.

Skirting St Huthy, I was soon bowling along a coast road ribboned by the azure sea; the skyline notched by dolmens and barrows. Within this narrow strip of territory was contained the very essence of early Cornish civilization—the witches' wishing stone and the foundations of the oldest Christian church in the Duchy. St Benyn's school, once a vicarage, was situated just beyond the ruins.

Queenie seemed surprised and not too pleased to see me, although she invited me into her sanctum, which was stacked with bed linen and trunks. She switched on the electric kettle and set out a tea-tray while listening to my complaints. 'I thought you'd be only too pleased to help Stephen, the poor lamb,' she protested indignantly. 'Tied down here as he is all day while these wretched people sit closeted with Mira, poisoning her mind against him. Oh, it's too cruel. And his teaching suffers. I've heard some of the staff say so.'

I began to wonder whether she was in love with him, and

repeated the basic question, 'But why pick on *me*?'

Her answer really astounded me: 'As you were brought up a Christian Scientist, I thought you'd know about faith-healing, and that kind of thing.'

'But, Queenie, that was *years* ago.'

It was perfectly true that my parents had been close adherents of that faith; but they died when I was ten years old and I was brought up by a humanist. For this reason, I had virtually no contact with any organized religion during the formative years; since when I had given the matter very little thought. Briefly, I reminded Queenie of my guardian's views and of the fact that in general terms I had accepted them. 'So if that's all you had to go on,' I concluded, more amiably, 'please explain to your friend that I don't really want to get involved with his problem.'

'If you say so, boss.' She pushed a brimming cup towards me with scant grace. I could see how seriously annoyed she was that her impulsive suggestion had so badly misfired. I confirmed that I would be expecting her at my hotel to lunch on the Sunday. She acknowledged the invitation with a curt nod and left me to see myself out.

The hotel at which I had elected to pass the week of my enforced solitude was picturesquely situated in a charming woodland glade. Yet my spirit was no longer attuned to the pleasantness. I hurried through dinner and as soon as possible returned to the lounge for coffee. The waiter mentioned that a visitor had arrived to see me. Inwardly I groaned. Queenie!

But the caller was Stephen. 'Mr Hallam,' I began as he came forward to greet me. 'I'm so sorry. . . .'

'No, please don't apologize. How could I expect you to spend a whole day of your holiday hanging around Lancevearn? . . .' He explained that the work on his car had taken longer than expected. It was past five o'clock before he reached the house, only to discover that 'the worst' had happened. Mira admitted that the faith-healers had been with her for most of the afternoon. 'I protested and accused her of caring more about them than for me. It was most unwise. She flew into a terrible rage and then, suddenly, she went quite calm and cold. She told me that she had decided to leave me and go to live with them if I interfered or criticized them any more. And I could see she meant it.'

'But how could she leave Lancevearn? She isn't well enough?'

'That's what I said. "Taunting" her, was what she called it.'

'You must see them,' I said, 'it's gone too far.'

'Then *you* will have to help me to find them.'

This time I raised no objection for suddenly I felt curiously uneasy and apprehensive about the situation. We went into the bar and carried our drinks over to a corner settee, trying to assess what little information we had to go on.

'There's just one thing I've suddenly remembered,' he exclaimed after a long pause. 'Quite soon after we came here we had a very heavy fall of snow and I nearly skidded getting my car round the farm-house. Mira seemed surprised when I told her because she said the faith-healers hadn't mentioned having any trouble. She was quite willing to talk to me about them in those days. It suggests they were familiar with the Lancevearn track or they'd have stayed away in such bad weather.'

I agreed. 'Oh, they must be local people. No doubt about that.'

I could only promise to do my best. Soon after midnight a gale blew in from the Atlantic rendering sleep intermittent. My dreams, too, were disturbed. In one of them I was with my parents, walking along a river-path, until suddenly they were drawn from me into a swirling torrent. I awoke, jaded and heavy-eyed, to an enveloping mist through which I could barely identify the golden landscape of the previous afternoon.

After an early breakfast I set off in my car, driving straight into a bank of fog so that soon I was completely lost. Presently, a grey stone building loomed ahead of me. This was a typical Wesleyan chapel. Placards affixed to the gate exhorted the sinner to repent while time was on his side. 'Hell-fire awaits the wicked. Ye shall be saved when ye see Christ.' At that moment the minister rode up on a motor-bicycle and inquired if there was anything he could do.

He was a genial man with an open rugged countenance. I mentioned my interest in the Wesley brothers, and he invited me to step inside. A woman was practising the harmonium; the atmosphere struck agreeably warm and musty. When we had spoken of

the eighteenth-century sectarian divisions in Cornwall I decided
to make a tentative inquiry about the faith-healers. And I gave
him, briefly, such details as I possessed.

' "Faith-healers ?" ' He seemed astonished; even resentful.
'No, I've never heard of any practising in these parts. Our mission
is to heal the spirit rather than the flesh, by the unquestioning
acceptance and acknowledgement of God's will. We would have
nothing to do with such people in our ministry.'

I realized that I had drawn a complete blank. The minister
had lived in the St Huthy district all his life, yet he could not
identify these people, nor any remotely like them.

And that was the uniform reaction I received throughout a long
sodden morning, during which I called at churches and chapels,
even at the Citizens' Advice Bureau. The nearest I came to a clue
was the casual mention in a village post-office of a bone-setter at
Tintagel, but it appeared that his remarkable 'cures' were due
simply to manipulation and he claimed no more for them. By
early afternoon, when the drizzle had become a steady down-
pour, I admitted defeat. The time by then was three o'clock. I
considered whether I should telephone Stephen at St Benyn's
from a call-box or wait to ring him from the hotel during the
evening, and decided on the latter course.

And then, as disconsolately I drew level with the Lancevearn
cross-roads, a new thought struck me. Was not this the very
hour at which the faith-healers usually called ? While I exhausted
myself running hither and thither on this inclement morning,
wasting my own time and everybody else's, the prize lay all the
while within my grasp. I had only to break in upon them, insist
that they remained until Stephen returned, and my unwelcome
involvement would be at an end.

The approach to the house was a quagmire. Rain fell with a
chattering sound on the leaves of the escallonia. The place looked
utterly deserted. An enamelled bin stood in the porch with an
order for bread scribbled on a piece of cardboard. Fortunately,
the front door was open and I stepped thankfully into the hall,
depositing my mackintosh and umbrella on the hat-stand. As I
did so I became aware of loud voices; at first a mere jangle of
conflicting sound, but presently identifiable as a man's vigorous

recital of a prayer, followed by a woman singing a hymn in quavering, falsetto tones.

'Shepherd, show me how to go,
O'er the hillside steep. . . .'

Hastily I withdrew, taking my mackintosh and umbrella with me; ignoring the rain and slanting wind, for I had decided to revise my tactics. It would be far more effective to waylay the faith-healers just as they were leaving, thus obviating any risk of Mira warning them against me. There was a gazebo on the far side of the drive, with windows facing the sea. Into this I retreated to watch the wind playing weird games with the oncoming tide. Far more time than I realized must have slipped away. Had I, while resting comfortably in a wicker-chair piled high with cushions, actually fallen asleep? I never knew; only that, when belatedly I glanced at my watch, the hands pointed to four o'clock.

The rain had almost ceased. As I hesitated for a moment in the porch I was conscious of the gentle ticking of the hall clock and the distant throbbing of a refrigerator. Apart from that, silence enveloped the house like a blanket. I could not bear the possibility that I had missed the moment of departure. I looked into the various rooms, not liking myself for doing so. But there was nothing to see—two guest apartments, a small library, Stephen's bedroom and a second staircase leading to the domestic quarters. Mira's sewing and a book lay on the escritoire in the window recess but she herself was asleep in her bed. From the doorway I stood for a full minute watching the rhythmic rise and fall of her breast.

Somehow they had eluded me. Bitterly I upbraided myself: but then, as I paused before a small window looking on to a kind of enclosed inner yard, the question slid into my mind as insidiously as an asp. When did they leave Lancevearn—and how? For it seemed impossible that a vehicle could have driven out through the main gates while I was in the summer house without attracting my attention.

At that moment I heard a car outside and hurried downstairs

to the porch. I could hardly conceal my disappointment when I realized that the sound came from the baker's van. The roundsman was the gardener whom I had seen working among the escallonias on the previous morning.

'Have you just passed a car in the lane?' I inquired breathlessly.

He shook his head. 'Who'd be out on such a day? I wouldn't myself, but people must have their bread.' He explained that he had a puncture just as he passed the St Huthy cross-roads and spent half an hour mending it.

I made a rapid calculation. If the faith-healers had driven up the track while I was in the gazebo they must have passed him.

'Is it possible,' I asked, 'that anyone could leave Lancevearn by some other route? Or even without a car? There's a foot-path to St Huthy, isn't there?'

He deposited a couple of loaves in the bread bin and glanced at me pityingly. 'On a day like this? It's every bit of five mile to St Huthy round by the cliff.'

'As much as that? Well, it certainly doesn't seem very likely. But I mustn't keep you,' I added, for he seemed to be waiting, though unwillingly.

'Good day to you, then,' he said, 'I'll be getting along. I've still most of the round to do,' and away he went up the track in a cloud of petrol fumes. I noted that I could see and hear the van until it reached the farmhouse.

When he had gone I concentrated my gaze on what could be seen of the foot-path from where I stood. The boundary of the Lancevearn grounds on this side of the estate was little more than a collection of leaning posts. I pushed aside a strand of trailing wire and stepped over it on to the moor. Bushes and thistles pressed around me as I followed the path until it terminated abruptly at a sheer cliff face. Far, far below, I could see white ribbons of foam as the incoming sea licked at the sides of the ravine. On the opposite side of the inlet, at a distance hard to estimate, the path reappeared, meandering towards the sky-line, against which a deserted mine-shaft provided a distinctive landmark. With the wisps of grey mist clinging to the vegetation and the leaden sky above it was the most desolate place imaginable, untrodden for months, even years by the look of it.

Clearly, the two faith-healers could not possibly have left Lancevearn by this route. The ageing woman, even with the assistance of a much younger man, would never have been able to negotiate it in the time. Somewhere, they would still have been visible from my vantage point above the ravine.

So where were they then, and what in heaven's name was the explanation of their disappearance? For a moment I waited, still scanning the forbidding landscape; and then, almost without realizing it, I answered my own question. They had never been on the cliff-path: nor in the house for that matter, *because they did not really exist.*

I could not possibly have explained by what means I arrived at this extraordinary conclusion. Yet once stated, it was unanswerable. A cold terror seized me then, so that I shivered violently while my body temperature seemed to drop to a degree far below normal.

I ran from the place in a kind of panic frenzy, averting my eyes from the house lest I should glimpse the phantom forms awaiting me there in the porch. I started up the car and covered the distance between Lancevearn and St Huthy with more speed than caution.

From the porter's desk I telephoned St Benyn's, leaving a message for Stephen that I had been unable to locate the two people of whom we had spoken, and that as I would be out the entire evening it would be useless for him to call or ring me at the hotel. In fact, I went straight to bed, fortified by two hot-water bottles and an electric fire. Yet still I shivered convulsively, as though suffering from malaria or ague. Release came only when, half drugged by aspirin, I fell into deep sleep.

As on the previous night, my dreams related to childhood. I was standing on a dark stairway leading from the Christian Science Sunday School which I attended while my parents were at the morning service. I feared they had forgotten me, but when my sense of abandonment and loss became unendurable a porter, with the face of the Lancevearn gardener, appeared to comfort me. 'Silly kid,' he chided me, 'your mum and dad won't be long. Listen, they've just started on the last hymn.'

And so they had. The reverberating swell of several hundred

eager voices rose to engulf me like a cool, lapping wave.

'Shepherd, show me how to go,
O'er the hillside steep,
How to gather, how to sow,
How to feed thy sheep.'

And I was warmed by a rosy comfort which, alas, was short-lived. For that incident, or something very like it, really happened a few days before the accident in which my parents lost their lives.

The trouble with dreams, as Jonathan Swift once remarked, is that they tend to leave us very much as we were before dreaming! I awoke abruptly some hours after midnight, still shivering. Nevertheless, the words of that hymn remained quite clearly in my mind, although I had not consciously thought of them in all these years. I recited all the stanzas unhesitatingly. By the time the sun rose, on a very chilly dawn, I was beginning to understand.

I dressed before anyone was up, roaming about the hotel garden in the soft bright light of early morning, while I attempted to analyse and assess the situation. That I myself was acutely sensitive to supernatural manifestations I already knew as a result of a very disturbing experience. This concerned a brooch purchased from a small antique-dealer in my home town. Whenever I wore it I was subject to moods of such acute depression and fear of the future that I thought it worth while to investigate the history of that brooch. I learned that it had belonged to a young woman who had committed suicide. This was my first intimation that an inanimate object could be permanently invested with the personality of the individual who had once possessed it—also that certain people, myself in this case, might unwittingly tune in, as though on a kind of one-way radio telephone, to span the limbo which separates the living from the dead.

My doctor, who insisted that he did not for one moment accept the possibility, none the less urged me to get rid of the brooch as quickly as possible and this I did, by throwing it into a pond.

I could not reasonably expect such tidy, conclusive proof in the present situation. All the same, I decided to seek some confirmation of my theory, if that were possible in this out-of-the-way locality.

Immediately after breakfast I drove into the nearest of the coastal towns and there by sheer good fortune discovered in the public library a copy of a book on faith-healers which I remembered reading some thirty years earlier. In it I found reasonable corroboration of my own grotesque conclusions.

I knew then that I must remain no longer in the St Huthy neighbourhood. For I dared not again risk brushing even the garments of the supernatural. I gave notice at the hotel, packed, and wrote a letter to Queenie saying that I had been unexpectedly called away and so was obliged to cancel the invitation to lunch. And early in the afternoon I drove off, feeling infinitely relieved, with the intention of reaching my own home sometime on the following day.

But as I passed the Lancevearn cross-roads a dark cloud of guilt descended on me. I alone suspected the true identity of the Lancevearn 'visitors': yet I had taken no steps to warn Mira either about her own occult sensitivity or of the 'other-world' influences to which she was being subjected. More important still, should I not have told her husband? For whatever principles the two faith-healers might have upheld when living and breathing in the material world, their motives seemed to have become frighteningly distorted while breaking the barrier between this universe and the next.

I could imagine Stephen's astonishment only too easily.

'But of *course* the faith-healers are real people. Certainly, they have a peculiar hold on Mira and I mean to put an end to it. That's why I begged you to help me find them.'

Rather than face a conversation along these lines I was putting distance between Lancevearn and myself. And yet . . . If I made no attempt to communicate my reading of the situation, surely I would always despise myself? So, torn by one of the strangest conflicts I have ever experienced, I reversed the car and drove back to the Lancevearn turning. The sun was stronger now; cotton-wool clouds floated high above my head. Away towards the sea a kestrel hovered: and I heard lark song on the still air. It would have been difficult to imagine a more tranquil scene, and deeply I regretted leaving it after so short a stay.

I reached the house just after four o'clock. Once again, the place seemed utterly deserted. The front door was slightly ajar, as before. This time a plastic container with an order for the butcher propped up against it stood just inside. Although not unexpected, the silence was uncanny, for there was something final and menacing about it. And yet on the surface, all seemed normal: the dining table set for supper and through the open conservatory window great gusts of clean, billowing sea-air made nonsense of my apprehensions.

I braced myself to ascend the stairs. Gently, I knocked on Mira's door, but there was no answer. 'Please may I come in, Mrs Hallam?' I called out, 'I have something very important to say to you.' But had I? Suddenly, I was no longer sure.

At last I looked into the room, not quite sure what I expected to see. Mira was not there. The bedclothes had been carefully folded back into position and several small toilet items removed from the dressing table. There were no clothes or books lying about and the thought struck me that Stephen must have prevailed upon her to leave Lancevearn for a while and recuperate elsewhere. He would have had no obligation to tell me of any such arrangement after my telephone call to the school and if this was really the case I need have no further feeling of responsibility.

I did not linger in this room, scene of so much suffering and acrimony, for suddenly I felt spent and exhausted after the anti-climax of finding her gone. I almost fainted as I crossed the landing and sank down on the rocking chair, resting my head against the escritoire, until the blood flowed slowly back to my brain. At that moment I saw them, in the diffused grey light which made a startling contrast to the brightness outside, yet distinct in every detail. A slight, elderly woman, plainly though expensively clad in a dark enveloping garment made of some kind of brocade with, at her throat, a diamond brooch in the shape of a cross. She moved with extreme difficulty; yet maintained an air of authority and purpose. The man who supported her wore an old-fashioned jacket and knee-breeches. His manner was solicitous and quietly deferential.

I have often wondered how eventually I found courage to

follow them down the stairs, although I felt certain they would be gone before I reached the hall. And I was right; not even a wraith of mist remained; although the conviction was hard to put to the test!

*

In the weeks that followed I sometimes speculated as to where Mira had been that afternoon and whether she was by now fully recovered. Yet soon, with the press of family and other interests, I forgot her. But before that happened I had found time to look up various biographies and reference books in an attempt to clarify my impression of the two figures who had appeared before me on the staircase at Lancevearn. From prints and reproductions I recognized without any hesitation the Founder of my parents' faith, Mary Baker Eddy; by her sparse, carefully waved white hair, the material of her dress and the diamond brooch. There was no picture available of her companion; but sufficient published information for me to identify him as one of the two principle 'disciples' who supported the closing years of her long, tempestuous life. In a photograph of one of the rooms at her last home, Chestnut Hill, Massachusetts, I noted pieces of furniture identical with those on the landing at Lancevearn, and the wonder was that they had ever come into the market, rather than the high price paid for them, which at first surprised me.

Gradually, I came to accept the extraordinary experience as a fact. I had no wish to arrive at a final judgement. Whether ultimately a force for good or the reverse, I realized that the projection had been trapped between cross-currents of time and resurrection at the most autocratic and doctrinaire period of a controversial career. I asked only to forget the Lancevearn episode as quickly as possible.

But this, alas, I was not permitted to do. My contact with Queenie had reverted to a state of suspended animation. I feared she must have been very annoyed at my abrupt departure and it might be that I would never hear from her again. But early in December a Christmas greeting arrived. Much information about her activities was compressed into a small space in almost illegible hand-writing. I was relieved that she bore me no ill will: although as I read the postscript on the back of her card, a kind of electric shock seemed to pass through me.

'I don't suppose,' she had written, 'that you ever heard about the tragedy the day you left St Huthy. Mira Hallam was found drowned in the Lancevearn cove. Later on, her suitcase was washed up farther along the coast and the coroner said she must have been trying to leave home while "the balance of her mind was disturbed". It was a terrible shock for Stephen. You see, he blamed himself. The only thing you can say is that in some ways it was a "happy release". . . .'

The room in which I sat seemed to darken. I crumpled the Christmas card in my hand, dropping it into the heart of the fire. . . .